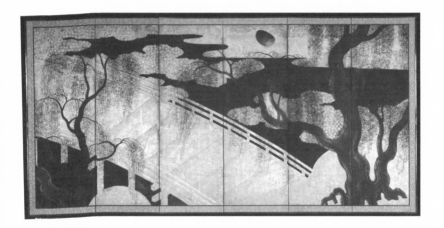

The Hidden Keys

ANDRÉ ALEXIS

Coach House Books, Toronto

first edition

Published with the generous assistance of the Canada Council for the Arts and the Ontario Arts Council. Coach House Books also gratefully acknowledges the support of the Government of Canada, and the Government of Ontario through the Ontario Book Publishing Tax Credit and the Ontario Book Fund.

LIBRARY AND ARCHIVES CANADA CATALOGUING IN PUBLICATION

Alexis, André, 1957-, author
    The hidden keys / André Alexis.

ISBN 978-1-55245-325-4 (paperback).

    I. Title.

PS8551.L474H53 2016   C813'.54   C2016-902856-9

For Nicola Alexis-Brooks

In a dream, the caliph al-Maʾmun saw a pale man with a ruddy complexion, a broad forehead and joined eyebrows. The man was bald, his eyes deep blue. He seemed approachable sitting on his dais. But I was directly in front of him, said al-Maʾmun, and I was afraid. I asked him: Who are you? He answered: I am Aristotle. I was delighted and I said: O, Sage, may I question you? He said: Go ahead. I asked: What is the good? He answered: That which is good according to reason. I asked: What else? He answered: That which is good according to revelation. I asked: What else? He answered: That which is good in the eyes of all men. I asked: What else? He answered: There is nothing else.

— Ibn al-Nadîm, *Kitab al-fihrist*

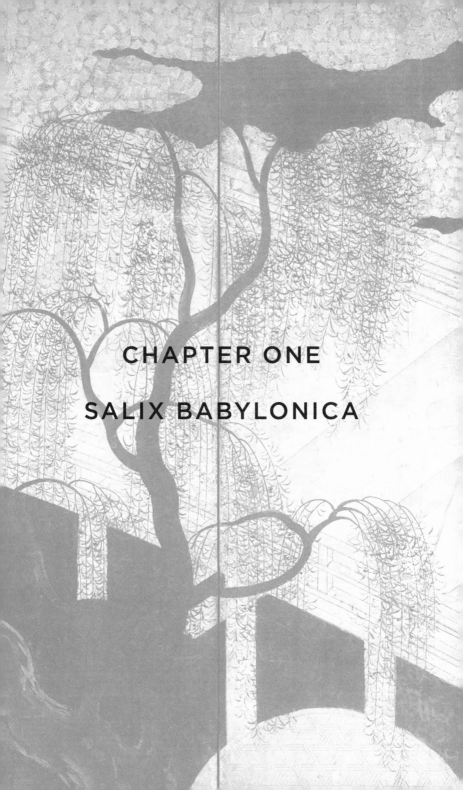

CHAPTER ONE
SALIX BABYLONICA

1 A Willow in Parkdale

Tancred Palmieri was sitting in the Green Dolphin thinking about how best to dispose of a black diamond he'd stolen from a house on the Bridle Path. He was twenty-five years old and he'd been a thief from the age of eleven, but this was the first time he'd had difficulty deciding what to do with a stone. It was as if the diamond had a personality.

Tancred was a tall and physically imposing black man, but he was also approachable. He could not sit anywhere for long without someone starting a conversation. This was, his friends liked to say, because his blue eyes were startling and his voice deep and avuncular. So, when he wanted to be alone without necessarily being alone, Tancred answered in French – his maternal tongue – when spoken to by strangers. Few who came into the Dolphin knew the language. But Willow Azarian did, and she took the fact that Tancred spoke it as a portent. They would be friends. She knew it and, touching his arm, she blithely began to tell him about her family.

Tancred interrupted her. In French, he said

– You know, I'm not really one for family stories.

In French, Willow answered

– What have you got against them?

– I just don't like them, said Tancred.

Willow nodded in sympathy and patted his leg. Then she carried on from where she'd left off, speaking about her family as if its story were something Tancred had to know. Willow was in her fifties, more than twice his age. As he was chivalrous by nature, he listened to her, skeptical but polite.

To be fair, there were a number of things that made Willow's story implausible. To begin with, she was a junkie. Tancred himself had seen her, either high or strung out, stumbling around Parkdale like an outpatient from Queen Street Mental.

Then there was what she told him. Though they were meeting for the first time, Willow expatiated on her family's wealth. The

Azarians – about whom Tancred had heard – owned property all over the world. Her father had been brilliant, generous, wonderful! He had always treated her – his youngest – as if she were a princess. She had millions, thanks to him. A fortune. Enough to last a hundred years.

– Of course, he didn't leave as much as he could have, she said.

It all sounded to Tancred like the daydreams of an orphan.

Then, too, there was her appearance. Willow was thin and pale. She was in her fifties but his impression was of someone older. Her hair was greying. There were crow's feet at her eyes and her lips were those of a smoker, puckering when she spoke. Her clothes were out of style: a green-and-white floral dress with padded shoulders, a felt hat with wilted green plumes curling around to the side, a white sweater and clunky black shoes. It was not a getup you'd associate with wealth.

Finally, there was the place itself. Why would a rich woman hang around the Dolphin? Tancred came to the Dolphin in the afternoons to think things through, to stand at the bar and withdraw. At night, the Dolphin was a different story: noisy, filled with regulars or stragglers or cops. He went then to be with people he knew – thieves, dealers, users and prostitutes. Seeking company, he would stand at the bar and talk to whoever was there. One night, for instance, he spoke to a Salvadoran refugee whose family had been wiped out by death squads. On another night, not long after, he'd listened to a Salvadoran refugee who'd been a member of a death squad. Neither had looked like victim or executioner.

Though he did not often drink alcohol, Tancred had been going to the Dolphin since he was eighteen. In all that time, he could not remember meeting anyone posh. The place was too rough for it. Even Willow's dealer – 'Nigger' Colby by name, though he was albino – preferred to drink across the street, at Jimmy's. As far as Tancred knew, the most common reason for strangers to choose the Dolphin was the price of beer: it was twenty-five cents cheaper there than it was anywhere else. But Willow did not drink beer. She drank vodka and orange juice, and it seemed to Tancred that if she had really been wealthy, she'd have frequented better places, junkie or not.

Then again, who could tell about the rich? In '03 or '04, there'd been a politician caught trawling for prostitutes on Queen Street, not three blocks west of the Dolphin. In those days, the most unfortunate women worked Queen between Lansdowne and Triller. The wealthy men who came around looking for sex must have been attracted to something in Parkdale: the lawless, the sordid, the unlikeliness of being recognized. For all Tancred knew, the streetwalkers' desperation was itself what turned these men on. It may have been something similar that brought Willow.

He found her difficult to credit, but she was also amusing and surprisingly sympathetic. He listened to her for an hour, listened until she spoke again about her father and then faltered and then stopped.

– I'm sorry, he said, but I've got to go. It was nice to meet you.

– You speak English, said Willow.

– Yes, said Tancred, but I prefer French.

– So do I, she said, but Japanese is my favourite.

She held up a hand, limp-wristed. Unsure what he was meant to do, he held it. He felt faintly ridiculous, but that was part of what made the encounter memorable.

Their second meeting was more memorable still.

One night, Tancred was at Close and Queen, walking home. Behind him, toward Parkdale Collegiate, he heard a cry. Turning, he saw three young men pulling at a woman. His adrenalin immediately spiked. He walked toward them. The woman called for help, as two of the men tried to keep her quiet.

The third and most imposing came forward. Tancred calmly said the first thing that came to his mind

– Are you guys holding?

before running at him, catching the man by surprise, punching him (accidentally) in the throat and then (somewhat purposely) in the face. The man growled and hit out but lost his balance, ending up on his hands and knees. Tancred kicked him, very hard – not in the ribs (where he was aiming) but only in the arse. The man swore and tried to get up but, as he did, Tancred kicked him (accidentally but with a physically pleasing *thuck*) in the face, breaking his nose.

The man stayed down, loudly cursing and holding his face.

Thirty seconds of close-quarter chaos that might have gone either way. But Tancred was fortunate. Fortunate, not only because he was unhurt (though his foot had hit the man's arse at a bad angle and would later swell slightly from the sprain) but also because the other two, seeing their friend incapacitated, backed away, forgetting about the woman – Willow Azarian! – as they prepared for Tancred's onslaught.

It was an onslaught that never came. It seemed to Tancred that a beating would have done them good – high school students, they looked like, five or six years younger than he was, thin as whippets. It would have given him pleasure to hurt them, but instead he helped Willow up and led her past the one who was groaning and complaining as he tried to stand up.

They reached Dunn, a block away, when Willow stopped. She could not go on. She stood shaking, her hat almost falling off.

– We should keep going, said Tancred. Where do you live?

It was a while before she could answer. Tancred waited, looking warily west to where they'd left her assailants and east at all the lights along Queen Street, the city stretching from the small desolation of Parkdale to the tall buildings and illuminations in the distance.

– I can't go home, Willow said.

What she meant was that she did not want to be alone, and Tancred understood. The problem was, he knew nothing reliable about her and nothing about what had happened. What had the three men been after? Were they after her still? Who could he trust to take care of her? All he knew for certain was the reality of the human being beside him: thin, a foot or so shorter than he was, her lipstick smudged so that it looked like a reddish cloud on her cheek, streaks of grey in her bottle-blond hair. Seeing her like this, by street light, it added up only to distress and need.

— I don't live far, he said. We can wait at my place while you decide what to do.

They made their way to King Street, then past old apartment buildings, rooming houses, big homes and corner stores to Temple, where Tancred rented an apartment. A fifteen-minute walk during which neither of them spoke.

There was a moment, as they climbed the stairs to his place, when Tancred questioned the wisdom of what he was doing. He allowed few strangers into his home. It was his sanctuary. He took pains to keep it as he wished it to be: four rooms (living room, bedroom, small kitchen, bathroom), white walls with ocean-blue trim. There was little furniture. He had a bed from IKEA, a table with four chairs, a blue sofa his mother had insisted on buying for him, above which hung a painting she had made for his home: a portrait of the goddess Oshun in the shade of a tall tree, the goddess – breasts bared – wearing a bright yellow skirt and an ankle bracelet, the whole scene set under a cloudless blue sky. He had lived in this apartment since moving out of his mother's home on St. Clarens. Though he could have afforded something bigger in a better neighbourhood, it had never occurred to him to move, the simplicity and warmth of his rooms being a tonic to the complications of his life.

On the landing, Tancred looked back at Willow, forlorn as she stood on the step, her hand on the banister shaking, blood on her knuckles. What was this person to him? Nothing, really, but that she needed help. He opened his door for her.

He made her tea, after helping to clean the blood and dirt from her hands, knees, elbows and cheek – the places scraped when she'd fallen. Her clothes – flimsy-looking – had not torn, despite being pulled about. Somewhere between Dunn and his apartment, she had lost her hat. Two or three of the hairpins she'd used to keep her hair tucked in dangled like clots.

Willow was in shock. The only words she managed – insistently repeated – were

— I won't forget your kindness.

Somewhere around two in the morning, after they'd spent hours quietly speaking of personal things, her words of gratitude gently met by his assurances that he'd been pleased to help, he asked if she wanted to sleep.

– I think I should, she answered.

So, Tancred gave up his bed and slept on the sofa.

He came to think of this as a second first encounter with Willow. This time, his impression was of a woman in distress. But there was more to it than that. As she recovered from the indignity she'd suffered, there were also moments when he sensed strength in her, a resolve. These were unusual things to sense in an older, frail junkie, but they struck Tancred the way the integrity of her clothes had: flimsy-looking was not always flimsy. The glimpses he had of her resolve and determination were what interested him most. He was not moved by weakness, though he felt bound by vulnerability.

This was a precept Tancred had taken from his closest friend, Daniel Mandelshtam, one of two friends he'd had since his childhood in Alexandra Park. As Daniel put it, weakness was a habit, one that led to a kind of contented incapacity. It made no sense to help the weak, because that was what people called 'enabling.' But as to the vulnerable – there was a different story. Anyone might, given the circumstances, find themselves in above their heads. And it was dishonourable, Daniel thought, to let such people sink. Tancred had agreed. But the distinction was neither clear nor absolute to the young men since, as Daniel said, the weak, too, could be vulnerable. A further twist: Daniel was now a policeman, paid to protect the weak and the vulnerable indiscriminately.

Early the following morning, Willow emerged from his room and thanked him. She would not hear of his accompanying her. She was not afraid of the boys who'd attacked her. It had all been a misunderstanding, she said, an accident for which she blamed herself. She'd spoken of her wealth to the wrong people, that's all. Tancred was not to worry about her safety. She would be grateful if he forgot the night they'd just passed. It was too humiliating for words.

Which was not to say she would forget what he'd done. How could she? He'd proven her right. They were destined to be close, and she never questioned destiny, whatever else she might dispute.

A long time passed before Tancred saw Willow Azarian again. Almost three full years. Nor was the time insignificant. His mother died.

Clémentine Fassinou, a non-smoker, died of lung cancer on a bright day in June, her soul leaving earth from her apartment on St. Clarens. She had been suffering for months, and her dark, African face had grown meagre and grey. Before she died, Tancred, her only child, had wished for her release from discomfort and exhaustion. After her death, he was contrite that he'd wished such a thing, though he had wished it out of love.

Then again, he and his mother had always had a complex relationship. From his childhood, they'd been as much friends as they'd been mother and son. This was just as well, because Clémentine had been a somewhat inattentive mother – unavoidably inattentive. Over the years, she had taken on any number of low-paying or temporary jobs to support them. And when she came home, exhausted from a day's – or night's – work, it was he who comforted her – keeping the house clean, preparing her meals once he was old enough to do so, washing the dishes. It was a role he had liked, one that he had jealously guarded against the occasional intrusion from men who stayed over from time to time before disappearing from their lives.

As it happened, his mother's absence brought great good to Tancred's childhood. When he and Clémentine lived in government housing near Alexandra Park, Tancred spent most of his time at the home of the Mandelshtams, who lived on Denison, and the Mallays, who lived around the corner on Carr. Baruch Mandelshtam, Daniel's father, had been like a father to Tancred as well. Daniel and Tancred, both born of African mothers, looked like siblings. The Mallays' son, Olivier – pale as winter – was almost as close to him as Daniel. The three boys had been inseparable from kindergarten until the end of high school, and they were close still.

Tancred had long forgiven his mother for any supposed damage his childhood had done to him. But it seemed that she hadn't entirely forgiven herself, that she blamed herself for his way of life. Before she died, Clémentine had made him promise to read the Bible in her memory. Tancred had agreed, because it would not have been possible to refuse her anything as she lay dying. And although he was not much of a reader, reading mostly to please others, it was an easy promise to keep. His mother had asked Daniel and Olivier, who'd been on death watch with him, to help her son change his life. A more difficult proposition. Daniel had said he would, when Tancred was ready to change. But Ollie said that he would not.

— I wouldn't know how to do that, he said.

Ollie being Ollie, he could not have answered otherwise.

But Clémentine had asked in earnest. She'd wanted to believe, before dying, that her son would find the right path. And Tancred had been hurt, not because his mother wished him to live a better life but, rather, because she knew he was living a life in the shadows. That she knew this, moreover, had been his fault. He had decided, at nineteen, to be honest with her, whatever the consequences. So, when she'd asked him where he got his money, he had defiantly admitted that he stole things for a living. At her death, he cringed at the brashness of it. She'd loathed thievery. He had put her in the position of having to choose, day after day, between her conscience and her son. That she had steadfastly chosen her son was no credit to him, and he knew it.

After his mother's death, it was as if Parkdale had turned away from him, all the familiar places seeming drab and pointless. This was not the worst of his bereavement, but it was unexpected. The worst was the feeling of irreality, like living in a state just before waking. Parkdale had been home to him since he'd moved there at eighteen, his first home as an adult. It was unbearable to feel as if he were suddenly estranged from the world.

For a while, nothing mattered to him. He went on as he had, stealing what was wanted by those who paid him to steal. But something was working its way out. He had become strange to himself as well and he began to question his way of life and his motives. Ironically, this was also the time when he most needed his skill – the planning, the cold carrying out, the algebra of thieving. It seemed to be the only thing to distract him from grief.

For three years following his mother's death, Tancred did not see Willow at all. The idea that they were destined to be close faded to grey, along with any number of assumptions and ideas that had preceded the death of his mother.

And then Willow walked back into his life.

It was a Sunday and it had rained. Tancred was wet and cold as he sat in one of the half-booths at the Skyline: orange leatherette seats on both sides of a white laminate tabletop. Sunday was now the day he spent alone. He would wake at seven, eat eggs and brown toast at the diner, return home, read from the King James Bible, make plans for the week to come, clear his mind and go to sleep early.

By now, he'd spent Sundays this way for years, and even some who knew him assumed there was a religious tinge to his discipline. But there was not. What there was was devotion to his mother. For the hour or so it took for him to read twenty pages, Tancred felt her presence. Or at least he thought of her. His reading of the Bible did not lead him to God or prayer or worship. It did not lead him to a new life. Though it was no doubt less than what his mother had hoped for, he simply grew more and more familiar with what was, for him, a mostly tiresome but sometimes entertaining repository of catalogues, tales and poetry.

He had ordered his eggs and toast, when Willow came in off the street. She saw him and, speaking to the waiter, asked that her coffee be brought to Tancred's table. She was neither spaced out nor flagrantly high. She was thinner than she had been, however, and she wore more makeup. She greeted him, took off her raincoat and sat down.

– I've been looking for you, said Willow. Freud Luxemberg told me you come here on Sundays. And Nigger told me you're a thief. Is that true?

– Why do you want to know? asked Tancred.

– You think I'm a foolish old woman, said Willow. And I am. I know it. But I'm more than that, Tancred. If you'll listen to me, I have a proposition. You don't have to say anything. I'll do the talking. But first, I want you to know how I ended up here.

– Where? asked Tancred. The Skyline?

– No, no, said Willow. *Here.* In this life.

She began to rummage in a purse that was black, cumbersome and capacious, with a clip that looked like two brass moths meeting, their entangled antennae keeping the purse closed.

– My name is Willow Azarian, she said. My family is well-known.

– You told me all this, said Tancred, when we met.

– Yes, she said, and you may have got the impression that I worship money and status. But I don't. I just wanted you to know who I am.

She took a bank statement from her purse and said

– This is from my expense account.

She pushed the statement to his side of the table. Tancred looked at it. Yes, it belonged to 'Willow Azarian.' Willow reached across and put her finger beside a number at the bottom of the page. For a moment, looking down, Tancred assumed he was mistaken about the figure he saw there:

$$\$15,011,957.07$$

– It's only my mad money, said Willow. I have much more.

– Why are you showing me this? asked Tancred.

– I want your help, she answered.

Her eyes were blue, not big or round, but set off by her thick eyebrows. Her face was pleasantly oval, her lips thin but expressive. Her ancestry would have been difficult to guess. Her clothes, on the other hand, suggested ideas of elegance whose time had long passed. She was wearing a black dress with padded shoulders, the dress's collar cascading from one shoulder like three dark ripples and coming to a point on the other.

Willow was out of place in Parkdale. It would have been difficult to say where she'd have fit in. But she was not weak.

— What can I do for you? he asked.

2 Willow's Inheritance

By her own account, Willow had had a wonderful childhood. It had been everything she might have wished for. Her parents had been loving. Her siblings had helped to take care of her, changing her diapers and feeding her when her mother was tired. They had all doted on her.

For her first eight years, she felt loved and precious. The world itself was marvellous. The Azarians lived in Toronto for most of the year but in winter they moved to Key West where Nicole, their mother, had lived as a child. Willow had had, she believed, the best of north and south: the dry quiet of Rosedale (wealthy, its big houses politely distant from the street) and the sea-shush of Old Town (thirty degrees Celsius in the morning, houses modest and close); the soft rain along streets with tall trees and torrential storms so vivid she was certain their house in the Keys would shake apart.

Though she would not have changed a moment of her early childhood, it was not without its shadows, shadows that lengthened until they blotted out her adolescence. The worst of them was her mother's illness: Creutzfeldt-Jakob. The eight-year-old Willow watched as the mother she loved was slowly taken from her, slowly becoming a woman Willow did not know. It took a year for Nicole Azarian to die.

This being the first and most frightening death in Willow's life, it would be fair to say that she never recovered from it. For one thing, her mother's death was the beginning of an anxiety about her father. For years she had nightmares in which her father succumbed to the same disease as her mother. Awake, the young Willow watched for symptoms of Creutzfeldt-Jakob in her father: dementia, changes in personality, the shakes.

Her father, for his part, had nothing but sympathy for his youngest. She was, maybe even to her detriment, the one child he indulged, the only one whose presence he always welcomed. Over the years, their bond was precious to both of them. She kept watch over him whenever he was home, while he came to think of her as a confidante.

This was a point Willow wanted to impress on Tancred: she was convinced that she'd known her father best – his personality, his deepest thoughts, his sense of humour, his playfulness, his strange ideas, his follies. Although she'd loved her father unconditionally, love had not blinded her to his flaws. That is to say, she had a realistic idea of who the man named Robert Azarian had been. It was crucial that Tancred take Willow's word for this, if he was to grasp a second point she wanted to make.

At her mother's death, Willow's father had been forty-three and extremely wealthy. He had inherited millions and worked to make countless millions more. When he died of cancer in 2005, he died a multi-billionaire whose main company, Azarian Holdings, was involved in any number of enterprises in any number of countries.

At her father's death, the last thing on Willow's mind was the state of Azarian Holdings or her father's will or her inheritance or anything of the sort. Her grief was such that her siblings were, rightly, troubled by her state of mind. Three years after her father's death, however, financial matters did begin to impinge on Willow's mind. Her grief gave way to an obsession with her father's legacy. Robert Azarian had left each of his children two hundred million dollars and a one-fifth share of his businesses and assets. He had made his eldest son, Alton, head of Azarian Holdings, but his five children were equally served by his will. In effect, each inherited almost a billion dollars.

Along with the money and assets, he also bequeathed to each a *memento mori*, each memento holding special significance for the one who received it.

> Alton inherited a mounted and framed poem,
> Gretchen, a model of Frank Lloyd Wright's Fallingwater,
> Simone, a painting of the Emperor Nero beside a man with
>   a raven on his shoulder,
> Michael, a bottle of Linie Aquavit,

and Willow inherited a near-faithful imitation of a six-panelled, Momoyama-period Japanese screen known as *Willows by the Uji Bridge*. Willow's screen had had its last panel replaced by a blank, lacquered, willow-wood panel. Toward the bottom of this last panel – on the same side of the screen as the reproduction – was a lozenge-shaped brass tag, two inches high and four inches long. Engraved on the tag were the words

Salix Babylonica
(Psalm 137: *By the rivers of Babylon ...*)

The screen was such a perfect memento of her father that it added to Willow's grief. She could not see it or even think about it without remembering him.

She'd studied languages at a number of universities. She could fluently speak English, French, Spanish, Arabic and Japanese. But she had taken Japanese, thanks to her father. Robert Azarian, knowing that Willow wanted to add an Asian language to her arsenal, had suggested it himself. He'd had a covert motive, it's true. Azarian Holdings – whose chief interest then was in cellphones – was opening an office in Osaka and he could not avoid spending time in Japan. So, he and Willow had travelled to the country together, Robert extending his stay so his daughter could complete her first course in Japanese.

During their months in Japan, they had – when both were free – travelled around the country together, taking trains to Kyoto, Nara, Kobe and Tokyo. She could still recall the small towns along the way, the baseball diamonds, the fields and houses, the tall buildings and neon lights. It was on these travels that Willow discovered her love for the painted screens of sixteenth- and seventeenth-century Japan: gesso, gold leaf, a season coming to life panel by panel as the screen is opened. Leave it to her father to remember her enchantment and remind her of the works she'd loved, to recreate a screen on which there were weeping willows, *Salix babylonica*, her symbol.

Three years after her father's passing, when she was again able to think of things other than his death or at least to think beyond her next fix, she remembered words he'd spoken in his final days. She'd been holding his hand as he lay on his bed. He had awakened briefly from his chemically induced sleep and, seeing her beside him, he'd said

– Willow, you, your brothers and sisters ... you'll all have more than I've left, if you want it. But you'll have to work for it. Promise me you will ... promise me you'll work for it ...

He'd repeated the word *promise*, more and more faintly as he was drawn back into his opiate antechamber. She had, of course, promised. But later, thinking about her promise to him, the words *work for it* struck her. At his death, her father had made each of his children near-billionaires. They would make millions more from their shares in Azarian Holdings. It was more than enough. What, then, was there to work for?

When she'd conveyed their father's words to her brothers and sisters, none had found them particularly significant. To her siblings, the words were banal, their meaning clear: they were all meant to help Alton run Azarian Holdings. It was their duty to work together as a family.

But that made no sense! Where Azarian Holdings was concerned, Alton was the authority. What's more, Alton was as prescient and talented as their father had been. And why not? Robert had taught Alton everything he knew about business, as his father, Avram, had taught him. The company was thriving. There was no work for the other siblings, save for staying out of Alton's way. This could not have been the work their father had in mind.

The third Christmas after her father's death, when she and her siblings had gathered at Gretchen's, Willow asked

– Is all of Dad's money accounted for?

The young children were in the playroom with their toys, watched over by their nannies. The teenagers were with boyfriends or girlfriends or they were in the den watching television. Willow, her brothers and sisters (and their spouses) were at the dining room table, a plate of freshly baked keta, still warm, before them.

– All Dad's money? said Alton. A lot of it went to charity. He donated hundreds of millions to causes all over the world. The rest he put back into the company.

– I know Dad was generous, Willow had said, but something doesn't add up. Why did he leave us so little?

The others had guffawed in unison – a strange sound, as if something were suddenly caught in a number of throats. How could she say that he'd left them 'little'? None in her family accepted that it was in any way 'little' to be left almost a billion in cash and assets. The conversation had almost immediately turned to other matters.

That was where things stood, as far as her siblings were concerned. Yes, perhaps, in theory, their father had been worth more than was disbursed in his will. But once you took his charitable donations into account, it was all above board and, frankly, not worth the bother.

But between bouts of heroin-brought stupor, Willow thought about her father's words. She was convinced that she and her siblings were meant to be doing something other than gathering money from their inheritance. The maddening thing is that there were clues this was the case, clues that her intoxication shrouded. For one thing, every one of the mementos her father left them was, in its own way, provocative. Take hers, for instance: the screen with its painting of willows by the Uji bridge was a message of some sort. It had to be. If her father had simply wanted to remind her of their precious time together in Japan, a reproduction of *Willows by the Uji Bridge* would have been more than enough. It would have been perfect. But her father, or whoever made the reproduction, had removed part of the screen – had removed a willow – when they'd replaced the final image with a blank panel of wood. Why ruin the work? To what purpose? To let her know that the trees painted were weeping willows? But that was obvious. Although Psalm 137 was lovely, it simply did not jibe with seventeenth-century Japanese art. And on the back of the willow-wood panel, the letters

a(ɯ)

had been imprinted toward the bottom in indelible black ink.

The most provocative thing was: all this was so like her father. Robert Azarian had loved to devise the clues – difficult clues – for his children's treasure hunts. As far as Willow was concerned, her screen – and each of the mementos – was a clue to something. And the work they had to do was in the uncovering of that thing.

Had she told her siblings her thoughts about their mementos?

Yes, she had.

Had she asked if they, too, had found anything 'playful' about the mementos their father had left?

Yes, and of her siblings, only Michael would admit his memento (the bottle of aquavit) was 'suggestive.' Well, why would their father leave someone who was teetotal – that is, Michael – a full bottle of alcohol? Then again, Michael had added that their father had no doubt been old when he'd chosen (or commissioned) the mementos he'd left them. So, one might have expected these incongruities. The other three – Gretchen, Alton and Simone – would not even admit that much, though their mementos were just as suggestive.

Had she examined their pieces for herself?

No. Willow had seen the other mementos, but none of her siblings would allow her time with their piece. In fact, it was as if they were colluding against her. Just as maddening: each one had privately encouraged her to keep on looking for answers. It was as if, in private, her siblings became reasonable, admitting the obvious, though none would help her.

The situation was bedevilling. It was almost enough to make her go cold turkey so she could think straight for longer stretches. She hadn't kicked, though. Instead, she lived with two things constantly at the edge of her mind: her father, his mementos.

Her story finished, Willow took a sip of coffee. She'd put a napkin beneath her cup – the mark of those who do a lot of sitting over coffee in restaurants. From her moth-clips purse, she took a chocolate doughnut from a Coffee Time bag and, putting her hand before her mouth, took a bite. Then, as if ashamed, she put the doughnut back in the bag and the bag into her purse.

— What does any of this have to do with me? asked Tancred.

— I want you to steal my father's mementos for me.

— From your brothers and sisters?

— Yes, from my brothers and sisters. But I don't want to keep them. I'll give them back. No one else has the right to have them, but I need to examine them and I know they won't lend them to me. I've asked all of them.

— So, if I've got you straight, said Tancred, you think your father left you something but he hid it. How much could this whatever be worth, if it exists?

— I don't know. I suppose it's valuable. But this isn't about money or wealth or anything like that. It's about finding what my father hid. If I had time with the other mementos, I know I could figure this whole thing out. I was always good at treasure hunts.

Tancred wasn't sure what to think. It had been impressive to see the fifteen million in her account, but difficult to think of so much as 'mad money.'

— Listen, he said, I'll think about it, but first I want to see the screen your father left you.

— Why? asked Willow.

— Put yourself in my place, he answered. You're an addict, Willow. You don't always make sense. I'd like to see the screen, just so we're on the same page.

— That's fair, said Willow. I'll see to it.

With that, she got up, pulled on her raincoat and thanked him for listening. She left a twenty on the table.

— I'm sorry, she said. I don't have anything smaller.

Tancred was about to say

— You don't have to leave anything

but Willow had turned away and the image that came to Tancred's mind was of a woman pulling up her skirt as she fords a river.

3 A Visit from Nigger Colby

There were a number of things Tancred found disconcerting about Errol 'Nigger' Colby. To begin with, there was his nickname. It was unpleasant for Tancred to hear, as he sat in the Green Dolphin,

– How you doin', Nigger?

or

– What's up, Nigger?

Adding to the strangeness was that, although Errol Colby was albino (white hair, white skin), he was of Jamaican descent. He was 'black under the white,' as he himself liked to say, so that calling him 'Nigger' seemed both offensive *and* considerate. Colby himself took pride in his nickname. He was more ashamed of being albino than he was of being black. In any case, Tancred refused to call the man Nigger, calling him instead Errol, his given name.

Colby was a drug dealer who seemed not to mind if people knew he dealt. He wasn't casual about dealing, exactly, but at times it was as if he took pride in his accomplishment. You could see it in the way he treated the junkies who came to him. He was like a vampire who had affection for his prey. Tancred had heard him speaking to junkies pale as death warmed over as if he were their therapist, warning them about the effects of junk, advising them to return to their homes and loved ones.

Tancred assumed most of them took Colby's advice for yet more humiliation, because his kindly advice in no way stopped Colby from being the usual monster: condescending, gouging, arrogant, refusing to give up a fleck of H or crack without being paid.

It was cruel to lecture junkies before exploiting them. It seemed to Tancred like cleaning the rust off pinching handcuffs while making sure their locks were still good.

Then there was Colby's friend, Sigismund Luxemberg, whom everyone knew as 'Freud.' Luxemberg was another man fond of his own nickname. He hated to be called Sigismund, feeling that it made him sound foreign when he was, in fact, proud of his birthplace:

Alexandra Park – the same projects Tancred grew up in, though Freud was of the next generation. He was twenty-two, six foot three, built like a bull, but he had a severely clubbed foot for which he wore a special black shoe, and walked with a limp. Tancred, who liked most people, could not stand Freud. Besides being sullen and prone to violence, Freud always made Tancred feel as if they had – he and Freud – unfinished business from their childhood, though Tancred scarcely remembered the young Freud, remembering, rather, Mrs. Luxemberg, her voice calling 'Siggy' home after school, her German accent.

For these reasons and perhaps deeper ones as well, Tancred was not pleased to find Colby waiting for him as he left his apartment. It was an afternoon, a day or two after Willow had asked him to steal her siblings' mementos. As usual, Colby was wearing the fedora and sunglasses he wore year-round to protect himself from the sun.

– Tancred Palmieri! he said.

– It's not nice to stalk people, said Tancred.

– I hear you, man. But I wanted to thank you.

Colby, in his early twenties, was a head shorter than Tancred. He was broad-shouldered with the build of a swimmer, his white eyelashes long. You could tell he was black, but his features were all slightly clouded by whiteness.

– You heading to Dufferin? he asked. I'll walk with you. I want to thank you for buying coffee for Willow. Freud and I try to keep an eye out for her, but Willow's a little difficult, eh?

Tancred said

– It sounds like you want to talk business, Errol, but we don't have business together.

– But we've got things in common, Tan. That's kind of like business. Anyway, I just wanted you to know that you don't have to worry about Willow. I heard you bought her breakfast the other day and I thought, 'That's generous.' But then I thought maybe you think she's your responsibility and I want you to know that's not true. We do a pretty good job taking care of her. How do you think a woman that dresses like Willow and wanders around high doesn't get assaulted every day of the week?

– What do you want me to say? asked Tancred.

– Nothing! I don't want to know anything. I was just wondering what did you and Willow talk about the other day?

– What is it, Errol? Do I look like a reporter?

– I think you've got the wrong idea about me, Tan. Maybe because we've never talked like this, man to man. I'll be honest with you. Willow's good for business. I'd hate to lose her and I like to keep an eye out for her.

They had reached Dufferin and King.

– I didn't do anything for you, said Tancred. You don't owe me anything.

– Well, I'm still grateful. Can I buy you lunch?

– No, said Tancred.

He crossed Dufferin, leaving Colby on his own.

The encounter with Colby made Tancred want to interfere in the man's business, made him want to help Willow Azarian. For one thing, it was dangerous to let hustlers think they could intimidate you. Nothing good could come of it. But shortly after he spoke to Colby, he was encouraged to steal a number of Lamborghinis. And for a while, he was not often home.

Not that he stopped thinking about Willow or about Colby.

There was one stretch in particular: he'd driven one of the Lambos to Vancouver with Olivier and they'd taken the train back. It was the first time they'd spent so long together since they were children. Both of them missed Clémentine and their mood led to thoughtfulness. It was on the train ride home, for instance, that Ollie had confessed his enduring love for Eleanor Bronte, a classmate who'd died when they were in grade school. When Eleanor died, Ollie had ceased to believe in the importance of anything: money, fame, property. After Eleanor, nothing meant what it had meant while she was alive. So, the nine-year-old Ollie had become a nihilist. Not that he knew what nihilism was at the time. It was, rather, that a habit of mind, like a seed, took root in hospitable ground. He was a nihilist still. He was also good-humoured, good-natured and loyal. If you asked him why he was these things, given that he did not believe in anything, he'd answer that it was boring to be foul-tempered, unpleasant and disloyal. As he did not like to be bored, he was what he chose to be. Nothing had value beyond what he provisionally gave it, even life itself.

It was strange to think that the death of a nine-year-old girl had been so influential on his friend's life. Stranger still to think that Eleanor's death was at the heart of what Tancred found admirable in his friend. Though he did not believe in anything, Ollie chose to be who he was. He was loyalty and honour exemplified, and though Tancred could not follow his example – Ollie being eccentric – he'd have done anything for him.

As if he were having similar thoughts, Ollie had asked if he regretted being a thief.

– No, he'd answered.

But his own answer did not satisfy him and, his conscience very much on his mind, he spent hours talking to Ollie about why he stole. And what had it come down to? Why *did* he steal? It was a matter of talent. He was talented. Maybe, in the beginning, he'd wanted attention. Or maybe he'd wanted to rebel, resenting as he had his father's refusal to acknowledge him. But those were all psychologists' excuses, if they were excuses at all, and they were none of his business, because he could not see himself from that angle.

The difficult thing to express was the feeling of it. Though Ollie had helped him steal on a number of occasions, it was not the same. On his own, Ollie would never have stolen anything. He did not feel the exhilaration, the humiliation or even the wanting to be caught. Tancred did. He understood the emotions. But none of those feelings kept him at it. What did was the thrill of getting things right.

It all had to do, no doubt, with how he'd begun. At the age of eleven, Tancred had been taught to pick pockets by Malcolm

Something-or-other, an Englishman, long gone but still the only one of his mother's companions he'd ever liked. Malcolm had learned his trade when he was a boy in Northampton, and he'd made Tancred aware of things like tradition, telling him often about the 'trade' he was passing on.

– You're not the first to do this, he'd say. Remember that.

Over the years it took him to master the art of stealing watches, wallets, passports and such, Tancred had found the idea of a 'trade' helpful. It gave him a sense of belonging. And as he moved on to breaking and entering and then to more targeted theft, the things that interested him most were rightness, doing work flawlessly, and tradition, doing work in the spirit Malcolm had passed on.

– If it's a trade, Ollie asked, how will you know you're good at it?

– When I've done it for as long as I want without being caught, he'd answered.

– Don't tell me you don't like the adrenalin, Tan.

Well, yes, that too.

As he thought about how calm he felt at the rush of adrenalin, Tancred abruptly recalled a photograph he'd found when he broke into the home of a man whose Lambo he'd stolen. The keys to the car had been left on a kitchen counter, right there for the taking. Beside the keys, a picture of a man and a woman. There was no way of knowing if it was their car he'd taken, but the memory reminded him of Errol Colby. He'd felt contempt for the way Colby treated the junkies who came to him, his victims. But how was he, a thief, any better? He simply refused to acknowledge those he stole from, as if he were playing a game to which everyone knew the rules.

– But everyone does know the rules, Ollie said. Nothing's permanent. You can't take anything with you. Why worry about cars?

Tancred had thought this way himself at one time. It now felt too convenient.

– Because they choose to worry about them, Ollie, he said.

– Too bad for them, said Ollie

as the train moved past brush and skinny trees like it had something urgent on its mind.

The next time Tancred spoke to Willow was the very evening he returned from B.C. He'd got a boneless chicken curry with a 'buss-up shut' from Ali's and he was walking home along Cowan. The street was its usual self: scruffy and untrustworthy at Queen, gradually more genteel as one walked toward the lake.

As he went by Masaryk Park – a patch of grass that sometimes had outpatients and junkies for decoration – he saw Willow sitting on the steps of St. John's Cathedral. She was sitting alone, staring straight ahead. She did not acknowledge him. So, he'd decided to leave her to her reverie when she called his name.

– I thought you'd forgotten about me, she said.

Before he could explain his absence, she began to tell him about Oshun.

It was a strange non sequitur, but Tancred had been moved. It was not only that Willow remembered the portrait of Oshun in his living room or that talk of the goddess brought memories of his mother – a Christian who'd delighted in stories of the goddess. It was that Willow seemed to know a good deal about Oshun: myths, folklore and all. He himself knew little. So, he'd sat with her and listened – the two of them on the steps of the church as the sun set. They even shared his buss-up shut, though Willow ate so little that, in the end, there was more than enough for another meal.

She did not mention inheritances or the screen her father had left her. So, it occurred to Tancred that she'd forgotten about them. And who knows, perhaps she had. It's always difficult to say what's on a junkie's mind, aside from junk. Yet here was one whose mind he could admire. Willow was brilliant, despite her sickness, despite her self-destruction.

He wondered why she had surrendered comfort and security for heroin.

– Why'd you start using? he asked.

Meaning: why would someone like you – wealthy, favoured, cultured – choose to live in such a terrible corner of hell? The answer was, naturally, complicated, but not so complicated that he could not understand.

4 A Task Accepted

The worst of it, when Willow was younger, was being told how fortunate she was, how thankful she should be, despite the death of her mother. She had been blessed with intelligence and beauty and wealth. She did realize, didn't she, that she'd been blessed? And she would say 'yes' and bow her head and accept the condescending praise she got for her good manners. It was almost a relief to grow up thin, with a mild case of scoliosis that gave her body a slight but noticeably eccentric curve. She moved from the realm of the beautiful to that of the 'elegant' – a realm of fashion, education and silence, things she at least aspired to master.

From early childhood, Willow had felt herself judged, held to standards that had nothing to do with her. Her parents warned them that, because they had money, they would be treated differently, that people would have unspoken and, occasionally, strange expectations of them. Her siblings, each in his or her own way, managed to deal with the feeling on their own, but Willow found foreign substances helped best. She began drinking and smoking from the age of twelve. She was discreet, always, where alcohol was concerned. But there was no great need for discretion with cigarettes. Her father smoked and was only dutifully annoyed when he discovered his youngest was a smoker, too.

In those days, Willow's most persistent habit was discretion. She found ways to hide her drinking and its effects. It was only when she drank heroic amounts that her intoxication was noticeable and, even then, she kept quiet and, mostly, to herself. Drink was not a means of losing her inhibitions. It was another way of being alone. It was joyless, but it did bring her relief from the feeling of being observed and, for the most part, it allowed her to function. She earned three doctorates while a drunk: Philosophy (summa cum laude with congratulations of the jury, École normale supérieure, 1976), Doctor of Letters (University of Tokyo, 1981), Comparative Literature (summa cum laude, Harvard, 1990). She was not alcoholic, not by her own measure. By her own measure, she was only a drunk – that is, someone who drank to pass out.

It was not until much later, back home and in her forties, that she discovered her drug of choice: heroin. This discovery was a surprise. The first time she'd tried it had been at Harvard. She had snorted it at some gathering or other and it had done nothing much for her, although, admittedly, it had not been as annoying as cocaine or meth, both of which tasted like laboratories felt. But the first time she shot it, heroin was like discovering that a legendary panacea actually existed. She'd loved it at once: the euphoria and its afterglow, the clean taste it left in the mind, the liberation from thoughts about looks, station, fears and neurosis. Yes, the things she loved – languages, philosophy – faded, too, but that was to be expected and, besides, it was tolerable to lose something when you gained such a pleasing alternative.

Willow could have remained a stay-at-home user. Her money allowed her that choice. Moreover, the first time she shot up had been with one of her mother's friends, Mrs. Fraser, a woman in her seventies who only ever used at home.

Strange moment: she had visited Mrs. Fraser and had, as she did when she was being discreet, turned down an old and rare whisky, when Mrs. Fraser brought out a black leather pouch with what looked to be a gold zipper. In the pouch was all the woman's paraphernalia: rubbing alcohol and cotton batten, sterile needles, a World War II naphtha lighter, a silver plunger, a silver spoon and long silk scarves to tie off an arm or leg. She was old-fashioned. She cooked her shots with citric acid. And she believed that silver, having medicinal properties, was good for her arthritis.

– I'm feeling a little flushed, Mrs. Fraser had said. I apologize for my manners. Would you like to join me?

Willow politely admitted that she had never shot heroin, though she had tried it.

– Oh, it's not the same when you sniff it, dear, said Mrs. Fraser. Let me show you.

With little more fuss or nerves than if she'd been serving ginger snaps, though with more precision, Mrs. Fraser herself had prepared a shot for Willow, using a disposable needle and plunger she kept for guests.

The afternoon was odd, its pieces not quite consonant: Mrs. Fraser's makeup – too much rouge, a skin-tone face powder that stopped at her neck so that paleness began at her neckline; the smell of an aggressively floral perfume; the way Mrs. Fraser's hands shook as she prepared Willow's needle; the feel of the living room – wall-to-wall white carpet, indigo-and-orange drapery, indigo sofa and armchair; an impression of pink or pinkishness; and then, while she was high, Mrs. Fraser's talk of redecoration, a subject that seemed to come up again and again, though really, Mrs. Fraser must have mentioned something about wallpaper or throw rugs once or maybe twice and Willow's mind had taken it in and held it so that, along with the ecstasy, there were thoughts about furniture.

Willow's introduction to the ritual of shooting up was unusual, but only slightly. There were not many like Mrs. Fraser, it's true. For one thing, few addicts – wealthy or otherwise – were as old, and very few old women were as open about their habit. Rarer still: those willing to share their paraphernalia and their heroin. It made Willow wonder if Mrs. Fraser had recognized something in her. On the other hand, Rosedale, where she and Mrs. Fraser lived, had at least as many addicts as Parkdale. They were better sequestered, but if you were a member of 'society,' as Willow had been, you were bound to know one or two. Though she was grateful for the introduction to junk, Willow no more wanted to shoot up with Mrs. Fraser than she would have wanted to shoot up with her own mother.

For years, she shot up in her Rosedale home, alone and in private. Her habit grew, but her discretion was such that, she imagined, few knew of her addiction. In fact, her family did know she was an addict. What they did not know was the extent of her addiction. She was careful to be herself – an innocuous version of herself – in their company. So, her discretion was at least partially effective. At her father's death, however, everything changed. Rosedale, her home, became a torment. All of it reminded her of him and she could not bear to be there – not even in her own house – when she was not high.

Which is where Errol Colby came in.

– No, we're not close in *that* way, said Willow

answering a question Tancred had not even thought to ask.

Willow had never been much interested in sexual congress of any sort. This was not said as warning to Tancred or as an excuse for what some called her coldness. Her libido had been low long before junk squelched it. She supposed that she was heterosexual. When she was much younger, she had been aroused by men. She was not aroused, in that way, by women. At least, not that she knew of. But, given her lack of interest in sex, the thought of an emotionally hectic union – billing, cooing, pecking – filled her with indifference.

She had never been in love, but this thought in no way saddened her. On the contrary, Willow found it amusing that she had devoted so many years to the study of literature – novel after novel, poem after poem – devoted to the thing she had never known nor much desired: romantic love. This did not stop her from being curious about Tancred's emotional life. On a couple of occasions, she'd asked if he'd ever been in love.

– I have been, but I'm not in love now, he'd answered.

But Tancred, as a matter of principle, never spoke of such things to anyone but Daniel or Olivier, and even then rarely. His discretion was a way of protecting the one he loved. He supposed it was old-fashioned, but he believed in the sanctity of love. Not only love but also the feeling, ever-different, that exists between two who might fall in love. He did not like to read fiction or poetry for this very reason. He had never found a work that spoke of the feeling with dignity. Most were a desecration of it, save *The Divine Comedy* – read at the behest of a woman he was seeing – which was sublime but over-the-top. It had been more entertaining, reading Dante, to imagine the circle of Hell he, a thief, would occupy: the eighth, with its snakes, ashes and humiliation. All that for taking toys from grown men!

No, with Nigger, Willow continued, it was all about the pharmaceuticals. Whoever his supplier, Nigger's junk was – at least in her experience – clean. Then, too, he treated her with respect. Yes, it was because she had money. But why should his motives matter to her?

In the beginning – that is, not long after her father's death – she would take taxis to Parkdale, get off at King and Jameson and walk up to the Dolphin. In those days, she dressed normally – that is, normal for Rosedale. Not a good idea, as people either mistook her for a social worker or called her a Dickless Tracy to her face. She then, briefly, dressed down. This was worse, as it drew the attention of drunks or men who wanted to fuck her. It was then she decided to wear her mother's clothes – that is, the fashion from her mother's youth. A variety of old-fashioned duds, day after day, a uniform of sorts. The clothes attracted attention, but most of those who saw her in, say, her black dress, elbow-length black gloves and a plumed hat assumed she was either 'artistic' or 'touched': not wealthy, not a worthwhile mark. She added to the impression of eccentricity by openly talking about her addiction. This was surprisingly effective. You could almost feel the cool breeze as people turned away. And once Parkdale knew who she was (or imagined it did), it left her alone. She would shoot up in the washroom at Bacchus or Ali's – plastic spoon, cotton batten, needle from PharmaPlus – and then, if she was able, stumble to the lake to zone out. More than once, she'd passed out on a bench and woken in the dark, the murmuring lake before her, the shushing expressway behind.

That's not to say she was never bothered. She was still a woman, after all. She'd had her purse stolen – grabbed in passing so they nearly took her arm off. She'd been screamed at by aggressive outpatients from Queen Street Mental. She'd been knocked into the street by people who'd have crushed her without qualms. But here, too, Nigger was helpful. As long as she was around him or Freud, people left her alone or paid immediately for bothering her. Freud, in particular, liked to hit. He was happy to sit with her at the Dolphin and quick to take offence on her behalf.

(Tancred said

– Freud's your knight in shining armour?

– No, *you're* my knight in shining armour, she said.

She was joking, but the idea – which she must, to some extent, have believed – made Tancred uncomfortable.)

Nigger, Freud, the lake, the Dolphin, the greengrocers at Queen and Jameson where she could buy sugary Indian sweets, the Coffee Time at O'Hara: these were the reasons she preferred Parkdale to Rosedale. Nothing about the neighbourhood reminded her of her father or of home. The faces, the languages she sometimes heard spoken, the accents, the slightly seedy buildings from Queen and Roncy to Queen and Dufferin – all of it reminded her, more than anything else, of somewhere south, of Key West or Freeport or Havana. At least, in summer. In winter, Parkdale was unpleasant. In winter, she preferred Rosedale, but she made the trek anyway, spending hours in the dog's mouth that was the Dolphin with its heat on – or, once the police shut the Dolphin down, hours in the Skyline.

Getting to know Willow as Tancred did – that is, in short bursts, from just before the Green Dolphin closed to sometime after Rob Ford's election – seeing her decline, her skin growing sallow as it clung to her skull – it was inevitable that he would come to mourn her passing: a brilliant woman with a sickness that left her incapacitated for long stretches, a sickness that sometimes brought out the worst of her and ate away at her already-meagre body. On those occasions when he imagined her passed out on a bench or sitting in the doorway to some business on Queen, he preferred to think that her soul had flown while the chemicals did to her whatever it was they did. But the thought of what she might have been troubled him less and less as he strove to accept the woman she actually was.

Days after their meeting by Masaryk Park, Willow asked him to come with her to an address on Chestnut Park in Rosedale. It being

Sunday, Tancred found the request inconvenient, but he went along, thinking she needed help with some domestic chore and that it could, whatever it was, be done quickly.

The address in question was Willow's, though she seemed ill at ease in her own home. The house was, for Rosedale, modest. A hedge formed a rectangle around a bit of lawn, a rectangle bisected by stone steps that led up to a landing. Between the top of the steps and the house there was a larger patch of lawn on which, to one side of the house, an ash tree sustained a cloud of leaves while, to the other, a dogwood – its trunk forked – shaded part of Willow's house as well as her neighbour's front walk.

Willow's house was three storeys high with what looked like a gabled attic on the top floor. All the windows seemed to be French, their slats painted white. The dark brick walls were partially hidden by ivy that ran up to the two chimneys, one on each side of the house. The entrance to the house did not face the street. It was on the side, hidden from view.

Tancred had the unpleasant feeling that he'd once broken into this very place. Each step toward the house gave him déjà vu.

– I apologize for the mess, Willow said as they entered.

But it was a peculiar kind of mess. The house was immaculate and smelled of nothing in particular. Yes, the kitchen was like a room lived in by transients. There were pots and pans about. There were empty containers here and there: boxes that had held chocolate bars, boxes that had held doughnuts, containers of Häagen-Dazs. But even the kitchen was oddly antiseptic, there being no sign of anything organic or rotten. The rest of the house was elegant. That, in any case, was the word that came to Tancred's mind, *elegant*. The floors were a polished, blond hardwood. There was very little furniture: Quakerish tables and chairs in the dining room, a single, ghost-blue sofa in the living room, no curtains or drapes anywhere, the windows spotless, the walls white and, from the look of them, recently painted.

– So, said Willow

pointing to the screen that stood facing the sofa

– Do you believe me now?

It was a moment before Tancred realized what she was referring to. Here was the six-panelled screen, one of the supposed clues to something or other, left to his children by a father playing games from beyond the grave.

The screen was beautiful and no doubt valuable in and of itself. It was some five feet tall and, when opened out, twelve feet wide. Its backing was thick, light-apricot-tinted paper. The front of it, a painting of willows by a bridge, was so well done that, when the screen was at its widest, the breaks between four of the panels were barely visible, unless you knew where to look. Five of the panels – thick paper – were done with black ink, coloured ink and gold leaf. The sixth and final panel was willow wood.

Had the screen been an original from sixteenth- or seventeenth-century Japan, it would have been invaluable. As authentic as it looked, however, it was not meant to deceive, not meant to pass for genuine. It was not flawed. It was what it was deliberately. But what was it, exactly? An exquisitely done memento? A work whose meaning was playfully obscure? Having seen the screen for himself, Tancred at last understood Willow's certainty that there was more to it than one could easily figure out.

– Now that you've seen this one, said Willow, will you steal the others?

– Won't your brothers and sisters be angry? asked Tancred.

Willow ignored this and, instead, went to get something from the kitchen: a circular, covered tin that had once held Royal Dansk butter cookies.

– Here are the others, she said.

Inside the tin there were four photographs, one of each of her siblings' mementos: a bottle, a painting, a poem, a model of Frank Lloyd Wright's Fallingwater.

– Now you know what you're looking for, said Willow, promise you'll do this for me.

The hepatitis that would kill her was beginning to do its worst. Willow's face was sallow, gaunt and frightening. The disease was changing her into an emaciated, waxlike version of herself. It was partly for this that Tancred promised to do what she asked. He felt pity. The other reason was that he did not believe there was any money or treasure to be found. He did not believe a proper businessman would deliberately bury millions of dollars – or anything of great value. Not on a whim. A treasure hunt, whatever else you might call it, was a whim. So, to his mind, he was doing this for Willow, doing something to bring her peace, a kindness to one who was in need of kindness.

He gave his word.

He agreed to steal the four other mementos.

He agreed to try to work out the significance of each.

He agreed to return the mementos to Willow's siblings along with most of anything he and Willow might find.

– You'll get my share, she said.

– You'd give me your inheritance? asked Tancred.

– There's nothing I need, said Willow. This isn't about gain, Tancred. I just want to know I'm right about Dad hiding something. I want to know what's hidden and I want to know why. That's all. I know you, Tancred. Even if you are a thief, you've got principles. I want you to promise me you'll take my share of whatever you find. And promise you'll give the rest to my brothers and sisters.

When he thought about her words, later, it seemed pointedly significant that she made him promise to take her share, as if she'd known she would not be around to see it. Whatever the case, he'd agreed to this, too. He again gave his word.

5 The Japanese Screen

It was odd to think of a death like Willow's as unexpected. Tancred had seen her gradually shrink into a sere version of herself. Of all the people he knew, she had been for some time the one most likely to die without warning. Yet, her death was a kind of surprise, because it interrupted the task they'd begun.

Shortly after showing him the Japanese screen, Willow had it moved to a loft she'd rented for him, a place bigger than his own where they could meet. There, late at night, Tancred – alone or with Willow – stared at the screen, breaking it down in his mind to its constituent elements, trying to find some hidden sense in it:

> – wood (from a willow tree)
> – gold leaf
> – inks (black and coloured)
> – dimensions when open: 5 feet x 12 feet x 4 inches
> – dimensions when closed: 5 feet x 2 feet x 2 feet
> – numbers associated with it: 5, 12, 6, 2, 137
> – names associated with it: *Willows at the Uji Bridge,*
> *Salix Babylonica*
> – biblical reference: Psalm 137 'By the rivers of Babylon …'
> – on the wood behind the sixth panel, the letters 'a(ɯ)'
> thickly printed in black

Tancred felt ridiculous peering at the screen's panels, searching for meaning. He had no idea which aspects of the thing signified and which did not. After a while, he left the speculating to Willow, though her words – those he took in – were not enlightening.

– There must be something important about Babylon, she'd whisper.

or

– Could he have meant Iraq?

Instead, Tancred did what he knew best: he prepared to steal the reproduction of Fallingwater from Willow's sister Gretchen and the painting from her sister Simone. Willow advised him to steal trivial things along with the memento, so as to disguise his (or, rather, her) intent. And, of course, he should work as efficiently as possible, so they could examine all five together before, as she herself put it, her health worsened.

Here, there was what Willow called a 'caveat' – an important detail is what she meant. It seemed Michael's bottle of aquavit would be very difficult to steal. He lived in Castle Rose, an exclusive, reputedly burglar-proof building on the lakeshore. Tancred had heard of the place, though he knew it as the 'Hidden Castle.' Though Willow had visited Michael, she could tell Tancred neither the number of Michael's condominium nor the floor on which it was to be found. Her only clue to its whereabouts – the only clue she herself possessed – was that Michael's neighbour was a one-legged military man who insisted on being called Colonel. Michael despised him. Aside from that, neither she nor anyone else had the least idea how to find Michael's place.

And here, too, there was a lure. Willow had already begun her own inquiry. In the time between their first meeting and now, she had discovered a few things: a possible solution that led, perhaps, to a cemetery, and the meaning of the 'a(ш)' on the back of the screen. This was the only detail she shared with him, because she was proud of herself. But she had found nothing else of which she was certain and she did not want to pollute his mind with her guesses. First thought, best thought, she believed. She wanted his first thought, when all the mementos were finally gathered together. Only then would she share the rest of her ideas with him.

Unfortunately, Willow's health worsened faster than either of them thought it would. Or, to put it another way, what had been a long time coming came at last. Her glacially paced suicide was finally accomplished, hastened in the end by a vicious pneumonia. Tancred saw her a week or so before he broke into Gretchen's home. She was anxious that everything go right.

– Remember, she said, take other things. But don't take anything too valuable!

She gave him money 'for your expertise and your expenses.' Twenty thousand dollars in hundreds – cash, so the two of them could not be linked by cheques or transfers. If anything went wrong, she would deny having anything to do with him. She'd have to. It would be too humiliating to admit to Alton, her eldest brother, that she'd stolen from them. She simply could not. She was sorry. She was very sorry, but Alton must not know.

Willow closed her purse and, referring to the twenty thousand she'd just given him, said

– It's awkward carrying around so much paper.

They agreed to meet after he'd stolen Fallingwater or Simone's painting. She got up to leave.

– I'm grateful you're doing this, she said. I'll see you in a few days.

But Tancred never saw Willow Azarian again.

CHAPTER TWO

FALLINGWATER

Mrs. Gretchen Azarian-Grau was embarrassed, it seemed, to have called the police. From the moment Detective Mandelshtam entered her home, she was apologetic. She and her eldest daughter, Adele, had prepared an afternoon tea for him – Moroccan mint tisane, butter cookies, wildflower honey. After he made a show of dusting for prints – not straightforward, because ashes had spilled from an urn and besmirched the living room – they both entreated him so earnestly to have tea that Mandelshtam accepted so as not to hurt their feelings.

Much had been done to spare their feelings. To begin with, a uniformed officer would usually have been dispatched, not a detective. Although, to be fair, Daniel Mandelshtam, twenty-eight years old, had only recently been promoted to detective. So, this, a low-level assignment, was a good way of easing him in. Then again, an officer would not normally have dusted for prints when so little was at stake. But he had been told to dust. The Azarians were well-to-do and well-connected, and he'd been sent as a favour to someone or other. Though he did not resent the assignment, he was slightly wary of the women before him.

The Azarian-Grau house on Lowther – not far from Avenue Road – had been burgled. As they were in the Annex, you could not call burglary unusual. The neighbourhood was largely middle-class with, here and there, pockets of the upper and upper-middle in renovated Victorians or renovated Georgians or strange hybrids meant to look stately. The Azarian-Graus were in one such pocket. Their house was big, old and impeccably renovated: red-brick exterior, teal doors and window frames, its antique and modern elements in harmony.

The house had been robbed twice previously and the Azarian-Graus had learned their lesson. Their valuables – documents, jewellery – were hidden in a safe in the master bedroom where Gretchen, a widow, slept on her own. The door to her room was thick and had a simple and effective lock. Their alarm system was new and, they'd been assured, trustworthy. So, it was disheartening to discover they'd been robbed a third time.

Having shown Detective Mandelshtam the alarm system – which the thieves had shut off, both women were certain of it, as they infallibly turned the system on every night at eleven – Gretchen came to the point.

– The thing is, Detective, Adele and I searched through the house and there's almost nothing missing. They took two laptops and a model of Lloyd Wright's Fallingwater. But nothing really valuable.

– That's not the point, Mother, said Adele.

She was exasperated.

– Whoever it was broke in at night when we were home. It could have turned out so much worse! And who knows if they're going to come back?

Detective Mandelshtam was sitting in the armchair that had been offered him. He was holding a teacup in one hand, an unbitten cookie between the thumb and forefinger of the other. He now found himself looking up at the two women, mother and daughter coming toward him as each made her case. Adele, a woman in her thirties, by the look of it, was holding a silver tray on which a white teapot, a clear-glass honey pot with its amber honey spoon, and a white sugar bowl stood. Gretchen, who was in in her sixties, though she looked much younger, held aloft a blue plate on which there were more cookies. Seeing the cookie plate and the tea tray moving toward him, like barges converging, Mandelshtam held up his cup and cookie, wordlessly indicating his satisfaction with what he had, and said

– When did you notice anything was missing?

– As soon as we came downstairs this morning, said Gretchen. Miou-Miou's ashes were all over. Fallingwater was gone and so were our laptops.

– And so was the toaster, said Adele.

– Yes, that's true, said Gretchen, so was the toaster. But we found the toaster in the alleyway.

– That doesn't mean it wasn't stolen, Mother!

– I'm sorry, said Mandelshtam, but what is 'Fallingwater'?

– Fallingwater? said Gretchen. It's a house by Frank Lloyd Wright.

– He means, said Adele, Grandfather's *model* of Fallingwater. Don't you, Detective?

– Yes, I guess I do, said Mandelshtam.

– We keep it on the mantelpiece, right here, said Adele. You can't miss it being gone. It was big and strange-looking.

– It wasn't strange-looking, said Gretchen. It was silvery because it was made from titanium and niobium.

– It *was* strange-looking, Detective. I'm sure you'd agree. We only kept it in the living room because Mother's so attached to it.

– I'm attached to it the way you're attached to the cat's ashes. And I *told* you that urn was going to fall.

– Could you tell me about the model? asked Mandelshtam.

– Oh, well, said Gretchen, there's a bit of a story to it. Do you mind?

Detective Mandelshtam did not mind, though the story began a little further back in time than he might have wished.

Mrs. Azarian-Grau – who preferred to be called Gretchen – had had a wonderful childhood. She'd been especially fond of her mother who had, poor woman, died tragically young. Her family – that is, her father and her four siblings – grew closer after her mother's death. If there was any good to be taken from the long agony her mother suffered, it was this mournful solidarity her family might not otherwise have shared. It goes without saying, of course, that they would all have surrendered even the most blessed of solidarities to have more time with their mother, whose portrait, by the way, was on the mantel in the living room.

Mandelshtam politely regarded the framed photograph. It was taken in the fifties, from the look of it, and somewhere in Yorkville. Mrs. Azarian was not smiling but not at all dour. Something of her warmth and humour was in her eyes, her long lashes, her white coat and the playful sombrero whose rim she held up so you could see her face. Blond in black and white, she was unmistakably Adele's forebear and Gretchen's mother.

When Gretchen was twenty-one, she'd not yet chosen a profession. Her father, Robert, thought her brilliant. He would have liked her to help him run Azarian Holdings. He'd taught her about business at the same time as he'd taught her older brother, Alton, and she'd been able to read a financial report from the age of eleven. But Gretchen wanted a profession in which she could express her own creativity. And she had options. She excelled in music and photography. But though she played the oboe exceedingly well, for instance, she could not imagine a life spent playing the music of others and she felt no urge to write her own. So, though she was infatuated with music, she turned down a scholarship to Julliard. The same hitch prevented her from pursuing photography. She felt no need to do it.

Then, one day, she found one of her younger brother's books lying open on the kitchen table. The book was oversized, beautifully bound, filled with striking photographs. It was devoted to the life, ideas and work of Frank Lloyd Wright. Gretchen could remember the pages at which the book lay open: 105 and 106, two impressive photos of the Great Workroom of the Johnson Wax Headquarters, with its so-called lily pads and columns and natural light. Seeing them, Gretchen knew at once she wanted to be an architect. In fact, as she looked through the book – which she begged Michael to give her and which for years she kept by her bedside – it seemed so obvious she was meant to be an architect that she felt almost foolish not to have realized this until faced with Lloyd Wright's exquisite work.

Her father was disappointed. He tried to dissuade her from architecture. It was a difficult profession, he said, one rife with treacherous competition. The most successful architects were not necessarily innovative or creative. They were the ones who gave the client what the client wanted, and most of the clients she encountered would be men who preferred vapid grandiosity to the play of form and light. Besides which, though he did not mind paying for schooling any of his children, he suspected that paying for her to become an architect would be like throwing his money down a well while wasting her time.

For months she pleaded with him and for months he refused to answer the simplest questions about her future. Then, when she had begun to make her own plans, looking into the prerequisites for admission to MIT (where another of her idols, Marion Mahony Griffin, had studied) and casting about for work that would pay for the tuition, her father asked her to accompany him and Alton to Pittsburgh where, he said, he needed intelligent advice on a delicate matter. She went with them but with a single purpose: to convince her father to support her in her desire to be an architect.

During the trip to Pennsylvania, her father refused to talk about architecture. Whenever she brought the matter up, he changed the subject, speaking instead about the business he'd brought them along to help him resolve – something to do with zoning laws and deciding if a certain real estate agent was or was not trustworthy. By the time they landed in Pittsburgh, Gretchen felt humiliated, barely able to look at her father. The agent in question picked them up in a Lincoln Continental. The car radio was tuned to some vacuous station that played the hits like 'Dizzy' – a song Gretchen still associated with anguish – until she asked the man to turn it off. Which he did, thus nurturing the dull talk that went on and on as they drove into the heart of a late-spring countryside.

By the time the car stopped in the middle of the woods, Gretchen was so relieved to get out and walk she scarcely took in the surroundings. The agent preceded them down a winding path. Then her father called her to his side while Alton and the agent went on ahead.

Suddenly solemn, her father said

– Gretchen, I love you very much.

He was not one to overuse the word *love* – at least, not around her – so she was taken aback.

— Whatever you want in this life, he continued, I want for you. Of course I'll support you if you want to be an architect. I just wanted to know you were serious.

Though she found this change confusing, she was almost immediately ecstatic. She hugged her father and they walked arm in arm along a beaten path further into the woods, the sound of water growing louder, the smell of spring overpowering. And it was as they came to a short bridge over a river that she finally understood where they were: Fallingwater, the house designed by Lloyd Wright! It was as if they had walked into the pages of Michael's book: the cantilevered terraces, the steps down to the river, the house descending by stages into the woods.

She wept that day and she wept again some forty years later as she recounted the moment to Detective Mandelshtam, the moment she began to think of herself as the architect she eventually became. Adele put her arm around her mother's shoulders and the two were quiet.

— So, said Mandelshtam, your father left you a model of Fallingwater. Was it valuable?

— Well, said Gretchen, it has great sentimental value and it's unique. But if you mean how much did it cost to make … I'm not sure, Detective. Maybe hundreds for the material. It was titanium and …

— Mother, said Adele, it was mostly titanium. The craftsmanship. That's what would have been expensive. I told you, you should have had it evaluated.

— I understand you lost something of personal value, said Mandelshtam, but …

— No, no, said Gretchen, this is why I hesitated to call you, Detective. Would you like another cookie? I'm going to have to talk about my family again. You see, my poor sister, Willow, died a week ago.

— She was a heroin addict, said Adele.

— She was my *sister*, said Gretchen, and I loved her. I won't have you saying unpleasant things about her. Yes, Detective, my sister was an addict. It wasn't a complete surprise that she died when she did. But she was a talented woman, much more intelligent than I could hope to be. Honestly, Adele, you have no business speaking of her like that to a stranger.

– I didn't mean anything unpleasant, said Adele. I loved Aunt Will as much as anyone, but she was an addict. The detective should know.

Mother and daughter sat side by side on the sofa, facing Mandelshtam. One really could not have taken them for anything but relatives: both of them blond with brown eyes and slightly hooked noses, both obviously fit and, one might say, defiantly unashamed of it. On this day they were dressed similarly as well, with one colourful difference: Gretchen wore a silk kerchief from Hermès, its border light blue.

– I wonder, said Mandelshtam, if we could get back to the things that have been stolen.

– Willow, said Adele, has something to do with what's been stolen.

– She might, said Gretchen. My father left each of his five children a memento, something to remember him by, in his will. He left Willow a lovely Japanese screen. Alton got a poem. I got a model of Fallingwater. I can't remember what Simone got. Oh yes, a painting. And Michael got a bottle of alcohol. Willow thought the mementos father left us were clues to some fortune or other. Sometimes she thought they were clues to money and sometimes they were clues to Lord-knows-what. To be fair, Detective, my father *wanted* Willow to think this. He thought the game would distract her from her addiction. You'd have to know my sister to know why this makes sense. You see, once Willow got an idea in her head ...

– That's why it's important for the detective to know about Aunt Will, Mother. So he has an idea of the kind of people Aunt Will talked to. We all know why Grandfather did what he did, but her addict friends wouldn't. They might take the treasure business seriously.

– Yes, yes, said Gretchen. Who knows to whom she told her story. I haven't thought about any of this too deeply, Detective. We knew there was no treasure, so none of us took the treasure hunt seriously. But when we went to Willow's home, Adele and I, and the screen wasn't in her living room where she always kept it, we both noticed. And we looked for it. I wanted to have it in memory of my father and my sister. But we didn't find it. That was two days ago now.

– Could she have sold it or given it away? asked Mandelshtam.

– She wouldn't have, said Adele. My aunt would never have sold her screen.

– My daughter's right, said Gretchen. Willow treasured that screen the way I treasured Fallingwater. It can't be a coincidence that both mementos are gone or that mine was stolen so soon after Willow died. What I think, Detective, is that Adele is right. Willow didn't always choose the best company and she never made a secret of her ideas.

– She was probably too stoned to keep a secret, said Adele.

Gretchen put a hand on her daughter's leg.

– Willow used to tell us about the places she frequented. 'Dives' is what we called them, in my day. And if some desperate person believed her about the things Father left us being clues, it wouldn't have taken much to find out where we live. Willow herself might have told them. In monetary terms, Detective, it wouldn't be a big loss if our mementos were stolen. None of us would suffer financially, but it's an invasion and, speaking for myself, I really resent losing this connection to my father.

Detective Mandelshtam rose from the armchair, brushing cookie crumbs from his jacket.

– That's an interesting story, he said. Have any of the other mementos been stolen?

– No, said Gretchen. I don't even know that Willow's screen was stolen. It's not where it was. That's all. But now that mine is gone, it set off bells.

– I understand, said Mandelshtam. We'll do what we can. I will say this looks like fairly competent work. Not the kind of thing you'd expect from heroin addicts. And, to be honest, I don't think we'll recover your model.

– You're not very encouraging, said Adele.

– I didn't want to call the police at all, said Gretchen. No offence, Detective, but I told my daughter, 'What can they do? What's gone is gone.' It's sad to have lost something my father left me. It makes me miss him even more. But when you get to my age you accept that things will go their own way. I really don't understand why anyone would take it, though. I suppose it was unusual. It was made of titanium and niobium. The titanium was pure and it would have been hard to work with, but the model wasn't worth a lot of money. Whoever stole it went through a lot of bother for very little. The paintings in the dining room are worth much more.

– I didn't mean to be discouraging, said Mandelshtam. But I try not to give people false hope. There's minimal chance we'll recover your things, unless we catch someone trying to sell them. But, out of curiosity, if you don't mind: do you think your father was the kind of man to leave money to be discovered?

– Absolutely not, said Gretchen. If there was a chance we wouldn't find it, he would have been horrified at the waste. At the idea of it. My father's parents were well-off, but they were always frugal. I think he would have died rather than waste money.

Adele said

– On the other hand, my granddad had a great sense of humour, Detective. You could never tell what he was up to.

– He had a sense of humour, said Gretchen, but not about money.

– One last question, said Mandelshtam. I'd like to know how expensive your model of Fallingwater was. Do you happen to know who made it?

– No, I don't know that, said Gretchen.

– I do! said Adele. Aunt Will found him a while ago. I remember his name because it sounded so grand: Alexander von Würfel. It sounds like a count in exile, someone who'd lived in a ruined castle. When I told Aunt Will that, she laughed at me.

Gretchen put a hand to her mouth, suddenly upset.

– I'm sorry, she said. My sister had such a lovely laugh.

2 Von Würfel's Animals and Birds

Much like his friend Tancred, Daniel Mandelshtam did not like family stories. Something about them reminded him of dreams – fascinating to the dreamer, dreary for anyone else. But the Azarian-Grau story had been unexpectedly interesting or, at least, puzzling. A treasure hunt to distract a heroin addict? A strange idea and, as the addict in question had died, of questionable merit.

Then, too, there was the burglary. Why would a professional – one who'd left no prints and shut off a sophisticated alarm – take on such risk for such poor return? The model of Fallingwater was made of relatively common materials and its significance was so specific it was difficult to imagine anyone hiring a thief to steal it. The laptops were not worth much more unless, of course, they were being mined for information. But why bother to take a toaster and then leave it outside the house? Contrary to what he'd told the Azarian-Graus, that was the mark of amateurs, of drug addicts. The theft left an odd feel in the mind. Was it that a good thief had made a mistake or was it that an incompetent one had inadvertently done almost everything right? Or was it that the front door had been left unlocked, the alarm off, and some opportunist had wandered in and, like a jackdaw, taken a few shiny objects?

He had written up his account, done all the paperwork himself, and yet, days after speaking with the Azarian-Graus, Daniel was still sufficiently intrigued to dig a little. He found out where a certain von Würfel – 'Preserver of Animals and Birds' – had his business and, on a day off, visited the place.

He saw at once why Willow Azarian had been amused by her niece referring to von Würfel as a count. The man's shop was in a dingy little building not far from a 'bike joint' and an establishment called Angst whose sign was in a silvery, gothic script that made it seem like the kind of place Europeans went to be punished. To be fair, the buildings along Queen from Moss Park to Ontario were all a little grimy so that von Würfel's shop – Von Würfel's Animals and Birds by name – did not stick out until you saw its unusual display window – a tallow candle dimly burning in it, surrounded by a muddle of objects vaguely resembling pieces of leather and dry stick, fronted by two preserved frogs fighting a small-sword duel.

The inside of the shop was unexpected, in that it was so different from its display window. For one thing, it was well-lit by banks of fluorescent lights that hung from its high ceiling. Its walls were a pleasing celadon. Or, rather, what you could see was celadon. The colour was obscured by shelving that was screwed into the walls themselves. On the shelves was a wide array of glass containers filled with gel or some vitreous fluid that magnified the animals (or animal skeletons) floating within: parrots, falcons, mice, shrews, lemmings, squirrels. All on the upper shelves. On some of the lower shelves there were aquaria – filled with the same or similar liquid – in which cats or dogs or (in one instance) a monkey were suspended.

The shop was both eerie and fascinating, the animals all – from shrew to monkey – as if caught in moments of pleasure or enterprise.

– Can I help you?

The question was asked by a young woman in a bright green dress.

– Is Mr. von Würfel in? asked Daniel.

– I think he's in the back, she said. Did you bring your pet with you or is it not dead yet?

Then, seeing that Daniel looked baffled, she motioned toward the shelves.

– Most of these are people's pets, she said. Instead of doing old-school taxidermy, my dad turns them into works of art. Don't you agree?

– They look … striking, said Daniel. But I really came to speak to Mr. von Würfel.

– Oh, okay, said the girl. I'll get him.

Mr. von Würfel was, in his way, as eccentric as his shop. He was a tall man – six feet three or four – and portly. He stooped slightly and his hands moved constantly as he spoke. The frame of his glasses was black-rimmed, thick, rectangular. A man in his seventies by the look of it, he dressed as if he were younger – plaid shirt, blue jeans – while grey stubble made his chin and cheeks look prickly. He walked as if he'd had a mild stroke or, perhaps, polio when he was a child.

– May I help you? he asked.

Von Würfel? The man's accent was English and his voice was soft.

– Are you Alexander von Würfel, the artist? asked Daniel.

– Yes, I am an artist, said von Würfel, and my medium is pets. As you can see, we give you so much more than a painting or photograph of your domestic companion. With my method, they're captured lifelike and – I'm sure you'll agree – happy. May I ask what your pet happens to be? For obvious reasons, we do not do Great Danes. Or, we do, but I discourage it.

– I'm sorry, said Daniel, I'm afraid I haven't made myself clear. What I meant to ask was if, in the past, you've made models or sculpture. I'm specifically asking about a model of Fallingwater by Frank Lloyd Wright.

– Oh, I see, said von Würfel. In the past, one has done a great many things, but one doesn't do these things anymore. I am seventy and my eyesight is failing. But I've done Fallingwater. Yes, I have.

– Do you mind if I ask you a few questions?

– I don't mind, said von Würfel, but I'm going to disappoint you. I no longer do painting or sculpture. I haven't done for quite some time.

– What would you say your model of Fallingwater is worth?

– What would I say? I would say it's worth what my client paid.

– I ask, said Daniel, because your work was stolen.

– Was it? said von Würfel. What an interesting development. Are you from the insurance company or the police?

– Detective Mandelshtam, police. But I'm off-duty. If you'd prefer not to talk about this …

– On the contrary! But if you don't mind, I have a workroom in the back. We can speak there and keep out of Sharon's way.

Von Würfel's workroom was different again. Though it was larger than the front room and its ceiling was just as tall, it felt like a more intimate space. At least, it did on first entering. It was well-lit and, at one end, there were two windows that looked out on a backyard with a green lawn. The walls were the same celadon as the front room but here the floor was cement, as opposed to wood. In the centre of the room there was a rectangular silver-metal table. Two large corkboards had been screwed into the walls and painted white. Hanging from pins in the cork were the immaculately maintained and numbered instruments of von Würfel's trade: scissors, callipers, secateurs, eye scoops, gouges, rulers, saws, knives, scalpels, pins, brushes and tweezers.

The room smelled of formaldehyde and vinegar. On a metal table beneath one of the windows, an impressively lifelike beaver looked on as if it were suddenly aware of the men who'd entered the room, as if it had just stopped chewing on something, curious to see what the taxidermist and the detective were up to.

Von Würfel sat in an armchair beneath a second window by the beaver.

– I hope you don't mind, he said. By mid-afternoon, I need a few minutes' rest if I'm to carry on. I want to hear about Fallingwater, though. Who owned it?

– A Mrs. Azarian-Grau, answered Daniel. Didn't you know?

– Why should I know? I made it ten years ago for *Mr.* Azarian. It was made around the same time as I made a painting to his specifications and created a facsimile of a bottle of aquavit for him. Mr. Azarian paid me a great deal of money for all three, but I never knew whom they were for. I assumed they were for him.

– They were for his children, said Daniel.

– Do you know, Detective, I'm not surprised to hear that Fallingwater has been stolen. And if I were you I'd be looking into the whereabouts of Mr. Azarian's daughter, Willow. At least, Willow was the name she gave when she came to ask me about Fallingwater and the bottle of aquavit. The woman was convinced there was some significance to them.

– I'm afraid Willow Azarian is dead.

– No need to be afraid, Detective. We all die. I haven't been feeling well for years. With my blood pressure, it is a miracle I don't fall over this instant. Still, I hope the woman did not meet a violent end. She was ... excitable. Pale and excitable. So, I told her I knew nothing at all about the pieces. Which was true, Detective. I built them to specification, then I forgot about them, until she came to my shop. About three years ago, now.

– So, you don't think there is any covert significance to them?

– I didn't when I made them, Detective. Mr. Azarian told me nothing about those pieces. But now, with you standing there asking me about it, I'm sure they had some significance. And do you know why I think so? Because last year my daughter Taylor finally married a Norwegian. No, that'll sound odd. I mean, she's married at last and to a Norwegian named Espen, and for Christmas he brought us a bottle of aquavit. Have you ever had aquavit, Detective? It's as foul as pigeon feathers! I was being sociable, so I had to drink a mouthful. And I was looking at the label thinking, 'Who do I have to kill to avoid another mouthful?' when I remembered the bottle I'd made for Mr. Azarian. I had a Proustian moment, you see. To make a little conversation, I asked Espen about the label on the bottle. The label's meant to have the date the aquavit left Norway and the date it came back to Norway after crossing the equator twice – once going, once coming. It ages at sea. But Mr. Azarian never had me write in proper dates. He had me write in numbers and he was very firm I should get them right. Well, when I remembered Mr. Azarian telling me to get the numbers right, it struck me as significant. And now you're here asking about it, it's curiouser and curiouser.

– Do you happen to have any idea what the numbers meant?

– No, I haven't. But if someone noticed the numbers on the aquavit, they might have the same thought as Willow did.

– You mean they might think these mementos are clues to something?

– That's my thinking, Detective. Mind you, who's to say they are clues and who's to say what they're clues to? If I were younger, I'd find all of this fascinating. I used to love a good puzzle. But I am old and I find this business only mildly diverting.

The interview with von Würfel had been the worst kind of frustration. Daniel had got no real answer to any pertinent question. His curiosity had been abetted, not satisfied. He was no nearer to finding Mrs. Azarian-Grau's Fallingwater and, worse, he now had grounds to think someone might try to steal the other mementos.

The remaining Azarians would all have been warned about possible burglaries by their sister Gretchen. It was up to them to keep an eye on their possessions. Ah, but what if something happened in the course of a burglary? What if one of the Azarians surprised a thief or thieves and was hurt? He would feel responsible, wouldn't he? It was a dilemma of his own making. He ought not to have gone beyond his responsibilities, ought not to have questioned von Würfel, and he had no business speculating about future predation.

As if all that weren't enough, Daniel also felt a twinge of embarrassment imagining the questions Baruch, his father, might have asked, had he still been alive.

– So, Danny, would you have put yourself out this way – on your day off, even! – if these people had been poor? You're a servant of the wealthy and you don't even know it.

Daniel strove always to live at the height of this question, ever ready to answer it. *Whom did he serve?*

– Whose dog are you?

is how Baruch would have put it. Now that the old man was gone, it was Daniel's way of honouring the memory of a man who – for political and emotional reasons – had not wanted his son to enter the police force.

Though he had been, in most ways, a great father, there'd been times when Baruch's sense of justice had taken precedence over those close to him. He had never been abusive but his disapproval had been painful to his son. The vestiges of that pain were manifest in Daniel's occasional self-doubt. Now, for instance.

No, he would not have put himself out this way had the Azarians been poor. He, a detective, would not have been assigned to the case had the victims been unconnected. Then, too, thieves did not waste their time stealing clues to fortunes from people who lived in government housing. In this instance, Baruch's question was not pertinent. But it still felt as if he were troubling his father's ghost.

Hoping to allay his unhappiness, Daniel decided to walk a ways before going home from von Würfel's shop. It was mid-afternoon, mid-week – his days off falling awkwardly – and the middle of autumn. The streets were busy. The lake was a thing glimpsed from time to time between buildings – fleeting segments of a grey-blue expanse. Reasoning himself into a need for *pain aux raisins*, he decided to walk all the way to Nadège, the patisserie. At Bathurst, he decided to go on to Dufferin before heading home. Why? Because he hadn't seen Tancred, his best friend, for months, duties at 14 Division and at home eating away at his time for friendship. If Tancred was home, they could have a drink together somewhere off East Liberty. If not, he'd still have gotten a good day's walk and he could hop on the Dufferin bus to get himself homeward. On top of that, he would feel virtuous, as he always did, for walking.

So, at Nadège he bought four *pains aux raisins* – one for him, one for Fiona, two for the fridge – a number of croissants and half a dozen macarons before calling Tancred.

– Am I speaking to the black Cary Grant? he said.

– *Miséricorde*, answered Tancred, *c'est les flics!*

– Time for a drink, Tan? I'm about half an hour away.

– I'll come down when you get here.

Daniel did not walk to Dufferin, however. He found it discomfiting to carry his goods in the oversized and showy paper bag from Nadège. He walked to King, climbed onto the King streetcar at Strachan and was at Dufferin in five minutes. Which is why – and the coincidence would trouble him – he was at the corner of King and

Dufferin at the same time as Nigger Colby and Sigismund Luxemberg. That is, as the light was green, he crossed Dufferin, then he crossed King without paying much attention to his surroundings. And there, in front of the bank, the two men were.

Colby was the first to speak.

– Nice to see you, Officer, he said.

Luxemberg looked away so as not to have to say anything. Daniel said

– Nice to see you, Nigger. You still dealing?

– Oh, no, Officer, said Colby. I cannot stand narcotics.

This brought a smirk from the so-called 'Freud.'

While Tancred could not stand to call Errol Colby 'Nigger,' Daniel – who felt sorry for Colby and took Colby's self-perpetuated nickname as proof of the man's yearning to belong – could not stand to call Sigismund Luxemberg 'Freud.' In part, this was because Luxemberg was a twenty-two-year-old good-for-nothing, one who'd been charged with assault more often than most of 14 Division's regular offenders. He was tall, club-footed, Nordic, and he'd grown up about a block away from Daniel's home. In no way did he resemble the father of psychoanalysis. What really rankled, however, was the fact the man's name was Sigismund, not Sigmund. It offended Daniel's sensibility that a Sigismund should be nicknamed 'Freud.'

– How about you, Sigismund? he asked. You keeping out of trouble?

– I don't like to be called Sigismund, said Freud.

– Don't you? said Daniel. That's too bad. Your name's your destiny.

– Mine fucking isn't, said Freud.

It suddenly seemed strange to Daniel that the man – only six years younger than he was – had come from Alexandra Park. So much separated them, temperament above all.

– As long as you're talking to me, he said, your name's going to be Sigismund, same as your parents called you. If you don't like it, keep moving.

– No one's unhappy about anything, said Colby.

– Let's all move along anyway, Daniel said. We're blocking the sidewalk.

They all did move but as if in lockstep, and Daniel had the unexpected idea that they were all going to the same place: Tancred's. The idea turned to near certainty as they walked wordlessly to Temple and then toward Tyndall. Nearing the corner of Tyndall and Temple, Daniel hung back a bit, expecting Nigger and Sigismund to go up the steps to Tancred's apartment. This they did not do. They did something more strange. The two turned right on Tyndall and walked back to King Street.

It was none of his business if they walked in circles or squares. Perhaps they'd forgotten something on King. Perhaps they'd only wanted to stretch their legs. Perhaps they'd been flustered at the sight of him and turned south when they should have turned north. None of that really mattered. The incident – if you could call it an incident – stayed with him only because he was convinced that Nigger and Sigismund had meant to visit Tancred but had not because the police – that is, he himself – had been behind them.

By the time he rang Tancred's doorbell, Daniel's mind was far from the matter that had been troubling him: the Azarians and their heirlooms. Now he wondered if Tancred ever had dealings with Nigger. More to the point, he wondered if he should bring the matter up. It was accepted by both of them that 'business' – thieving or policing – was not a proper subject for conversation. Tancred never asked about police matters, while Daniel avoided the subject of crime. There was a certain amount of grey area, however. Anecdotes that did not amount to snitching were fair game.

(How could you *not* tell someone about the man who broke into a home and tried to blindfold the German shepherd guarding it? Why blindfold the guard dog? Because he didn't want it to witness what he was doing. This circumspection cost the thief – Chester Broegaard, an unforgettable name – two fingers and some blood.)

As it happened, however, the subject of Colby and Sigismund did not come up. He and Tancred had so much to talk about that

Daniel forgot about them. Tancred was now one of the few people alive who had been almost as close to Baruch as he had. Although these days, neither he nor Tancred set out to revisit the past, neither of them knew how to avoid it. Their lives were intertwined. Each was a witness to important moments in the other's life.

It was more than that. It wasn't only that the past had more weight for Daniel than the law. There was also a kind of defiance in his love for his friend. Though he might not have put it in these terms, his friendship was a way of showing Baruch – the Baruch inside him – that he was not a slave to power. Tancred and Ollie were his brothers. No book of laws and statutes, no rules and ordinances, could change what was in his heart.

How difficult it had been – how difficult it was still – to please his father. Baruch had often quoted with scorn E. M. Forster's dictum 'If I had to choose between betraying my country and my friend, I hope I should have the guts to betray my country.' There, Baruch would say, was the bourgeois animal at its most arrogant, preferring its own to the survival of a country from which it took all it wanted. What's more, it was always easier to choose the concrete over the abstract. If guts were needed, they were needed to help choose the collective, an abstract and more fragile thing. But Daniel could not – did not – agree. Short of destroying his country, Daniel would choose his friends, his family, a shared past. These were what made life bearable.

Then, too, the past was a place where he and Tancred had both been happy. (Who would *not* be happy rushing home from school to watch TV before eating, if they were lucky, the akara – or falafel! – their mothers used to make?) Sharing that lost world as they did, they did not always speak about things they should have – Tancred's way of life, for instance.

Fiona, Daniel's wife, often asked
– You know him better than anyone. Why is he a thief?
And he'd answer
– I have no idea. We never talk about it.

It was an answer Fiona resented. She could not imagine not knowing something so important about a friend. In fact, she did not believe he didn't know. And she was right. He and Tancred no longer talked about it. But Daniel had a very good idea why his friend was a thief: the exhilaration and the skill. When they were sixteen, Tancred had shown him how to pick a pocket. By then, Tancred had been an accomplished pickpocket for some time. But there was more to it than the accomplishment. There was pride and, at times, an ecstasy. One day, they'd been downtown together, walking on Yonge toward College, when Tan had pointed to a police officer outside a coffee shop – Daniel remembered the officer's face still – and said he would steal the man's wallet. Bravado, you'd have thought. No one could be so stupid. But as Daniel watched, Tan had asked the officer for directions to the Y and then taken his wallet, his watch and a pen he'd had in his shirt pocket. If he had not been there himself, Daniel would not have believed it. Just watching the performance had been thrilling.

What had Tan done with the wallet, watch and pen? He'd given them back to the officer.

How? He had followed the officer into the coffee shop and stood behind the man, exchanging words with him until the officer ordered his doughnuts and coffee. Daniel had watched as Tan returned the pen to its pocket and then, with timing that a concert pianist might have envied, put the wallet into the man's hand as he reached for it and put the watch into the pocket from which the wallet had come. For Daniel, it was like witnessing a display of pure magic: enchanting, mystifying, exhilarating. That day, he'd felt sheer admiration for his friend.

It was an admiration he felt still, despite himself. Tan's way of dealing with pressure, drama and nerves was exemplary. Daniel had learned from him, imitating him as one would an older brother, though they were the same age. As they grew older and Tan kept on thieving, however, Daniel came to understand that his friend needed the exhilaration. Tan sought out moments that would be distressing to most people. From Daniel's perspective, Tan's talents and character – his quickness of mind, his reflexes, his devotion to his friends, his kindness – were wasted on thievery. It wasn't only that theft was immoral, inconsiderate and ignoble. It was that Tan's thieving was entirely self-serving, a means to adrenalin, a selfishness that Baruch would not have respected, despite his affection for Tan.

Ah, but there were enough nuances here to give you a headache! To begin with, Tancred knew very well that what he was doing was wrong. For ages he refused to show Daniel how to pick a pocket. Daniel pestered him until he acquiesced. But Tan gave in only on condition that if Daniel ever picked a pocket 'for real' he would have to repay Tan by working with him. Daniel was diligent and learned the art extremely well. He was eventually able to steal a wallet from Tan's pocket but, as Tan must have known, he was too circumspect to steal anything for real. That is to say, Tancred was perfectly able to be considerate of those he knew. It was mystifying that he had so little consideration for those he did not know.

Another nuance: before he died, Baruch knew that Tan was a thief. He did not approve but neither did he ever say anything to Tan directly. At some point, Daniel asked his father about this silence. Baruch had never been the type to keep his feelings hidden.

– Tancred's misguided, Baruch had said, but he's honourable.

– So, you think he's a good man?

– Not good, said Baruch, *honourable.*

That was all he would say about it. Which was annoying, because when Daniel decided to join the police force, his father was vocal, indeed. He would not condone Daniel's decision, arguing against it as passionately as he could. Baruch – Winnipeg anarchist from Winnipeg socialist parents – refused to accept that the police worked for any but the wealthy. Nor did he believe that his son, much as he loved him, could affect the good while working for one of the thorniest branches of an oppressive system of government: the police department.

– Whose interests will you be serving, Danny? Think about that while you're bullying the homeless or breaking up a strike.

– At least I'm not going to be a thief, Daniel had said bitterly.

– I'd prefer it if you were, his father had answered.

It had been a slap to the face. It was a testament to Daniel's love that he forgave his father. He understood Baruch's feelings. It took him a little longer to forgive Tancred because – and no getting around it – Tancred was one of those from whom he'd sworn to protect his fellow citizens. Forgive him he did, though, because he knew the good in Tancred and, in the end, accepted that it was his duty to protect that as well.

3 In Retrospect: A Theft and a Concussion

The task Willow had set him was going to take resolve to see through. Tancred had suspected as much the moment she asked him to steal from her siblings. He knew it for certain, however, after the debacle of Fallingwater.

He stole the model of Fallingwater with Ollie's help. He and Ollie worked well together, in part because they were close, in part because although Ollie was not a thief, he was good at it: conscientious, knowledgeable, nerveless as if born without them.

It had been difficult to persuade him to help. Not for moral reasons – Ollie had no problem with theft – but for practical ones. The bakery where he sometimes worked – and where they paid him next to nothing – needed him to cover for one of the owners who'd gone to the Ukraine to visit family. As Ollie had agreed to it, nothing could persuade him to change his mind. So, Tancred had had to wait for him.

That aside, the task appealed to Ollie.

– You mean we're stealing things so you can give them back? he asked. That's wonderful.

– Yes, said Tancred, we'll be stealing some things and giving them back. But we'll be stealing other things, too, so no one knows exactly what we're after.

– You had me at 'give them back,' said Ollie. This is how all thieves should work.

– At least for the first one, we're trying to make it look like it could have been stolen at random. If the others know we're after their mementos, they'll hide them or make them harder to get at. And I've got to do this. I gave my word.

– Then it's got to be done, said Ollie. What do you want me to do?

Willow's siblings all lived in wealthy neighbourhoods. They'd have alarm systems or dogs or whatever peacocks the wealthy used these days. He and Ollie would have to reconnoitre. Also, it being important that the Azarians not know what he and Ollie were after, it would be good to agree on what else to take before entering the homes to steal.

– Nothing of value, said Ollie.

– It's not so simple, said Tancred. If we take worthless things, it'll be suspicious. So, things with *some* value.

– What, like a toaster?

– Depends on the toaster, said Tancred.

On top of that, they had to decide which place to hit first. To do this, they tried to worm their way into each of the four homes. They were successful in two of them. Ollie got into the house of Gretchen Azarian-Grau by pretending to be a member of a local group committed to the restoration of churches in the Annex. Tancred got into the home of her sister – Simone Azarian-Thomson – in similar fashion. He asked Simone to sign a petition. This she would not do. Instead, she tried to contribute a single hundred-dollar bill. Tancred would not take it because (as he said) he'd come with no receipts. He promised to return for it.

Neither of them could gain admittance to the homes of Willow's brothers. One, Michael, lived in the Hidden Castle. Too much trouble. The other, Alton, lived in Moore Park, not far from Simone. But his manservant would not hear of allowing Tancred in while 'Mr. Alton' was not home.

– And Mr. Alton is *never* home for vagrants or parasites, I'm afraid.

As Gretchen's house was convenient – her alarm system providing little difficulty – they agreed to steal the model of Fallingwater before they took Simone's painting. That is, Ollie would handle the model while Tancred stole a few other things.

There ought not to have been any difficulty. For hours during the days beforehand, Tancred and Ollie sat in a car with tinted windows, noting the comings and goings of the women who lived there: Gretchen and her daughter, Adele. The house seemed never to be empty. There was always someone within. But the women held to a schedule that was obvious. At ten o'clock, night after night, the downstairs lights would go off and the lights on the top floors would come on. After ten o'clock, there was variation. On some nights, all the lights in the house were off by eleven. On others, the lights on the upper floors would stay on until midnight or one in the morning.

There were other unknowns. For instance, there was no way of telling if, after ten, any of the women descended in darkness to get water or food from the kitchen. Then, too, the house was not far from Avenue Road, a street that was busy until late. Lowther, the Azarian-Graus' street, often had pedestrians walking west from Avenue at all hours: drunken students, conversing couples, people who had parked their cars nearby. So, even if they avoided Gretchen and her daughter, Tancred and Olivier might still run into nosy citizens or drunken frat boys looking for trouble.

On the other hand, there were things very much in their favour. Ollie had drawn a plan of the house's first floor from memory. So, they knew, more or less, which rooms were where. And then – praise be to whomever – the model of Fallingwater was out in the open: on a mantelpiece beside a photograph. Finally, the alarm system was in the same room as Fallingwater – the living room – and could be disarmed in seconds. So, on balance, they could count themselves fortunate.

Their chosen night – a Tuesday at three in the morning – came and, early on, things went smoothly. Getting into the house unobserved was no problem. The front door's two locks – a deadbolt and a standard key lock – were dealt with in moments. Before you could say word one, Ollie was in, the alarm was disarmed and they stood in front of the thing they were looking for, their eyes adjusting to the dark.

Minutes. It would take them minutes, Tancred thought. But then there came a dull sound, halfway between a church bell in the distance and a nearby clang. At virtually the same moment, Ollie, who was not three feet away from him, collapsed with a floor-shivering thud. He was unconscious, his body a limp encumbrance.

As always in moments of distress, a calm came over Tancred. Having made certain his friend was alive, he left him on the living room floor and, rising, tried to figure out what had happened. Something had hit Ollie hard, but what? It was a while before he discovered the thing: an urn of some sort – elegant and squat, ten inches in diameter at its widest, cast iron with a pebbled metal surface, and surprisingly heavy. It had been dislodged from somewhere above – a shelf or niche, most likely – and struck Ollie on the head and then, rather than falling to the floor, it had bounced onto a sofa, scattering ashes, its small, round cover falling soundlessly onto the carpet.

Two thoughts occurred to Tancred at once. First: that it was unfortunate he hadn't been the one knocked out. Ollie had seen the house in daylight. He had not. He was in the dark in a place he did not know. His eyes had adjusted to the darkness, but you wouldn't have called the meagre light that came in from the street illuminating, exactly. Second: he wondered if Ollie was badly hurt. He was not dead, but he was not moving. Cradling his friend's head, Tancred gently slapped his face before leaving him behind the sofa and moving toward what he thought was the kitchen, looking for water.

He made it to what was indeed the kitchen, carefully pushing a swinging door, gratified to see silvery taps and a spigot glimmering in light that came through the pale curtains of a window above the sink. His gratification did not last long. He had opened a cupboard in search of a cup when a light went on outside the kitchen – it came beneath the swinging door and lit part of the kitchen. The light was followed by the sound of someone descending stairs. Tancred had moments to decide where to hide or how to hide or if he should hide at all.

There were two other doors in the kitchen. One was narrow and led to what Tancred assumed was a closet of some sort. The other led – again, he assumed – to the basement. This second door had a deadbolt on it: brass or some alloy that was yellow-ochre, an oval knob and a button beside the knob to keep the bolt either locked or unlocked. Tancred opened the door quietly, pushing the button up, and went out of the kitchen, holding the door closed as he listened with his ear against its cold wood.

It occurred to him, as he stood on a step down to the basement, that should Ollie come to, he might not know where he was. He would be confused and stand up and show himself. The longer whoever it was stayed downstairs, the more likely it was that Ollie would reveal himself – that is, if he wasn't already visible. The thought that Ollie had been seen was not alarming per se, but if it were true it would mean intervening. He would have to walk through the kitchen, help Ollie up and walk out of the house with him. Perhaps he should do that now, regardless? He listened for voices but heard none.

He decided to wait.

It was the right decision. Whoever it was in the kitchen – he assumed, for no good reason, that it was the daughter – shuffled about, drew water from the tap, shuffled about some more, then turned off the lights and left, the swinging door's rhythmic crepitations quickly fading until there was again only silence. The interruption must have lasted two minutes at most. Nor was there any commotion or noise – no voices raised – to suggest Ollie had been discovered.

Tancred pushed the door to the basement open, went into the kitchen, got a cup of water for Ollie, took up the antique-looking toaster on the counter beside the sink and went out to look after his friend.

It was testament to the steeliness of Ollie's nerves that though he was conscious he kept still until he was certain it was Tancred leaning over him. Then he sat up slowly, took the cup of water and drank it.

– Can you stand? Tancred whispered.

Rather than answer, Ollie rose, first getting onto all fours, then to his knees and then onto his feet. He was not steady. Tancred helped him to sit down on the sofa. In the backpack he'd brought, Tancred put two computers he found in the living room. Along with the toaster and the model of Fallingwater, that made four moderately expensive things. Not much camouflage for their intentions, but it would have to do. He was not sure how far Ollie would get on his own, let alone what he might be able to carry.

When time enough had passed for Ollie to orient himself, Tancred helped him up from the sofa. He took the model of Fallingwater himself. He put the toaster beneath Olivier's arm, as if it were a football. They left by the front door, unmindful of the noise they made, though Tancred closed the door quietly behind them.

As if the click of the closing door were a release, Olivier stumbled down the front steps, fell to his knees and vomited on the dark patch of lawn. He had to be taken to the nearest emergency ward. Encumbered though he was, Tancred helped Olivier to his feet, holding Fallingwater beneath one arm, pulling his friend – whose face rested on the lawn as if it were a pillow – up with his free hand. He did not forget the toaster. He left it where it had fallen.

– Someday, he thought, this will all be funny.

It was not funny. They stumbled like drunks, conspicuous until they got to the car Tancred had stolen. Mount Sinai was the closest hospital. In any case, it was the first one that came to mind.

Was this the end of their misfortune?

No, it was not.

Tancred decided to keep the model of Fallingwater with him when they went to Emergency. Ollie had brought an oversized and awkward travel bag that they'd left in the car, a bag like an old lady's accessory or something for Felix the Cat – houndstooth fabric, black-leather handles, two feet by two feet by two feet when wide open. Tancred put Fallingwater in it and kept it by his side. This was fortunate. Eight hours later, Ollie looking deranged with his head bandaged, they came out to find that 'their' car had been towed or stolen. So, there were the laptops gone. In fact, the only things they had to show for their work was a concussion (Ollie) and a model of some supposed architectural marvel, Fallingwater (Tancred).

Despite his concussion, Ollie seemed pleased with how things had gone.

– I can go to work tomorrow, he said.

Which is not what the doctor had suggested. The doctor had, in fact, cautioned him about going to work, warned him about headaches, nausea and the damage that could come from further trauma. Ollie was meant to take care of himself.

– Work should be the least of your worries, said Tancred.

– Tan, said Ollie, all my worries are the same.

Yes, true: in Ollie's mind, crossing the street carried the same weight as playing Russian roulette or waiting for a soufflé to rise. Was this a good thing or a bad one? At that moment, Tancred could not have said.

It was a few days later that Tancred and Daniel were drinking at An Béal Bocht, the Irish bar off East Liberty. They'd walked together through Liberty Village, only moments after Daniel had run into Colby and Freud. (Not that Daniel had alluded to the encounter.)

The neighbourhood, which had once been factory-filled and ominous at night, was now like a bad dream of condos and young people with dogs. It was unpleasant in a new way, having been turned into a kind of warren: no place for parking, no open spaces, no view of the lake, no capacity to accommodate the numbers rushing in to buy shoddy condominiums.

They had left the bar when Tancred, looking out at Liberty Village, said

– This is what you get when you have dishonourable people in office.

– No, said Daniel, this is what you get when you live in a capitalist society. These condominiums are badly built. They'll be rundown and undesirable in no time. The alpha professionals who've moved in will move out after making a profit, then the beta professionals will move in and lose money when they sell, and that'll mean the gamma crowd comes in and all the things that aren't a problem now – like no open spaces and no wide roads in – will make it harder and harder to police. In twenty years, it'll be like Jane and Finch and someone who wants money will vote to improve Liberty Village and the whole process will start again.

— How is that not the fault of dishonourable people? asked Tancred. Isn't this all about business over honour?

— You mean, said Daniel, if the city hadn't elected a hoodlum, things would be different? But, Tan, this neighbourhood was betrayed by previous administrations. And none of them were run by hoods. Okay, Rob Ford's an idiot, but he didn't plan this or make this and he's not going to be in office to see people afraid to walk here after dark.

— I didn't mention the mayor, said Tancred. He's not the only dishonourable one in the world, but the city's already starting to feel like his and it's only been a year.

— Meh, said Daniel. It'll pass.

— Well, I'm glad the city has at least one caring policeman, Tancred said.

— I'm supposed to be protecting you from people like you, said Daniel. Look, there's the bus. You sure you don't want to come with me? I don't know what we're having for supper, but I've got the dessert: *pains aux raisins*.

— No, no thanks, Dan. I'm dead tired. I'd be bad company.

— You're never bad company, said Daniel. Fiona likes it when you steal her watch. She thinks it's magic. It's not the same when I do it. By the way, how's Ollie doing? I haven't seen him in months.

— He's doing okay. He's got a concussion but he's still going to work.

— Because he told those people paying him minimum wage that he would, right?

— There you go, said Tancred. Ollie's Ollie from the moment he wakes up to the moment he falls asleep.

— I've been thinking about him a lot these days, said Daniel. Maybe because Fiona's pregnant. I mean, I love Ollie, but I can't imagine him as a dad, because I can't imagine him making the choices you have to make. You know what I mean? He's never even voted! He doesn't choose democracy or civilization, left or right, good or evil.

— I think, said Tancred, he'd be a great father, if he chose to be.

– But how do you choose something like that? How do you choose to be a father? Then how do you choose it day in, day out for the rest of your life? You can't be a nihilist dad, you know.

– You only have to choose until it becomes a habit, said Tancred.

– That first step's a big one, though.

– Are you worried you're not going to be a good dad?

– Yes, I am, said Daniel. I'm glad it's happening and all, but I don't exactly feel mature.

– Baruch was about your age when you were born, wasn't he? He did a pretty good job.

– It might surprise you to hear it, said Daniel, but Baruch wasn't perfect.

Their conversation was cut short by the 63's brakes: a strangled whinny.

– Later, said Daniel as he climbed onto the bus.

– Later, said Tancred.

He'd thought to walk straight home, but Daniel had reminded him about Ollie, and the thought of Ollie had brought thoughts of Willow. He had not seen her in days, but he was now willing to be convinced there was something about the mementos Robert Azarian had left his children. Willow had rented a storage space on Winnett just north of Vaughan. No, not a storage space – a well-lit, thousand-square-foot loft not far from a school. On a whim, as he watched the 63 take Daniel north, he decided to go to the loft. Perhaps, he thought, Willow would be there herself, examining the model of Fallingwater. He waited for the next 63 and when it came he sat by a window at the back.

Was it true that the city resembled its mayor? No, that was an exaggeration. The Victorian houses along Shaw, the grounds of the mental-health facilities ('Queen Street Mental,' as he'd always known it, though it was now CAMH), the restaurants and businesses on Queen then Ossington – they resembled no one man, no one group, no one place even. The city had been built by people from innumerable elsewheres. It was a chaos of cultures ordered only by its long streets. It belonged to no one and never would, or maybe it was three million cities in one, unique to each of its inhabitants, belonging to whoever walked its streets. Whatever the case, as Tancred watched it go by, he could not imagine himself anywhere but here. It did not disturb him to think that this was the only place he loved. It was home. But he did wonder whether it was the people or the place itself that made Toronto his. Or was home something stranger still – an idea or a feeling within him, one that could only be expressed by pointing to people and places?

Having walked to Winnett from Dufferin, Tancred turned on the lights in the loft. Willow was not around. Her screen was open to its fullest length. The model of Fallingwater was where he'd left it: beside the screen, on a wooden table Willow had bought for it. (The only furniture in the loft: three tables, an expensive easel, a futon, a fridge, a chair.) Seeing the Japanese screen and the model of Fallingwater side by side, Tancred at last understood why she believed they added up to something. They were odd in similar ways. You could feel that Mr. Azarian meant something by them, though what he meant was not possible to say. Not yet.

For a time, he stood looking at what he now thought of as two pieces of a map. There were three more to go.

4 An Unwanted Trip to Etobicoke

Colby and Freud had been spooked by Mandelshtam's presence. Without a word, the two had walked by Tancred's home and circled back to King Street. They hadn't given up on talking to Tancred, though. They'd returned twice that day and then again in the evening. On all three occasions, they'd rung his doorbell and the doorbells of the other apartments in the house. No one had answered.

Colby knew of Willow's death while Tancred, who was used to going days without hearing from her, did not even suspect it. Colby was afraid that Willow's death left Tancred as the only one who knew as much, if not more, about the Azarian mementos as he did. Willow, in various phases of intoxication or sickness, had shared with Colby her conviction that a reward was there for whoever could interpret the mementos properly. He'd believed Willow's story, and because he believed, he needed to know everything Tancred knew.

The following noon, Colby and Freud rang at Tancred's door.

Seeing who was there, Tancred felt a wonderful calm. He could, he thought, take both men: Freud first, then Errol. He would have to inflict real damage in the quickest time possible. But if he did, he would not discover why they were there. No one had ever come for him like this before. Something was up and it was probably best to let them tell him what it was before breaking limbs or having limbs broken.

He stepped out.

– What do you two want? he asked.

– Oh! said Colby. It's good to see you, Tancred. You know Freud, don't you? And just so we're on the same page: we all know how much you hate people bothering you at home. But we're not here for ourselves. We're only messengers. Mr. Armberg would like to see you. You know John Armberg, don't you, Tan?

– I do, said Tancred. I'm surprised he sent dogs to fetch me.

Colby took this well.

– I wouldn't say we were dogs, he said. Just messengers.

Tancred hesitated but curiosity again got the better of him. Given Colby's presence, this get-together could only be about Willow, and he was perplexed at the thought that Armberg could be involved.

– I hear you, he said. So, let's go then.

Mr. Armberg called himself a businessman but he liked to say that what he did was none of your business, even when it was your business. A friend of mobsters, bikers and pushers, he had a bit of a name but he was not as powerful as he imagined. He was what you might call middle management, and this rigmarole with Colby and Freud was proof of it. Powerful men didn't send dealers for people like Tancred. There was no need. Tancred was a known commodity, someone whose services could be used: a man good at what he did, one who kept his word. Had Armberg been really dangerous, Tancred would have been more careful. Still, Armberg was connected enough that it was worth at least hearing what he had to say.

Then again, had he known the meeting was in Etobicoke, he'd have resisted. Etobicoke was soulless and shiny, an encroaching wasteland, a tree-barren edge of the world. Tancred sat unspeaking in the back of the car – a Volkswagen – beside Freud, who listened to Drake at such volume that 'Headlines' bled from his earbuds. Colby drove along Etobicoke's version of Dundas: malls, tar, cement and glass.

Somewhere around Kipling, they turned onto another street and then into the parking lot of a tall building. It occurred to Tancred, as they were buzzed into the building, that they had entered a mausoleum: the fountain in the lobby a scene from some gruesome mythology – a dragon spraying water upward as a knight plunges his sword in the beast's side – the lobby itself so pungent with chlorine his eyes stung as they crossed it.

As they entered Armberg's apartment or office or whatever it was meant to be, Tancred was momentarily bewildered. The place was beyond crass. It was a Rona-catalogue version of luxury. To begin with, the floors were covered in white shag carpeting.

– You should take your shoes off, said Colby.

Then, all the tables in view were silver and glass – that is, soldered, silvery frames on which heavy panes of glass rested. On the walls there were paintings, their wooden frames carved into patterns of leaves. The paintings were reproductions of religious subjects: putti cuddling the infant Christ, angels hovering above the Virgin.

Colby led him into an office where, mercifully, the floor was varnished wood. They sat in silver-frame chairs with clear plastic backs and white cushions for seats. Before them was a desk – silver-framed, of course, with a thick glass desktop. Behind the desk, a chair very like the ones they sat in.

– How you doing, Nigger? said Armberg as he came into the office.

The man was somewhere under six feet, not particularly fat, though you could have called him paunchy if you were being critical. His skin was pale with reddish blotches beneath his chin and on his forehead. His hair had receded, but only a third of the way up his scalp, leaving something like an inlet. Nor did he comb his hair over to hide where he was balding. His hair was cut short. What was not short was his moustache: a full walrus that was darker than the hair on his head. In principle, he was well-dressed – dark-blue Hugo Boss two-piece suit, white shirt, orange silk tie – but everything on him looked about half a size small, save his shoes – oxblood Hush Puppies – which looked incongruously wide. Overall, there was an off-kilter stylishness, a not-quite-style that Tancred found surreal.

– You're Tancred? Armberg asked. Strange name, eh? Never mind. I heard you're a stand-up guy. Even Nigger thinks so and I can't tell if Nigger even likes you. You like him, Nigger?

– I haven't had any trouble with him, said Colby.

– Well, it's a start, said Armberg. Okay, that's enough small talk. I invited you here, Palmieri, because we maybe have an interest in common. I'm saying, maybe, because now Willow Azarian's dead, maybe things are changed.

This was the moment Tancred learned of Willow's death. He showed no emotion but he briefly saw – of all things to recall – Willow raising a hand to cover her mouth as she bit into a chocolate doughnut.

Armberg continued.

– Nigger here's told me everything about Willow Azarian, especially the business with what her father left her. I got to be honest: to me, it sounds like a fairy tale. But Nigger thinks it might be real. I heard a lot about Robert Azarian when he was alive. He wasn't that cute, you know what I mean? Not the treasure-hunt type. So, I'm on the fence about all this. But the man had more money than chinks got Chins and if he didn't leave all of it to his children, who else did he leave it to?

Tancred said nothing because there was nothing to say. Armberg was so obviously insincere, it would have been ridiculous to take him seriously. This was all a performance for his benefit, but it was not good, more comic than threatening. Armberg pulled out a cigar and lit it. He seemed to contemplate something as he drew on his Schimmelpenninck. He was not a gangster, thought Tancred. He was somebody's idea of a gangster.

– We're going to be partners, Tancred, you and me. It's like we're on an expedition, like looking for a sunken ship. You like that idea?

– Of course, said Tancred.

– You do? said Armberg. If you don't mind me asking, why do you like it?

– Now that Willow's dead, said Tancred, it's good to know I've got someone who'll put up the money I need to start my expedition.

– Money? said Armberg, What money? I'm not giving money. Who knows if there's anything to all this? This could all be a wet fart. Why am I going to give you money for that? You're out of your mind.

– Then we've got nothing to talk about, said Tancred. Without money, I'm done.

Armberg again fell into a sort of reverie, puffing on his cigar. After a moment, he said

— I looked into you, Palmieri. I know what you're about and I get it. This was a long shot, anyway. To tell you the truth, a man like me doesn't have time for fairy tales. I'm only talking to you to keep Nigger happy. But I've got a sense of adventure. And I see your point about investment. You've got to give something to get something. I get that. So, just out of curiosity, what would it cost to start you off? Keeping in mind this could be pennies in a jar we're talking about, this treasure.

Tancred looked the man in the face: crooked nose and large, brown eyes, the kind that must have been lovely when he was a child but now made him look as if he were part doe. Tancred was not for a moment interested in Armberg as a partner or associate.

— Fifty thousand dollars, he said.

Armberg took this in and thought about it.

— Is fifty thousand enough, he asked, or do you want to fuck my wife, too?

Behind Tancred, Freud and Colby laughed. But Armberg didn't.

— That's too much, he said. Too much.

— Without money, said Tancred, I've got no interest in this. And I'm not going to use my own.

— I think you do have an interest, said Armberg. And if you're going to keep going, I want to be part of the expedition. So, I was thinking we'd just go old-school on this one. I was going to have the boys bring your friend … What's his name?

— Olivier, answered Colby.

— That's the guy, Armberg said. You two are always together. So, I'm guessing you wouldn't want Freud here to slap your friend around. Am I right?

— You're right, said Tancred.

— Good, said Armberg. We're on the same page. So, let's put it this way: of course, if you need a reasonable amount of money as a get-out-of-jail-free kind of deal, I'll help out if I can. In exchange, whatever you find with this Azarian business, half of it's mine. And because Nigger knows the story, I want you to consider him my emissary. You know what that means, right? From now on, he'll be close to you. You find nothing, I won't be disappointed. Things don't always work out like we want. We'll be all square, if you've been square with me. You understand me?

— I do, said Tancred.

— Good, good, said Armberg. Let's shake on it.

— No, said Tancred, rising. I see where you're coming from. That's enough.

Armberg had already risen and put forth his hand.

— Shaking hands means we came to terms, he said. Haven't we come to terms?

— I'll let you know when I've got something to show you.

— Well, happy hunting then, Palmieri.

As he, Colby and Freud drove back to Parkdale, Tancred was not amused. Colby, who now sat in the back with him, would not stop talking. He was, it seemed, filled with enthusiasm for their project.

— We should stick to Willow's idea, he said. We steal her brothers' and sisters' things and then we can figure this out. I feel good about this, Tan. No reason we can't work together. Just tell me what you need.

Tancred kept quiet. He had wasted his time, learning nothing, save that Willow was dead and Armberg and Colby had no idea he'd already taken the model of Fallingwater. Then again, how would they know that? They were not the kind who had access to police reports. Armberg was — and here he remembered the man's shoes — a clown.

— I'm sorry we had to do things this way, said Colby. But I knew you'd listen to John before you'd listen to me. Yeah?

— I need to think, said Tancred, about Willow.

— Oh, sure. No problem.

For a moment as they passed the Humber Bay Arch Bridge, Tancred wondered what his duty to Willow was, now that she was dead.

But Willow's death changed nothing. If anything, it strengthened his resolve. He'd given his word. In the absence of any who could speak for Willow, in Willow's absence, he had no choice but to keep it.

Beyond that, there were vaguer impulses and curiosities. He truly wondered about what lay at the end of Robert Azarian's hunt. He did not think it could be money. Azarian's children already had pots of cash. (Nor was he himself interested in it. Baruch had taught them to think of money as 'the spoor of the ruling class,' and some part of him still thought of it that way.) So what was it that Robert Azarian had sought to pass on?

His curiosity did not mean he'd leave Ollie hanging, however. As they drove along the lakeshore, Tancred decided to move into the loft on Winnett and ask Ollie to stay with him for a while.

5 Von Würfel Almost Deciphers Azarian

One of the many unusual things about Alexander von Würfel was that, technically speaking, he did not exist. He was the creation of Alex Luck, an artist born in London, England, in 1941. Coming to Toronto in 1968, the twenty-seven-year-old discovered a city in the throes of what was called a 'youth movement.' It was a time of explorations in poetry, art and music, a time when reinvention seemed not only possible but desirable. So, the young man from south London became a German artist who'd fallen on hard times. He wandered around Yorkville in a progressively rattier three-piece suit and a scratched-up monocle. He referred to himself as Alexander von Würfel III, formerly of Mainz.

Alex Luck – who, at the invention of von Würfel, ceased somewhat to exist – had no idea he was an artist, but his alter ego took to the role with pleasure and passion. In the early seventies, von Würfel became what was called a performance artist, known for his 'happenings.' For instance, for two hours a day (from noon until two in the afternoon) he would hold up a large, freshly hand-painted sign that read

Wer sind Sie?

that is, 'Who are you?' in German – a language he did not actually speak. Von Würfel would hold the sign above his head whenever he was addressed or whenever a bus of tourists chanced to stop near him or, at other times of the day, when women in whom he had no interest asked him to say a few words so they could admire his accent – an English accent that he had, he said, acquired while studying at Oxford.

By dint of thinking about art and talking to other artists and living the life of an artist, Alexander von Würfel became an artist. Beginning with an awareness of how he painted cardboard signs, he progressed to the study of painting and sculpture. In the end, he finally saw in himself something that was there all along: great skill as a draftsman and the ability to stick with a project until it was done to his perfect satisfaction. By 1980, he had graduated from the Ontario College of Art, his paintings and installations were in group shows around town, he was respected by his peers and, of course, he was on the verge of starvation.

Ever practical – and having fathered four children (all girls) with four different women – von Würfel began to take commissions: portraits, landscapes in the style of A. J. Casson, still lifes in the manner of Lubin Baugin, canvases painted in colours that matched a living room, here, or a dining room, there. As he was good at this work and as he had no scorn for canvases done shocking orange (meant to set off the blue eyes of their owner), he soon had more work than he could manage. For a while, it even became fashionable to have von Würfel 'do a little something' for your home.

These commissions led him further and further from his own creativity. He ate well and his business brought in more than enough for him to support his children and their mothers. But his attitude changed. He began to speak of 'Art' with a certain disdain. After a while, he spoke as if the word itself could only be said ironically. Finally, he used the word *Art* only in order to get better prices from his patrons. He became like the fox with its sour grapes. Art existed, he would admit in private, but rarely. It was a false lure, something futile to pursue. What counted was pleasing a patron, as Michelangelo or Raphael once had.

It was at this point in his life, somewhere around 2002, that he met Robert Azarian.

Why Mr. Azarian asked him to make the four – not just three – pieces, von Würfel never knew. He'd had no idea whom they were for or what purposes they'd serve. Each of the works was precisely described. Each had exact requirements, specific dimensions and materials. Some of the pieces – Fallingwater, for instance – were difficult in themselves. Others were intriguing because of their content. He had not asked about the meaning behind the pieces because Mr. Azarian let him know at once that he was to do as he was commissioned to do and ask no questions. That, in itself, had been intriguing. Most of those who wanted portraits of their wives or marble statues of their husbands were avid answerers. Azarian had been resolutely uninformative. For all of these reasons, von Würfel never forgot the pieces, nor ever destroyed the plans and descriptions Mr. Azarian had given him. Unsure what to do with them, he kept them in his safe, in a folder marked 'Taxes 1998.'

Azarian having a small place at the back of his mind, von Würfel was not altogether surprised when Willow came to him seven years later, asking what he knew about the work her father had commissioned him to do.

– How do you know I'm the one who did those pieces? he'd asked.

– I didn't know for certain until this moment, she said. I guessed. On the back of the screen you did, there was a signature.

– I didn't sign any of the pieces, he said.

– Yes, you did, Willow had answered. On the last panel, there are two letters. One letter and another one in parenthesis: a(ɯ). I've asked every artist in town whose last name begins with W if they'd done work for my father.

– Well, congratulations, he said. You've found the right man. But that isn't my signature. I made a number of pieces for your father, true, but I didn't make a screen. So, I couldn't have initialled any panel.

Von Würfel found this bit of pure chance intriguing. Just as fascinating: for some reason, Azarian hadn't trusted him to make all five pieces. It made him curious. Nevertheless, Willow Azarian was the first of three to whom he lied about his involvement with her father. She was the first to whom he said

– I did *three* pieces for your father.

– Not five? There are five pieces.

– No, no, he'd said. He commissioned three from me. Someone else must have done the others.

Why had he kept his involvement with the fourth piece secret? Call it instinct, a sense that something interesting was afoot and he wanted some kind of leverage. Willow Azarian was also the first to whom he lied about keeping a record of the transaction between

himself and her father. He told her he'd destroyed the plans her father
had given him. Again, you could call this instinct or, perhaps, caution.

Yes, but he should have inquired about the fifth piece, the so-
called screen.

Immediately after Willow left his shop, von Würfel began to
take the Azarian puzzle – or conundrum or mystery or whatever it
was – seriously. Though Willow had told him nothing of what she
suspected or knew, he now took as given that the pieces he'd made
for Azarian were meant to lead somewhere or point toward something. So, not one hour after Willow had gone, he'd begun the work
of exactly reproducing (for himself) the four objects he'd made years
before. A painstaking and expensive process, but one that had
brought him diversion from his troubles – that is, from what he
swore would be the last of his divorces.

Von Würfel took it for obvious that the framed poem was the
place to start:

> None of the dead are lonely,
> or so the breeze would have it.
> Rather, far, the civilized wit
> than fortunes won without it.
> Hours from you, my porcupine, though
> four of your quills pierced
> three of my vines.
>
> When your fingers have plucked
> each of the strings
> south of my dying equator,
> the oceans will wave their
> seven blue veils but
> nine will comfort you, later.

As he'd done with the original, von Würfel copied Azarian's
poem in black ink on a page of pale-blue handmade paper. The
paper was the colour of faded chicory. It was smooth and thick and

just fibrous enough that one could have spoken of its grain. It was pinned to a two-inch-thick rectangle of African blackwood, as if it had been a specimen of something that had once lived. The whole – page, wood and pearl-headed titanium pins – was then enshrined in a Plexiglas case to which the wood was secured (from beneath) by four stubby, flat-headed screws.

It was difficult to tell what had meaning and what had not. Was it significant that the titanium pins were pearl-headed? Did Azarian's insistence on African blackwood point to something? What did it mean that the paper was blue? Not knowing anything about the poem's meaning or origin, von Würfel ignored all but the obvious acrostic. The first letters of the first words of the first stanza made the word

North

while the final couplet gave you the number 43.

The first letters of the first four words of the second stanza made the word:

West

while this stanza's couplet gave the number 79.

It took no skill at all to recognize that these were coordinates of latitude and longitude. On their own, they led to a point on Grand Island, New York. Von Würfel travelled to Grand Island and found absolutely nothing of interest, vacant space beside a highway. For a year – desultorily, occasionally – he tried to find other clues in the poem. Nothing. There were no Africans on Grand Island. There was nothing particularly blue about it and pearls were not on offer anywhere thereabouts. 'North 43°, West 79°' led him to a dead end.

It was not until he began thinking about the other pieces that he made what he was convinced was progress. The model of Fallingwater, for instance. How did it help find whatever was to be located at '43° N, 79° W'? For months von Würfel explored hints and possibilities. He drove to Fallingwater to look around. He added the numbers he got from Frank Lloyd Wright's birthday (June 8, 1867), his date of death (April 9, 1959), variations on those numbers and any number related to Lloyd Wright to the poem's coordinates:

> N 43.681°, w 79.867° (this was in Brampton)
> N 43.6801°, w 79.8607° (more Brampton)
> et cetera … (mostly Brampton)

He got nowhere significant, though he conscientiously explored each of the many dead ends.

Then it occurred to him how unusual it was to commission a reproduction of Fallingwater made from titanium and niobium. What were the elements' atomic numbers, again?

> Niobium 41
> Titanium 22

Adding these numbers to those from the poem, he arrived at either

> N 43° 41', w 79° 22' (Evergreen Garden Market on Bayview)

or

> N 43° 22', w 79° 41' (somewhere in Lake Ontario, near
> Burlington)

What good luck! And as soon as he arrived at the Evergreen Garden Market he knew (he simply *knew*) that he was onto something. He explored the market as no one before him had ever done, and he found nothing of use. But the impression he had of the mind behind the puzzle was thrilling. The invisible creator – Robert Azarian – was suddenly with him. The place he sought was somewhere in Toronto. It was as if Azarian had told him this himself.

It seemed to von Würfel that all of the mementos would be needed to find the proper spot, that no single Azarian heir could get to it on his or her own. This created problems for him. First, the painting of the Emperor Nero standing beside a man with a crow on his shoulder did not have any numbers on it anywhere. (Azarian's elaborate and precise description of the scene to be painted mentioned no figures or dimensions either.) And then, though he could find numbers related to three of the pieces – the poem, the model of Fallingwater, the bottle of aquavit – he was not certain what order the numbers should take. (Eldest to youngest made sense, but which piece had gone to which child?) Finally, there was the most difficult problem of all: he had no idea what the fifth piece looked like, no idea what kind of screen it was, no idea how it might contribute to the solution.

One day, as he was in the front of Von Würfel's Animals and Birds, thinking about the painting of Nero, trying to divine what numbers might be hidden in a portrait of the emperor, two men came into the shop: an albino and a physically imposing young man who looked as though he meant to break something.

– Can I help you? he asked.

– Are you Alexander von Würfel? the albino said.

– Who wants to know? answered von Würfel.

– We're friends of Willow Azarian, said the albino, and we just wondered, now that she's dead, if you could help us with something.

– I met a Miss Azarian once, some time ago, said von Würfel. I doubt there's anything I can help you with.

– I'm sorry, said the albino, I should have introduced myself. My name is Errol Colby. I was a friend of Willow's. We were very close and she told me once that you'd made a few artworks for her father. When she died, the work her father left her was stolen. So, we were wondering if you could help us recreate the piece her father made for her. It'd be a reminder of Willow.

– Oh, I see, said von Würfel. I'm afraid I'm going to disappoint you. Miss Azarian came to me years ago asking about those pieces. I made three of them for her father but I have no idea which piece was for whom. Mr. Azarian didn't tell me. And why would he? It was none of my business. He paid me and that was that.

– But you remember what they were?

– Do you know how many commissions I've taken for artworks? Hundreds and hundreds. The only reason I remember what these three were is that Miss Azarian *told* me. Beyond what she told me, I don't know a thing. I don't even remember making them: a painting of something, a poem mounted in Plexiglas and a model of a building.

– You didn't make a Japanese screen?

A *Japanese* screen? Despite himself, despite not wanting to betray any interest, von Würfel said

– A Japanese screen? What do you mean? Something that folds out?

The albino, who was wearing dark glasses, seemed to stare at him a moment, as if there was something he couldn't bring himself to say.

– Sorry to bother you

is what he said at last and the two left without another word.

A strange encounter, in the end. Nothing untoward had happened and yet there'd been a barely hidden threat in it. The Azarian business now had an unpleasant edge. The encounter was frustrating as well. The albino had brought von Würfel confirmation of the fifth piece but told him nothing useful about it.

No, that wasn't quite true. After hearing about the 'Japanese screen,' von Würfel felt as if he'd got an insight into Robert Azarian's logic, his playfulness. What a range of references! When, shortly after the albino's visit, the numbers hidden in the 'musical painting' of Nero and Consul Corvinus (the man's name meant raven!) suggested themselves to him (the 58th consul serenaded by Bach's 48), it was again as if Robert Azarian had spoken. Von Würfel took it as granted that the poem and the numbers associated with Fallingwater were in order, because they led to somewhere in Toronto. He then slotted in the numbers associated with the painting and with the bottle of aquavit, juggling them, changing them around until he got the exact coordinates – latitude and longitude – of a plot of ground in Mount Pleasant Cemetery. An electrifying moment! A eureka moment that only a dedicated puzzle-solver would understand.

It was at this point, however, that a (metaphorical) shutter came down. Without the fifth piece, with no idea what the fifth piece looked like or felt like, von Würfel could get no further than this:

'Plot 22' in the rectangle of ground bounded by Merton Street (north), Moore Avenue (south), Mount Pleasant Road (west) and Bayview Avenue (east), a little north of a parking lot, north of the Garden of Remembrance's conservatory, north and east of the cemetery office, by the graves of Millers and Smiths, and close to a mausoleum over whose door the name Weiden was carved.

By the time Detective Mandelshtam came to ask him questions – that is, a week after the albino – von Würfel had already spent hours in Mount Pleasant examining headstones and ground, pacing around the Weiden mausoleum, wondering what, in the patch of land around Azarian's coordinates (N 43° 41' 48.1889", W 79° 22' 58.4185"), was meant to be precious or to lead to something – if something there was.

In fact, von Würfel spent so much time among the graves and by the Weiden crypt that he struck up an acquaintance with Delmer McDougal, a man he saw there often and who he assumed worked at the cemetery.

– Recently bereaved? the man asked him one day. I'm sorry for your loss, eh.

– Not recent, answered von Würfel, but I'm paying my respects.

– It's the thing to do, for sure, said the man.

He was much shorter than von Würfel, stocky with a modest paunch, and his hair – what was left of it – was wispy and greying. Strands of it sometimes rose up – spidery – in the wind. Von Würfel took him for a contemporary and, as it turned out, they were around the same age, but the man was evidently from the Ottawa Valley, his accent sounding vaguely Irish. Had they been in England, Alex Luck might have looked down on him, but Alexander von Würfel was pleased to be reminded, however vaguely, of his homeland.

– Well, said the man, life's one of those things, eh.

– Thank you, said von Würfel

not knowing what else to say.

After Detective Mandelshtam's visit, the problem for von Würfel – the source of his anxiety – was the idea that he had rivals for

Azarian's secret. Was Detective Mandelshtam a rival? No, not Mandelshtam so much. He seemed legitimate. But the albino was almost certainly looking for whatever Robert Azarian had hidden, and if the albino was looking, there could well be others, others who might have had access to the final piece, the Japanese screen. If he – that is, von Würfel – had guessed that Mount Pleasant was part of the solution to Azarian's puzzle (if indeed it *was* part of the solution), others could guess it as well.

On a Saturday, two weeks into his (as he thought) absurd vigil – absurd because he was not in the cemetery long enough on any given day to effectively watch over the graves and crypt – von Würfel asked McDougal if he was always around the Weiden crypt.

– Well, hereabouts, said Delmer.

– You mean you work here?

– I do. That I do.

Von Würfel then asked if Delmer had seen anyone around the Weiden crypt 'lately.'

– If I seen anyone? said Delmer. Jeez, I don't think so, buddy. I see all kinds a people, but I can't say I seen any 'round here lately. You're not counting yourself, eh? So, no, not really. I mean, I see more people 'n you can shake a stick at. It's a cemetery, so people're just dyin' to get in, eh? But, like, 'round here? Today? It's just you, buddy. I don't think your Weidens were all that popular. That's what I tell myself when there's graves nobody goes to: Jeez, I bet youse weren't dancing at the prom. But then you come along and I had to apologize to your people here, 'cause now at least they've got someone. I'm not sayin' anything weird or anything but you get a kind of feelin' for the dead, eh, like you know 'em.

– I mean anyone suspicious-looking, said von Würfel, interrupting him. Not mourners.

– Suspicious? You know, there's mostly two types that come here, eh. It's the ones that're in mourning or it's the ones that come for to do what nature makes 'em. Them's pret' near the only suspicious ones. You're just mindin' your business and all of a sudden there's young people just goin' at 'er on people's graves. I don' know what's wrong with 'em! I guess mostly they're drunk, so I don't like to judge 'em. But jeez an' aitches! It puts you off the whole idea a dyin', havin' some guy puttin' the blocks to 'er, right on top a you. Not sure that's suspicious like you mean but that's as suspicious as she gets 'round here. Course that's summer I'm talkin' 'bout, eh. No one likes to do 'er outdoors in winter.

As if winter were a thing to contemplate, Delmer was suddenly quiet.

— I wonder, said von Würfel, if you'd do me a favour?

— Somethin' legal? asked Delmer.

— Yes, said von Würfel, legal. I'll give you a hundred dollars a month if you keep an eye out for people coming around here. To be honest, part of the reason I started coming here so often is that someone told me the Weidens' mausoleum was vandalized and I wanted to see for myself. It hasn't been vandalized, but now I come around so that people won't think no one comes around. If you could look out when I'm not here, I'd pay you for whatever you saw.

— Well, that *sounds* like a deal, said Delmer. You sure that's all there is to 'er?

— Yes, I'm sure. I'm interested in anyone who comes to the mausoleum or any of the graves around it, especially if you haven't seen the person before.

Apparently satisfied that von Würfel was no kind of deviant, Delmer agreed and von Würfel gave him a hundred dollars on the spot, to show his good faith. He also left Delmer a cellphone number at which he could be reached.

Their arrangement was, thought von Würfel, only slightly less absurd than his coming to the cemetery himself. Delmer, too, could miss important incursions by … well, by whoever else was on the Azarian trail. Handing over the hundred dollars was, however, a great relief to von Würfel. He had now done something. He was being what his daughter Frieda called 'proactive.' He was taking the next step along a road that had become a kind of obsession. He wanted – perhaps even needed – the answer to this puzzle. If the answer came at the cost of a few hundred dollars, fine. Having puzzled over Azarian's clues for what now amounted to years, he felt compelled to do all he could to find what Azarian had left to be found.

As he walked away from Delmer, Alexander von Würfel experienced a sort of communion with Robert Azarian, seeming to recall the man's features and voice, though he'd seen him only briefly, two or three times, a long time gone. He felt as if he and Azarian were now bound in a spiritual sense. It was suddenly clear to him that he was accomplishing Azarian's will by working this puzzle out.

– I'll get there, Robert, he said aloud.

His words were a brief warmth in the cold air. The sun was out. The sky was blue. The leaves had changed colour, making all of Mount Pleasant Cemetery more picturesque than it usually is. Pleased with the arrangement he'd made with Mr. McDougal, Alexander von Würfel stopped at the cemetery's glass-roofed conservatory to admire the plants within.

CHAPTER THREE

THE RAVEN

1 Errol Colby Goes Too Far

Errol Colby would have preferred to have as little to do with Tancred Palmieri as possible. He'd had what could be called a premonition, a feeling that Tancred was dangerous, and it nagged at him.

He hadn't wanted to be better acquainted with Tancred. Willow Azarian had forced his hand. It was Willow who'd told him about her father's 'treasure,' and it was she who'd told him her secret: she'd got a promise from Tancred to steal the clues to her father's fortune. Though Willow had been out of her mind when she told him, he'd believed her. From that moment, his and Tancred's acquaintance became inevitable because, more than anyone else, Colby believed in the fortune that awaited him and believed it was his due.

There were reasons to believe. Though Willow had been a junkie, she'd been a rich one, and Colby had seen very few of those. In fact, Willow had been the only wealthy person he'd known at all. As such, he'd respected her. Certainly, his respect had been tempered by reality. He'd seen the woman so out of it she could not sit, stand or fall down. He'd seen her piss herself a number of times or accidentally burn the clothes she was wearing with cigarettes. Once you'd seen someone in that state, it was not easy to maintain respect. But then again, Colby had been born poor, and part of the burden of poverty – at least, for him – was a gnawing, resentful esteem for the rich. Despite having seen Willow at her worst, despite knowing she was a junkie, he could not shake the foul habit of admiration. So, where Willow was concerned, he was not as skeptical as he would otherwise have been.

Not that Colby was a thoughtful man. Thoughtfulness was a luxury for those with money.

He was born in Jamaica of Jamaican parents, moved with his family to Canada at the age of four and was raised in government housing at Jane and Finch. Most of the kids he'd grown up with now worked the same side of the street as he did. They were dealers or small criminals and most of them were worse off than he was.

He'd been to jail twice, both times for under a year. It was a point of pride that he'd never served real time. Given his childhood, you could even say he was doing well.

Childhood? Now, there was a misery all its own.

A father who hated the sight of him – hated the colour of his skin – and a mother who – alcoholic and strange – accepted his whiteness but rejected him as she rejected all of her children. It was hard to say which had caused more damage – the cold, distant planet or the fiery one nearby. With both, avoidance was safety. But perhaps his mother just shaded it because when she was drunk, she was self-pitying and hateful, and it was best to stay out of the house until she passed out.

And yet, he had been loved. He and his siblings had relied on each other for the affection and guidance they needed. At times, it seemed as if he, his two brothers and three sisters had only each other in the world. He, the youngest, grew up with brothers who would fight for him and sisters who looked out for him while he did the only thing his younger self could: he loved his brothers and sisters unconditionally. But then, his oldest brother, Horace, was shot to death and his brother Simon was jailed for murder. All three of his sisters got married and though two of them stayed in the neighbourhood, it meant his siblings had all left home by the time he was twelve. He was the one expected to care for the father who despised him and the mother who, though diabetic and, by the time Errol was last one left in the nest, one-legged, still drank herself into a state once or twice a week. Only once or twice a week? Yes, and that was progress. Before she lost her leg, Errol's mother was drunk most nights. His father, too. Both of them were so often soused, it made you wonder where they got money for the parade of twenty-sixers (rum, gin and Scotch) and if alcohol was the only thing that kept them together.

They never drank on Sundays. Sundays were different. Sunday was the day Mr. and Mrs. Colby attended mass and lived, for twenty-four hours, as if they cared about God. It was a day of nervous peace.

And as he grew older it seemed to Colby that Sunday was the worst of days. Being devout on Sunday was how his parents convinced themselves they were responsible people and good parents, though they were irresponsible and some distance from 'good.' Sunday was also their sword. On the Sabbath, they forced their children to church, cuffing the kids to keep them quiet, listening to hymns at home on a stereo whose speakers were so blown that, even at low volume, it was like listening to saintly tractors. No one who knew him would have been surprised to hear that Errol Colby loathed Sunday.

(His feelings about 'God' were even less nuanced. 'God,' in whatever form or version you liked, seemed to him an obvious and ridiculous device, something used to gain an upper hand. Even the so-called meek, with their mewling piety, were out for unearned juice. In fact, the only times he grew irrationally angry were those when junkies dared to mention God in his presence. Any who did would find him dry for weeks.

– It's okay, he'd say. I'm sure God'll comfort you.

None of them mentioned God in his company twice.)

No doubt, given his origins, he was doing well. Yet, he was at the mercy of those who supplied him and he resented giving his money to those whose territory he worked. He resented having to live at home. (He was twenty-two. He'd lived with his parents his whole life.) Most of all, he resented junkies. It was like social work, this helping the weak to die. Were it not for the money it cost him when one of his regulars croaked or hit the skids, he would have missed none of them had they all vanished from the earth, Willow excepted.

Willow was a different matter, because along with Willow came Willow's dreams, and Colby was susceptible to them. Convinced that Willow's father had left a hidden fortune behind, he could not stop himself from daydreaming about its value. Robert Azarian had been a billionaire. It was a matter of public record. At his death, the *National Post* had reported his estimated worth to be somewhere around five billion, putting him among the wealthiest Canadians. It was obvious that such a man not only could have left a billion behind for each of his children but that he should have. Hundreds of millions was nothing to a man with five billion. It was almost a slap in the face, difficult though it was for Colby to accept (or even understand) that hundreds of millions of dollars could ever be paltry or unfair. So, when Willow had suggested there was a 'finder's fee' for anyone who helped her find 'the rest of her inheritance,' he'd been very interested. Tancred is whom she'd had in mind for the fee, it's true. But still. Now that she was gone, why shouldn't he be the one to find the rest of her money?

And what would he do with millions? He'd give up dealing. That was certain. He wasn't one of those who loved the life. His self-esteem did not entirely depend on the misery of others. He would travel, maybe leave the country, maybe move to New York or Paris or Rome. Not that he knew any of those cities. He'd never been out of Toronto. The closest he'd come to travel was one day when he'd taken the subway to its farthest point east (Kennedy) and its farthest point west (Kipling) to see what was there. He had found, at the edges of his world, nothing but a brick-and-steel desolation that seemed to go on forever. It was one of his greatest hopes that New York and Paris, London and Rome were as wonderful as those who'd come from them inevitably said they were.

Not surprisingly, all of this – his home, his albinism, his longing for money – influenced Colby's feelings about Tancred. He hated the man. To him, Tancred was no better than any of the hustlers in Parkdale. But he carried himself as if he were, as if what he did were somehow noble, while dealers like him and Freud worked the gutters. Other people liked Tancred. For Colby it was unpleasant to watch the whores make eyes at him and tell him their life stories, giggling like virgins while he pretended to care about all the abuse they'd suffered. He wouldn't even sleep with them! He remembered one of them saying

– Your dick's not made of glass, is it? I won't break it.

And Tancred had said something about how he was in love with a woman and how even if she wouldn't know he'd cheated, *he* would.

Love? Oh, please. The people who used that word most were Mr. and Mrs. Colby, his parents. He doubted Tancred had any idea what it meant.

None of that mattered, though. His feelings didn't matter. Tancred was his ticket out of Jane and Finch. He would have to deal with the man. Unfortunately, Mr. Armberg was not convinced that Tancred had been the least bit intimidated by their little interview.

– You won't get anything from him without force, Mr. Armberg had said.

As if he'd known Tancred would go into hiding.

They hadn't been able to find Tancred for days. Which meant that the second part of Mr. Armberg's thought was likely true as well.

– If you're going to threaten someone like Palmieri, you got to be ready to carry through.

Here Mr. Armberg would not go. He'd done what he had for Colby's sake – that is, out of consideration for a young man who was the only creature on earth who valued him as much as he valued himself. He would not help them rough up Tancred or Olivier, because he simply did not believe Willow's 'ravings,' did not believe anything lay beyond the so-called clues Robert Azarian had left behind. Hurting people was not a problem, but one had to have a reason.

– I've got principles, he'd said.

Which meant that Colby would have to do the roughing up himself. No, not himself. The roughing up would be done with Freud. But now, of course, they couldn't find Tancred. He and Olivier both seemed to have vanished.

Really, he should have left the Azarian thing alone. He should have dropped it. Let Tancred go on this wild goose chase by himself. None of his friends would have cared or minded. The world would have carried on spinning.

Yes, but he would have been miserable. It would be excruciating not to know the end of the story, not to know the reward that waited once the puzzle was solved. Was it cash? Jewels? Stocks and bonds? And why should he, Errol Colby, be cheated out of a share?

What was so special about Tancred Palmieri, anyway?

Colby assumed there was nothing special about Tancred, an unsound assumption that led him to a dangerous question: why shouldn't he steal the Azarian mementos himself? Willow had, fuzzily but repeatedly, described her father's mementos to him. He knew what to look for almost as certainly as Tancred did: a poem, a painting with Romans in it, a silvery model of a fancy building and a bottle of something called aquavit. That left Willow's screen, of course. It was strange, given his connection to her, that Willow's should be the heirloom he knew least. She'd never even properly described it to him. But he'd worry about that when he had to, if he had to. Given how Willow had spoken of Tancred, he suspected the man had hold of it already.

Furthermore, he'd done a little breaking and entering himself. He could devise a plan of attack as well as the next person. Then, too, when you thought about it, all he had to steal was one of the pieces. If he had one, Tancred would be forced to co-operate with him. His biggest problem, really, was time. He ought to have thought of this before. Palmieri was no doubt well along with his thieving. Which meant he'd have to get on with it, if his plan was to have any hope of success.

As Tancred and Olivier had before him, Colby cased the houses from which he'd be stealing. He wanted to know, as the two before him had, the layouts, whether or not there were alarm systems, the best points of entry for him and Freud – if, that is, Freud could be persuaded to help. He also needed to know what was left, which pieces, if any, Tancred hadn't yet taken.

For two days, Colby left his regulars in Freud's paranoid care. On the first day, he diligently scouted the four neighbourhoods he'd be working: Rosedale, the Annex, Moore Park, the harbourfront. On the second day, he dressed in good clothes and knocked at the home of Willow's sister, Simone Azarian-Thomson.

– Yes? said Mrs. Azarian-Thomson, answering her door.

– Good morning, Madam, said Colby. My name is William Sanger and I'm here on behalf of the Save Our Children Foundation.

Colby thought he heard men's voices from inside the house, but he carried on, feeling that the important thing was for him to get inside for a bit – to get a good look around – and it made no difference who saw him, as they would never see him again.

– We're a non-profit organization, he said, that's trying to end child poverty.

– Are you? asked Willow's sister. That's a good cause.

– I wonder, said Colby, if I could have a few minutes of your time?

– Would you like to come in?

– Thank you very much, Colby said.

Oddly, given his good instincts, he did not feel the least bit uneasy. He entered Mrs. Azarian-Thomson's home, pleased with how smoothly things were going. As they walked into the living room, however, he saw there were two policemen. One, unfortunately, was Detective Mandelshtam.

– Errol, said Mandelshtam. What are you doing here?

– Errol? said Willow's sister. I thought it was William.

– I misspoke, said Colby.

A more ridiculous answer he could not have devised if they'd given him weeks to think about it. If he could, he'd have sunk into the carpet.

– So, what are you doing here? Mandelshtam repeated.

– He's working for charity, said Mrs. Azarian-Thomson. Just like the man I was telling you about. Maybe they work for the same charity.

– Tell me about it, Errol, said Detective Mandelshtam. I'm interested in this new leaf of yours.

2 A Digression (with Simone Azarian-Thomson)

Tancred, having abandoned his own apartment, was now staying on Winnett with Olivier. He spent time contemplating the two Azarian mementos he'd brought together – those belonging to Willow and Gretchen. Willow had paid a year's rent on the loft. So, he had leisure to gaze at them and think, to look for a connection between them: an idea, a logic that would make the next (missing) piece in the sequence both necessary and superfluous. Necessary, in that it would be a confirmation that he'd grasped the true thought behind the clues. Superfluous in that, if he had grasped this thought, the remaining pieces would add nothing essential.

Ollie was, in his way, helpful. He was good at these sorts of games. But he'd recently rediscovered an interest in Buddhism, so he could not be counted on to think, as opposed to meditating. He'd sit on the floor before the model of Fallingwater or the Japanese screen, his ability to sit still in itself admirable. Once, after hours of looking at the screen, he'd calmly said

– There are willows in Psalm 137, with harps on them

before returning to silence. A gnomic pronouncement: just on the edge of sense, frustrating because it led Tancred nowhere definite.

When the time came to steal the painting from Simone Azarian-Thomson's home, it was a relief for Tancred to think about concrete matters. He'd seen the painting while casing the home. It was four feet wide and three feet tall, an awkward size. It looked heavy. Its frame – a dark hardwood – was, in front, unexceptional: six inches wide all around. But it was also six or seven inches thick and had a backing that made it seem as if the painting was in a kind of box rather than simply framed. The painting would be difficult for one alone to carry, no doubt about it. And, it seemed to Tancred, the work would be better done in daylight when you could see where you were going, though daylight, of course, would bring other difficulties.

The painting's size and integument were not its only awkward aspects. Its frame contained a motion detector and audio speakers.

Whenever anyone approached, the painting would play the first Prelude of Bach's *Well-Tempered Clavier*. That is to say, the painting was ensconced in a kind of music box. And the music was not exactly soothing. The painting played Glenn Gould's recording of the work. So, not only did a piano sound when one got close but, as well, with Gould's constant humming, it was as if a vagrant entered the room at the same time.

Finally, there was the painting's subject matter. It was both a double portrait and a landscape. Occupying two-thirds of the painting were two men in Roman togas, side by side. The men were on the summit of a green hill. The one on the left was shorter, bearded, wore a golden laurel wreath and in his right hand held a violin by the neck. The man on the right was grey-haired, his tunic was short, his thighs pale, and on his left shoulder there was a rather large raven, painted in three-quarter profile. The third of the painting not devoted to the men – that is, the third on the viewer's right – depicted a burning city: Rome. The conflagration was skilfully done. One could see, though the city looked to be some distance from the hill where the men stood, a number of fleeing figures, their robes in reddish-orange flames. It was like an ancient nightmare, not the kind of thing a loving father would leave as a memento, you'd have thought. On the other hand, the painting had been done by a talented artist. It was as striking as it was odd. If it were stolen in daylight, it would almost certainly be memorable to any passersby who saw it. So, they would have to cover the painting with canvas.

In any case, the important points were these:

1. that there should be a strong person to carry the painting (Ollie most likely)
2. that the painting's motion sensor be disabled so *The Well-Tempered Clavier* would not play
3. that the home's alarm system be turned off or made irrelevant

Willow's sister, Simone Azarian-Thomson, was a talker. When Tancred, asking her to sign a petition, had bluffed his way into the house to see where the painting was hung and what the alarm system was like, Mrs. Azarian-Thomson kept him there for half an hour, talking about her life and interests. Without prompting, she had told him how often she was home alone and how rarely she had company during the day. She'd told him so much, he'd felt like both taking notes and warning her to be more discreet.

Tancred was convinced it would take very little to get her talking again.

Ollie agreed to steal the painting on an afternoon he had off and Tancred set out how they'd proceed. Tancred would ring at the front door, remind Mrs. Azarian-Thomson that she'd offered to make a contribution to Toronto Western Hospital. While she was talking and signing a cheque, Ollie would enter from the back of the house, take down the painting, put it in a van they would steal beforehand, then blow the van's horn to signal that he had it. So, there it was: relatively uncomplicated, a job that could be done by amateurs.

Two days before they were to steal the painting, Tancred stole a van parked off Eglinton not far from Yonge. That night, in a storage garage Tancred rented at Kennedy and Sheppard, he and Ollie used a stencil and black spray paint to put

McCaltex Restoration

on both sides of the grey-blue van, Mr. McCaltex having been their grade-school art teacher.

The following day, with Ollie dressed in dark overalls, because that is what he imagined restorers wore, they set out for the Azarian-Thomson house on Edgar Avenue.

The house itself was impressive: red brick, with two chimneys. It was three storeys high, with a long front walk – precisely cut and laid shale – leading to cement steps. The entrance was through a brick porch over which there was a room with tall transom windows. It was the kind of house you would notice, but it was not ostentatious. It brought to mind old and polite money. If, in his professional capacity, he were going to break and enter anywhere on Edgar Avenue, Tancred would, he imagined, have chosen the grey, mock Tudor monstrosity down the road. Though, these days, he did not often break and enter unless, as now, he was looking for a specific valuable thing.

Though he'd spent time in Rosedale, it still felt to Tancred like walking through a rumour of Toronto. Unreal. How difficult it was, at times, to square these big-roomed places with their walkways and green lawns – no bald patches! – with the reddish-brick warrens where he'd grown up. For most of his life, 'home' had meant row houses, one home distinguished from the next only by a satellite dish or a window flower box or the butt end of an air-conditioner hanging from a second-floor window. Down the street or across Dundas: Asian grocery stores and restaurants, endless traffic till late at night, no quiet until three in the morning when the older kids had had enough for the night and would go home, their voices trailing after them.

Tancred parked the van on Roxborough by a modest, well-kept triangle of park space: wooden benches beside sparse plots for flowers, thin trees here and there. They had agreed that Ollie would go to the back of the house fifteen minutes after Tancred had entered it from the front. If the back door was unlocked, Ollie (who knew the layout of the house because Tancred had drawn it for him) would go in and take the painting at once, quietly and carefully, in case Tancred hadn't been the one to unlock the door. Tancred would, of course, distract whoever was inside.

If the back door was locked, Ollie would wait for Tancred's signal – a knock at the back window from inside the house. Having got the signal, he was to open the door and go in while Tancred distracted whoever needed distracting. If no knock came and the back door remained locked, he was to leave after twenty minutes without taking anything.

They were clear on what was to be done.

Less clear were Tancred's feelings. He felt exhilaration and pleasure, the usual. He imagined it was what actors felt going onstage.

But beneath the rush of adrenalin, he also felt distress. It was as if they were stealing from Willow, and that idea was disturbing. He'd felt the same when they'd broken into Gretchen's home. He was not made to steal from friends or to betray a trust. But how strange that he should feel this while honouring Willow's wishes and keeping his word. For the first time since he was a child, he found the difference between right feeling and right doing difficult to ignore.

Tancred was dressed much as he had been on first calling at the Azarian-Thomsons' home: navy-blue Canali two-piece, pale chicory-coloured shirt, light-orange tie. He looked, he thought, as those asking for money should look: clean, not desperate. In any case, Willow's sister had invited him in the first time and offered him a hundred dollars. There was no reason to think she'd be less accommodating now.

— Yes?

— Mrs. Azarian-Thomson? I wonder if you remember me.

She smiled, as if he'd said something ironic.

— How could I forget? she asked. You were collecting money for charity, wasn't it?

— Yes, said Tancred. And you were kind enough to offer ...

— A hundred dollars for a new wing at the Toronto Western! But you wouldn't take my money. Such an insult! Why shouldn't I turn you away now?

— I'd be disappointed, said Tancred.

— Well, said Simone, we can't have that. Come in, Tan. What did you say your name was?

For a moment, Tancred could have sworn she'd called him by name.

— *Ben*, he said. Ben Connolly.

Again, the enigmatic smile.

— A lovely name, she said

and stood aside so he could enter.

From there, things went almost precisely to plan. But if the chaos of the first theft had been stressful, the precision of this one was unnerving. It felt as if, at any moment, someone with a microphone might pop up and cry out that he was on television.

After fifteen minutes of talk about hospitals, fifteen minutes during which Willow's sister did most of the talking, he'd asked to use the washroom and she had pointed toward it.

– Through the next room, she'd said

and let him go on his own.

Glenn Gould had come on as he passed the painting. He'd gone through to the kitchen and unlocked the back door after tapping on the kitchen window. On returning through the room with the painting in it, with Bach still sounding and Gould going tra-la-la, he'd taken a small can of hairspray from his jacket pocket and sprayed over the painting's motion detector, disabling it. Once again in the front room, he tried to pick up the conversation from where they'd left off, but Mrs. Azarian-Thomson seemed to have talked the subject of hospitals out.

– Do you like the painting? she asked.

– It's unusual, Tancred answered.

She laughed and rose from her chair.

– It reminds me of my father, she said. He was an unusual man. Then she added

– I wonder if you'd come upstairs with me a moment, *Ben*.

He could hardly have refused. To take her farther away from the room with the painting was ideal. But spooked by this unsought advantage, he said

– Have I come at a bad time?

– You've come at the perfect time, she answered.

She walked toward the stairs and, looking back, nodded. She went up, no doubt assuming that he would follow – which he did, thinking, 'What's the worst that could happen?' At the top of the stairs, he was disoriented, unsure which room she'd entered, until she called out

– I'm in here

and Tancred entered what was, obviously, the master bedroom: pale wooden floors, darkly stained Mennonite furniture (a bed, a chest of drawers, a cabinet) and a large Persian rug that looked ancient but still vivid with a crimson border in which Arabic script was woven. The rug, elaborate and beautiful, was in contrast to the rest of the room, which was spare and simple. On top of the chest of drawers, in vials of ivory and coloured glass, unstoppered, there lurked strange, synthetic perfumes.

Mrs. Azarian-Thomson stood on the Persian rug, her back to him.

– I hope you don't mind? she said. I know it's a cliché, but I'd like to change into something comfortable.

He was meant to help her undress, it seemed, to pull down the zipper at the back of her dress. This he did, only to discover that she wore no underclothes, a fact of which she seemed blithely indifferent. She kept her back to him as she opened the chest of drawers looking for something. What that might be, Tancred did not know. He'd averted his eyes, paying exaggerated attention to the carpet beneath him.

– I gather the script is from the Koran, she said. 'O true believers, give alms of that which we have bestowed on you ...' That's as much as I know. I'm not actually Muslim. I just love the carpet.

– It's beautiful, said Tancred.

– Is there anything else you find beautiful?

– Yes, said Tancred, but it wouldn't be polite to say.

Simone began to laugh. Tancred looked up to see that she had put on navy-blue track pants and a grey sweatshirt. She sat on the edge of her bed looking at him.

– Oh, Tancred, she said. My sister was right about you! You *are* old-fashioned!

– *Ben*, said Tancred.

– *Tancred*, said Simone. And I knew it was you the first time I saw you. You're exactly as Willow described. You didn't think I'd offer a hundred dollars to just anyone, did you? I don't throw money around, Tancred. But Willow insisted you were an honourable man. 'A knight in dirty armour' is how she put it. So, I wasn't too worried you'd take my money. My sister didn't always have the best judgment, but I knew the moment I saw you that she was right. It's strange but you almost reek of devotion.

She touched the place beside her on the bed.

– Come sit beside me, she said. I'm sorry I put you through all this. Willow told me so much about you, I could have picked you out of a police lineup. But I like to judge people for myself. And I didn't know exactly what kind of person you are.

Strange behaviour if true, thought Tancred.

Reading his emotion, she said

– Don't worry. I can defend myself. I have a number of these all around the house. My husband's a fanatic and he's American. No home without guns.

She lifted a white pillow on the bed behind her. Beneath it, there was a pearl-handled Derringer, delicate-looking, as if it were a child's toy. She let the pillow fall back.

– The other thing about my sister, she said, is that she couldn't keep a secret. If there's anything about Willow I'd have changed, it would be her big mouth. God keep her soul.

– So, said Tancred, you think she was right about your father's mementos?

– Yes, I do think so, she answered, even though our father told us there was no so-called treasure.

– I don't understand, said Tancred. If she was right, why didn't you help her?

– Tancred, said Simone. Tancred Palmieri. Your father was Italian?

– Yes, but I never knew him.

– Lucky you. My father was Armenian: second-generation, old-school, the kids call it. Willow thought the sun shone out of Dad's behind, but that's not true. I remember how he treated our mother. He brought women into our home, right in front of her. I bet Willow never told you any of that. Or that he used to beat the hell out of Mike. For no reason. If Mike even looked at him wrong. My brother was an alcoholic by the time he was fifteen. Did Willow tell you that? I'm not saying my father was evil, but it was better if you stayed on the right side of him. One thing I'll say for him, though: he never fooled around with money. Money was his religion. I don't remember a single day in my childhood when he didn't tell us how important money was. That's why none of my siblings believed there was anything to Willow's idea. No one believes he was the kind of man to leave a bundle of it around, hidden somewhere on the off chance his children could solve some silly puzzle. Then there's the fact that he *told* us there was nothing to find.

Simone patted Tancred's knee.

– Something's not quite right, she said, and I'm not sure what it is.

– But Willow was right about the pieces being clues?

– Oh yes, she was right about that. They're obvious clues. And they lead to Mount Pleasant Cemetery, to a specific spot in Mount Pleasant Cemetery where the Weidens are buried and where he had a mausoleum built in their honour. But that's the end of it. That's the point of the whole charade. My father believed the Weidens were the best kind of family. He'd tell us we should stick together like they did. The kids took care of Mrs. Weiden when she had a stroke and they took care of their father when he had cancer. And even after Mr. and Mrs. Weiden were gone, the kids looked out for each other. They were good people and my father wanted us to be like them. All these clues, the whole business was his way of reminding us about what's important: family. After money, that was the thing my father talked about most. Do you know Psalm 137, Tancred?

– By the rivers of Babylon ...

(Here, Tancred heard the van's horn sounding.)

– That's the one. You know what it's about, don't you? It's about being in exile and missing home. When you take Willow's screen into consideration, I mean really take it into consideration, it points to Willow's relationship with Father and it points to Psalm 137. And Psalm 137 is the last piece of the puzzle.

Once again, she patted his knee.

– Anyway, she said, that's what my brothers and my sister Gretchen believe. That everything leads to the Weidens and the

Weidens are about family and that Willow needed something to distract her from heroin and to get her to think about her family. All very neat and sensible, but I don't buy it because I don't trust my father. I'm just not sure Willow's wrong. So, I don't mind you carrying on. Especially now that I know you.

– Thank you, said Tancred.

– You've come this far, said Willow's sister, you might as well keep going. But I'm going to call the police if you steal my painting.

– You don't believe I'll return it?

– I'm sure you'll return it. But I don't want my siblings or my husband to know that I think Willow might be right or that I'm on your side. I won't tell them who you are or where to find you, but if you manage to steal it I'll call the police at once.

– I wonder why Willow didn't tell me about Mount Pleasant, said Tancred.

– I'm not sure she ever worked it out, and Mike and I never told her. We would have, eventually, but we both thought it was good that she had this puzzle to keep her busy. Mike especially. He was an addict. So he knew what she was going through. This treasure business gave her something to occupy her mind. It's like Sudoku for addicts. The old Willow, the one you never met, would have worked it out in two shakes, but drugs took everything away from her. We knew she was doing drugs before Dad died, but she kept it under control. It's only after his funeral that she really went off the rails. She was barely herself in the end.

Simone rose from the bed.

– I'm going to go out for a run now, she said. Is there anything else?

– Yes, said Tancred. There's one thing. I know it's personal, but I wonder if you'd tell me what the painting means?

3 A Further Digression (with Glenn Gould)

Despite Simone's reservations about her father, she'd loved him as deeply as Willow had. Where Willow's love for her father was unalloyed, however, Simone's was not. Occasionally, ambivalence (even dislike) crept in. Her father's cruelty to her favourite brother – Michael – was one reason for it. His infidelity to her dying mother was another.

Although, as to infidelity . . . Simone was now older and she was herself married to a man who was infirm. As a result, she could appreciate her father's frustrations. She did not intend to betray her husband, but she now fully understood the temptations and wondered if she could resist them indefinitely.

She'd said to Tancred that her father had been 'old-school.' What she'd meant was that a part of him had been Armenian to the end. He'd been the true child of his parents, one foot metaphorically planted (or metaphorically stuck) in Yerevan. Simone assumed that this was a cross her father had had to bear. But Robert Azarian had also taken strength from his roots. He had inherited wit, determination and money. Beyond all that, however, he had been, in her experience, a sensitive man, one who cried easily and was not ashamed. He'd also been, with her, considerate and loving. The painting he left her was, whatever else it might be, proof of this.

There were, of course, two aspects to the painting, both equally meaningful: sound and image. Sound first: when Simone was seven or eight, her father had been friends with a man named Azriel Burkett: a name she could not forget, in part because it sounded to her younger self like a woman's name, in part because Mr. Burkett was the first man from Alberta she'd ever met and that fact had seemed exotic and attractive. Then again, Simone remembered the man as being troublingly handsome, the first man she'd been attracted to, though he'd been – what? – thirty? And she seven or eight.

She wondered now if her father hadn't known about her crush on Mr. Burkett. On a number of occasions, he'd taken her, Willow and Michael with him to Mr. Burkett's apartment on St. Clair. The most memorable occasion had come one summer evening sometime in the sixties. They had gone to the apartment and, as sometimes happened, they heard piano music. Simone could not remember anyone asking about the music before that night. In fact, though there was no doubt about what happened, there was some dispute amongst the children about who it was who asked about the music. Each of the children remembered being the one to ask, being the one Mr. Burkett had gratified by taking them all to the roof of the building to hear the music more clearly. Simone remembered the night still. The moon above them was white and full – not a crescent, as Michael remembered. There had been wind, a wind that blew Willow's dress this way and that. There had been the smell of tar and pine. And then, of course, there had been the music itself: each note clear, the piano stopping and starting unpredictably, then going on for long stretches, like magic. Mr. Burkett lived in the same apartment building as Glenn Gould and, from time to time, on a warm night, Mr. Burkett went to the roof to listen to the man play, the music rising from Gould's apartment whenever he practiced. Years later, Willow would swear she remembered Glenn Gould humming along. But that was impossible. Simone would have remembered it. In fact, she was convinced that Willow did not so much remember the evening as she recalled the innumerable times the three of them – Simone, Michael, Willow – had spoken of it together. The night itself was now as mythic to them as the Children's Crusade or the Battle of Roncevaux Pass.

In any case, it was obvious that Simone had been the one most affected by the occasion. She never again listened to Glenn Gould as they had that evening, but during her adolescence he became a kind of shibboleth for her. She bought all of his records, wearing out several copies of the *Goldberg Variations* and *The Well-Tempered Clavier*, listening to them alone in her room, dressed all in white as was, in those days, her predilection.

Simone had assumed her father knew nothing about her passion for Glenn Gould. When she thought about it, when she considered that for years none could pass her room without hearing Gould playing, it was clear he'd have had to have been deaf not to know. Still, she'd thought her father too busy to notice her predilections. So, it had been enchanting, at the reading of his will, to discover that he'd kept this time in her life in mind. That said, it had been years since she'd listened to Glenn Gould. She'd worn out his recordings ages ago.

But if the Gould was proof of her father's memory, the painting was something else. It was, at first glance and obviously, a depiction of the Emperor Nero Germanicus. But her father was teasing her. Simone, with her doctorate in history, could not have felt anything but amusement on seeing the violin in Nero's hand. Nero, as the popular saying went, had 'fiddled' as Rome burned. But, of course, the fiddle had not yet been invented in Nero's time. Nero, however, was not the most striking subject in the painting. Beside the emperor stood Marcus Valerius Messalla Corvinus. Corvinus's likeness was fanciful. There were no faithful portraits or statues of the man in existence, but he was identifiable by the large raven perched on his shoulder. The raven was particularly well done, each feather clear from its pinions in. The bird was at rest, but it was also as if on the verge of flight. Obviously, it was a clue to something or part of a clue, *Corvinus* being the Latin for raven and Marcus Corvinus – known as Consul 58 – having assumed his consulate in Nero's reign.

Of all the children, Simone was the one most likely to know these details. So, one could have said that the painting was as personal as the music, that it was meant for her. But the portrait of Marcus Corvinus was so obviously a clue to something, the painting became, in her mind, a thing not quite meant for her. The clue – the number 58 – was there for anyone to see or grasp, for anyone to use.

For anyone? No, not really. It was as if her father were playing a game not with her but *through* her, a game meant for Willow. She could not help resenting this evidence – she took it for proof – that Willow had been dearer to their father than she had. The painting being a clue, it turned the music into a clue as well: *The Well-Tempered Clavier* is, among musicologists, known as 'the 48.' So, her father's memento could be reduced to numbers: 48, 58.

This teetering between the intimate and the impersonal was unpleasant. It made her feel unsure of the painting's personal significance – as if her childhood had been ransacked for numerical correlatives – and, so, slightly unsure of her father's affection. Each of the mementos must have aroused something similar in her siblings but, of course, each of them took it in his or her own way.

Willow, for whom the whole charade existed, had been enthralled, the proverbial optimist digging in horse manure to find the horse. Gretchen ignored the clues in her model of Fallingwater. She knew they were there, knew their significance, but she held to what was personal: she and her father in Pennsylvania. Alton, the eldest, was amused by the whole business. He took it as one of their father's strange ideas, a flight of fancy. And though the poem he inherited bristled with personal significance, Alton refused to take it personally. Finally, there was Michael, whose memento – a bottle of aquavit – was a kind of rebuke.

A *kind* of rebuke? No, it was a rebuke pure and simple. Before going teetotal, Michael had gotten blackout drunk with some wealthy friends – or wealthy idiots, if you like – who'd got him on a private jet to Oslo and abandoned him there: naked, with a bottle of aquavit and a beach towel for succour. The experience was so traumatic that Michael gave up drinking for good. You could say his so-called friends inadvertently cured him of his drunkenness. Robert Azarian certainly thought so. But the bottle of Linie Aquavit he left his son was as much a reminder of humiliation as it was of salvation. Was there aquavit in the bottle? Was it meant as temptation? Michael never opened the thing to find out. And Simone was convinced he would not care if Tancred stole the bottle from him.

Simone sighed.

– I suppose these mementos are proof of my father's brilliance, she said. All this: the things he left us being personal at the same time as they have some other use. It may not lead to much but it's oh so brilliant.

– Willow . . . , said Tancred.

But Simone would not let him continue.

– No, she said. Willow was obsessed. I'm sure she was thinking about the treasure hunts we used to have as kids. Dad hid really great gifts. Alton found a gold bar one year. So, I think Willow just assumed these clues Dad left would lead to some fantastic thing. Poor Will. If she hadn't been so messed up with drugs, she'd have got all the clues as easily as the rest of us. If I ever thought about doing heroin, all I'd have to do is think about Will and that'd be that.

Simone rose from the bed.

– So, she said. I've got to get going now.

– Thank you, said Tancred.

– Don't mention it, said Simone. And good luck stealing my painting.

They were at the bottom of the stairs when Tancred said

– I've taken it already.

Simone turned her head back toward him, uncertain she'd heard him correctly. She was about to say, 'What's that?' when she walked into the middle room and saw that her painting was gone. She stopped, almost mid-stride. Far from being upset, she was delighted. It was as if she were witness to some extraordinary legerdemain.

– How did you do that? she asked.

– I'm not sure, said Tancred.

– You have trade secrets! How wonderful! I still can't see you stealing anything from Michael's condo but – do you know? – I'm not as sure about that as I was a few minutes ago. I've got to report this theft of yours, Tancred. I don't want my husband or my siblings thinking I'm in cahoots with you. I'm going to go out for a run. Then I'm going to call the police. I won't tell them anything about you. But I expect my painting back and I expect it back soon.

Simone let him out the back door, locking it behind them.

– You're an interesting young man, she said. I can see why my sister trusted you. She must have wanted to. But remember, Tancred, I'm not my sister.

4 Mandelshtam Suspects

And so, as Detective Mandelshtam was staring at the place where the portrait of Nero and Marcus Corvinus had been and an officer from 53 Division poked around the kitchen, Simone Azarian-Thomson brought Errol Colby in.

It would be difficult to say who, of Mandelshtam and Colby, was the more surprised.

– He's working for charity, said Simone. Just like the man I was telling you about. Maybe they work for the same charity.

Mandelshtam said

– Tell me about this charity of yours, Errol. I'm fascinated by the new leaf you're turning over.

Colby's mind worked furiously to come up with a credible story. Any number of doubtful things came to him: that he was in the wrong home, that he had an appointment elsewhere, that he had only just begun this charitable work and was no good at it, that his conscience had led him to charitable work and he sincerely hoped he'd done nothing wrong. But then a kind of dignity overcame him. What had he done wrong? Nothing. He'd come into a woman's home asking for money. Big deal. He hadn't forced his way in. No money had changed hands.

– There's nothing to tell, he said. I'm interested in buying this house and I was wondering about the price. I might have mentioned a charity so I could get a look around. But I didn't do anything wrong. What are you going to do? Arrest me for house hunting?

– But my house isn't for sale, said Simone.

– Well, now I know, said Colby. Thank you.

He turned around and left the place, surprised that no one tried to stop him. He heard Willow's sister say

– But ...

By which time he'd almost reached the front door.

Behind him, Mandelshtam lightly touched Simone's arm.

– Is he the one who was here yesterday?

— No, answered Simone.

— Then don't worry about him. I know where he lives. Let's get back to the painting.

There were a number of reasons why Daniel did not mind Colby's quick exit. To begin with, Colby was right. He hadn't done anything wrong. He'd been invited into the home. Then, too, Daniel did know where to find Colby if he was needed. Finally, there was Simone Azarian-Thomson herself. Something was off where she was concerned. She had done everything she was supposed to do. She'd reported the theft and mentioned that her sister's model of Falling-water had also been stolen, suggesting there might be some connection between the thefts. It was thanks to this mention – and her status as an Azarian – that Daniel had been sent to investigate, though Rosedale was out of 14 Division's district.

The two thefts almost certainly had something to do with each other. But about this connection, Simone Azarian-Thomson was, in person, strangely vague. It was as if on second thought she no longer found it significant that her and her sister's mementos had been stolen. Though he couldn't have said why exactly Daniel was convinced Mrs. Azarian-Thomson knew more than she was letting on. To his mind, it was even possible she knew the thief.

And there it was: another reason Daniel did not mind when Colby fled. Colby's presence had immediately brought Tancred to Daniel's mind and he suspected, without of course being certain, that Tancred had something to do with this Azarian business. It was an upsetting prospect: after his five years in the force, he might have to deal with Tancred in an official capacity. He might have to deal with his friend as he would any thief – impersonally, ruthlessly. It was not clear to him that he would be able to do this.

Had there been more to Mrs. Azarian-Thomson's story, Daniel might have questioned her further. If he'd believed her story, he might also have explored her house more carefully. But he did not believe and, on top of that, her story was ridiculously basic: she had been in her room preparing to go out for a run. That was not three hours gone. She'd come down the stairs and noticed that her painting was missing. Nothing else had been taken. She was adamant about it. The painting and the painting alone.

She'd seen nothing, because she'd been on the second floor.

She'd heard nothing.

— You're sure no one in your family ...

— I told you, Detective, my husband's in Ann Arbor seeing a specialist. My sons are away at school. Sam's at Columbia and Robert's at Stanford. Anyway, none of them has ever cared about my painting enough to steal it or have it stolen. Someone broke in to take it and I was very lucky that whoever did this wasn't interested in me or in anything upstairs.

— And you think it could be whoever stole your sister's memento?

— How would I know that, Detective? It's your job to tell me who took it.

— You don't think there's any connection?

— It's not that, Detective. It's that I don't know. All I know is that someone stole my painting and someone stole my sister's model of Fallingwater. If you think there's a connection, I believe you. But I'm just telling you what I know. I was upstairs. I came down and my painting was gone.

— Thank you, said Daniel, for your time.

It wasn't difficult to tell when someone was not being honest. Daniel had had a great deal of experience with liars. Though he could not exactly pinpoint a lie, he could feel its presence. It was like knowing there are mice in the house, though one hasn't seen any, nor even their droppings. Occasionally, however, class complicated things. Certain members of the upper class behaved as if candour were something they hadn't mastered. In those cases, it sometimes happened that a man or woman was not lying, though everything in their demeanour and tone suggested they might be. As Simone Azarian-Thomson was upper class, there was some doubt in Daniel's mind. Was she hiding something or was she peremptory and defensive by habit?

Mrs. Azarian-Thomson had seemed determined to report a crime and she'd tried to do this with minimal involvement. She hadn't been supercilious exactly, not like some in Rosedale who treated the police like liveried servants. But it felt as if she'd resented his questions, resented the small details he'd got out of her, resented the whole business, though she was determined to carry on. Her attitude had so struck him that Daniel decided to speak to his wife about it. Fiona – posh, London-born – might, he thought, have some inkling of why Azarian-Thomson had behaved as she had.

As it happened, that evening they had guests who helped bring the question up: Miguel Ferreira, his wife, Nira, and, unavoidably, their dog. Daniel had forgotten the Ferreiras were coming, but then they were not his friends. Nira and Fiona were close, having been at Cambridge together. He and Miguel, who worked in television, got along fine, but if it had not been for their wives there'd have been little incentive for them to hang out. Their interests were too different. Then there was the dog: a black poodle. Nira was as attentive to the creature's moods as if it had been a close cousin or an old friend. (She had first named the dog Jim but, after a time, its 'real name' – Majnoun – had come to her. Or so she claimed and, to his credit, even her husband rolled his eyes at this.) Daniel found Nira's attitude toward the dog pretentious. But the dog itself was impeccably well-trained.

That's not to say that the Ferreiras' company was a burden. It wasn't. Nira, copy editor that she was, was a fount of stories about writers and, above all, poets. It was amusing to imagine that poets might be, as Nira called them, the country's 'unacknowledged legislators.' It brought to Daniel's mind the curious idea that Toronto might have been different if it had managed to produce different poets. What would the city have been if it had made Robert Frost or Emily Dickinson? Could it have elected Rob Ford if it had been home to Sylvia Plath or John Donne? Then, too, what was Toronto that Gwendolyn MacEwen should be its legislator and conscience?

(Daniel had seen her once when he was a boy. Baruch, who'd admired poets since reading Mayakovsky when *he* was a boy, had pointed MacEwen out to him: a thin woman, birdlike, riding a clunky bike along Brunswick, her face pale, her hair greying. To Daniel, she'd seemed both noble and mysterious. Did his city derive its secret sense from her? But what remained most vivid, what moved him now that Baruch was gone, was the surprise he'd felt at his father's belief that poets meant something. And although, even in reverie, 'poet' was too fussy an occupation for him, he wondered if it was not from this fleeting encounter with MacEwen that he began to imagine what it might be like to write novels, say, or a memoir.)

After Nira had told a story about a poet and after Miguel had quipped his usual quip about copy editors being the unacknowledged legislators of the unacknowledged legislators, Daniel said

— What about some of the *acknowledged* legislators?

— Like who? asked Fiona. Politicians?

— No, said Daniel, the rich.

— You sound like your father, Fiona said.

Which was true, as Baruch could never resist talking about the rich.

— There's no such thing as '*the* rich,' said Nira. What rich are you referring to? Those born with money? Those who are wealthy through enterprise? The wealthy from Hong Kong? From Russia? How about the criminal rich? Those who are rich on the black market and have to hide their money? Toronto has all of them.

— Yes, said Daniel, but I'm trying to say that someone like Robert Azarian had more real influence than someone like Margaret Atwood ever could.

— I'm not sure that's true, said Nira. Money does what it wants to, irrespective of who owns it. When Mr. Azarian died, his money went on without him. Anyway, Atwood *is* rich, isn't she?

— I know you have trouble believing this, Fiona said, but the rich aren't that powerful.

Miguel smirked but held his tongue. They'd had this conversation before, any number of times. He and Daniel inevitably ended up arguing for the authority of the rich, while their wives – both born into wealth – pointed to the political influence of the poor.

– Allie Azarian was in my class at UTS, said Nira.

– You knew her? asked Daniel.

– I *know* her, said Nira, even if I don't see her as often as I'd like.

– Was Robert her father?

– No, Alton's her father.

– What's the family like? asked Daniel.

Nira thought about it before answering. Her poodle sat up beside her, tilting his head to one side, staring at Daniel.

– I like them, she said, but they're very intense. They play old-fashioned games like Botticelli and they used to have incredible treasure hunts, but they're super-competitive. The first time I was at Allie's, Allie and her brother got into a fight because they lost to their mom and dad at Botticelli. They were shouting at each other because Allie didn't know who Telly Savalas was. I still remember it. Allie was red in the face, she was so angry. I never would have guessed. At school, she never raised her voice. But she hated losing to her brother or her parents. On the other hand, they're the most generous people I've ever met. Once he knew I was Allie's friend, Mr. Azarian was very kind. He invited me for Christmas Eve one year, and they'd bought a present for me so I wouldn't feel left out: a gold necklace with a ruby pendant, because ruby is my birthstone, apparently. Very thoughtful and extravagant and sweet. I miss them, actually.

– I wonder, said Daniel, did you ever meet Simone Azarian?

– Who hasn't met her? answered Nira. You can't go to a fundraiser anywhere within fifty miles of Toronto without …

Fiona interrupted her friend.

– Why? she asked. Have *you* met her?

The question was clearly less significant than the tone in which it was asked, and the tone invited caution. So, Daniel said

– I've never met her socially, but she's the kind of wealthy person we were talking about, isn't she?

– Well, said Nira, she's just as complicated as the others, but she has a reputation.

– Yes, said Fiona. She's kind of scarlet.

That, for discretion's sake, was as far as Daniel ventured.

Whether Simone Azarian-Thomson was or was not 'scarlet' – whatever that meant – was none of his business. Nor did it make sense of her attitude. The thing that stayed with him was the idea of competition. Could it be that he'd stumbled onto a game Robert Azarian's children were playing against each other? If so, what were the stakes? And what did Colby and Tancred have to do with it?

It was difficult to imagine anyone less likely to be involved with the Azarians than Tancred. Tancred had always been wary of the rich. In that sense, he was more like Baruch's son than Daniel and, not for the first time, Daniel wondered if Tancred might not have been a better son to Baruch than he had. Then again, it was impossible to predict how two beings who are obliged to get along would actually get along. Had Tancred and Baruch been father and son, it's possible they would not have been so close.

Whatever Tancred's involvement with the Azarians, however, Daniel felt in his soul that Colby was a key to the whole mystifying business. Colby was crucial. That meant he'd have to keep an eye on the man. For anyone else, this would not be difficult. An albino who called himself Nigger and hung around Parkdale would be hard to miss. Unfortunately, Colby knew him well, knew him to be Tancred's friend. It would be impossible for him to keep track of Colby by himself. Not to mention that, the Azarian thefts being among his first cases as a detective, he did not want to work outside official boundaries. He'd have to call in a favour.

As it happened, Tom Paulsen-Puig – 'Puli' to his friends, though he did not resemble the dog – owed Daniel a number of favours. And he was good at his job: private investigator. Puli usually did skip tracing or spying for spouses. So, he could follow a man without being seen and, as it happened, Colby did not know him.

– So is this a personal thing, Dan?

Puli was looking out at the world. The trees in Cabbagetown were leafless and the street had taken on its late-autumn hardness, looking almost severe.

– I'm not sure, Daniel answered. I don't know what I'm looking for or what I expect to find.

– But you're sure there's something to find? Look, Dan, of course I'll do this for you. But if it's not personal or urgent I'll start in four or five days. Is that okay? I'm following a real pig around. His wife thinks he's having an affair but it's more like he's doing the entire population of Rathnelly. It's a good neighbourhood, but my god, it'd be easier to take pictures of the few people he *isn't* fucking.

Daniel, who up to that moment had been peering out at the street, turned to his friend. Puli was blond, his hairline receding: a man nearing forty. His nose, which had been broken sometime in childhood, was high bridged. He was in good shape but he drank too much and he was, as they say, unlucky in love. Puli himself admitted that, were he airlifted into a city of a million wonderful women among whom there were two who were 'unhinged,' he would have found and dated both and proposed to one inside of a week. Yet the man himself was sane, kind, even-tempered and generous. What was it in people that needed the sentimental confusion?

– A few days shouldn't make much difference, Daniel said. But the sooner the better.

5 A Mausoleum in the Cemetery

Tancred had made a promise to Willow and he *would* not consider his promise fulfilled until he'd done his utmost to discover any hidden significance to the mementos. His quest, as he understood it, was not about money or gain or status. It was about honouring his word and finding the truth.

But Simone Azarian-Thomson had muddied the waters.

There was a contradiction at the heart of the woman. She was at least somewhat convinced that the mementos were part of a treasure hunt whose reward was a kind of homily – 'cleave to your family' – meant for Willow. All the Azarians except Willow believed this. But either from faith in Willow or out of mistrust for her father, Simone also believed there might be more to it, that it would be just like her father to give the thing a final twist, to have a sting in the tail. So, she'd allowed Tancred to keep her painting and, by extension, her sister's model of Fallingwater. She had, in effect, given him permission to complete his task.

All of this left Tancred feeling as if he were in a fog of thought. Had Willow previously arrived at the same conclusion as her siblings and rejected it? Or was it, as Simone believed, that Willow had been too stoned to put the clues together? Did the 'clues' really point to a spot in Mount Pleasant? He hadn't solved the puzzle for himself, so the so-called solution had no hold on him. Should he, then, reject the Azarians' solution until (or *if*) he discovered it for himself? Or should he go to Mount Pleasant and look around?

How uncertain things had become! Since his meetings with Willow and the death of his mother, the world had become unreadable. It now felt as if a question lurked behind any action he contemplated. He was living in a world of Ollie's devising, it seemed, the value of everything open to doubt. But where Ollie could blithely live with uncertain value, he found it excruciating. How was it possible to know the important thing, under such circumstances?

He chose to go and look around the cemetery. There was no reason for Simone to invent such a specific solution to the clues her father had left. So, the place no doubt held something of importance.

It had snowed, but not heavily. A wind troubled the flakes on the ground as if they were sand, creating white whorls on the roads and walkways through the cemetery.

Tancred thought of Mount Pleasant as a kind of hospital, an extreme hospital, if you like. Its occupants were obviously beyond medicine, but the cemetery was so quiet, its atmosphere so serious, it was as if the dead depended on silence the way patients do: for sleep, for rest.

Simone had not given him the coordinates of the Weidens' graves. So, Tancred went to the cemetery's office and asked if there were a plot where a number of Weidens were buried. There was: plot 22, very near the office itself, though, because the grounds were so strangely laid out – plot 35 beside plot 39, 17 beside 22 and so on – it took Tancred a good fifteen minutes before he found plot 22 and a few minutes more to find the graves of the Weidens.

When he did find the graves, he was disappointed. He hadn't expected to find anything obvious. In fact, he wasn't sure what he'd expected. But the Weidens – generations of them – were buried beneath dull, grey stones. Here and there, carved into the gravestones, were putti, ivy leaves, praying hands or, simply, the name WEIDEN, beneath which the barest particulars were engraved.

Harvey Weiden
1924 – 1926

Winfried Weiden
1926 – 2011

There were, in total, nine gravestones – three rows of three – bearing the names of somewhere around a hundred Weidens. On either side of the Weidens, as well as before and behind, there were stones bearing other names: Homer, Lobden, Sylvester, Attal, Modeste, Borde. These surrounding gravestones were even more bland: polished rectangles on which the various surnames were engraved.

After allowing the other surnames to resonate with Weiden – wondering what, if anything, connected 'Lobden' or 'Sylvester' with 'Weiden' – Tancred finally noticed what he should have seen at once: the mausoleum just beyond the nine Weiden gravestones. The mausoleum was wide as a two-car garage – twenty feet by twenty, say – but built of thick and solid stone, its sides almost entirely covered by leafless vines. It was some fourteen or fifteen feet tall and in the lintel above its wrought-iron door the name WEIDEN was carved.

He stood before the mausoleum a while before he noticed that, from a certain angle, a glimmer of light came from beneath the door. Tancred pushed, and though it was heavy, the door opened without a sound, as if it had been recently oiled. Inside, the enclosure was empty, faintly lit by a gas flame. That is, in the centre of the mausoleum, on the ground, there was a copper circle, two feet in diameter, with a darker metal lip or border around it. The copper circle rose slightly at its centre, like a volcano with very little elevation. From the mouth of the volcano – a hole two inches in diameter – a seemingly endless supply of natural gas flowed, sustaining a reddish flame that lit the mausoleum's interior.

It was a few moments before Tancred's eyes adjusted to the light, but when they did he saw that what he'd taken for blank walls were not quite so. To begin with, the walls were of white marble and, from floor to ceiling, it was as if there were squares cut into the marble itself: each square about five inches by four, as if the inner walls of the mausoleum were the dullest mosaic imaginable. But that wasn't quite true either. At the centre of each square, more *feel*able than visible, the name WEIDEN was engraved. That is, there were thousands and thousands of squares engraved in the white marble walls, each square apparently containing the name WEIDEN.

Nor was the mausoleum floor a blank. Aside from the fountain with its flame, there were words engraved in the floor's granite. These words were more easily legible than the names on the walls but they were done so that they encircled the fountain, one leading into the other. As it happened, Tancred recognized the words at once. There were two quotes from the King James version of Proverbs. The first was from chapter fifteen:

> *He that is greedy of gain troubleth his own house . . .*

The second was from chapter eleven:

> *He that troubleth his own house shall inherit the wind . . .*

It was odd, being in that place. The mausoleum seemed to bear a message. The place itself meant something, but it felt, to Tancred, as if its meaning were just out of reach. Clearly, the mausoleum pointed to the idea of home or family. But, all the same, Tancred did not feel he had taken in the place's full significance. He was not convinced he ever could. The mind behind this room was so foreign to his own.

As was perhaps natural, given the quiet, the marble and the small light from a restless flame, Tancred's thoughts turned briefly to church and to God. How much he would resent any god that had the presumption to exist! But the Christian number, with its greybeard symbols and signs, was particularly galling. Why fill a world with clues if the only thing of significance was death, if all sacred signs pointed to nothingness? Then again, perhaps the world was, in terms of meaning, various, and it was this that he resented, forced as he was to choose what mattered and what did not. None of these thoughts helped him here, of course. This place had been designed by a man, Robert Azarian. It pointed to something in the world. The question, for Tancred, was if any but the one who'd designed the place could know what its meaning actually was.

Tancred had left the mausoleum and was walking away from the Weidens when he was stopped by an older man.

– She's a cold one, eh? the man said. You could use three or four long johns and it'd still freeze your tackle off. But you got t' visit the dead or the dead visit you, my mom'd say.

Tancred nodded and kept moving. He did not want to speak to anyone. The man put a hand on his arm and said

— You're here for those Weidens, aren't you?

The man was five feet seven or so, ruddy-faced, his grey hair sticking out from beneath a black toque, most of him hidden by a large blue overcoat that was so shiny it seemed to be made of plastic. It was difficult to tell how old the man was: sixty-five, at a minimum, it seemed to Tancred, but then he was a poor judge of people's ages.

— What do you want? Tancred asked.

— Nothing, said the man. The name's Delmer.

Delmer McDougal held out a hand, which Tancred did not shake.

— I guess you're thinkin', 'Jeez, who's the old fart?,' eh? I got t' tell ya, son, I don't even know how I got so old. It's not like it happened all of a sudden, eh? Not like one day you're young and the next your teeth are gone and you're pissin' yourself if ya don't get to the john on time. It's a terrible thing and it comes slow, but we can't none of us help it. Anyways, I'm sorry if I came at you out of nowhere. I didn't mean nothin' by it. I just thought it was interesting you comin' here for the Weidens. It's like a bunch of people just found out these Weidens here are their best friends.

— And you like to keep track of people? said Tancred.

— You put it that way, son, it's like you think I shit in someone's milk. That's not how my parents brought me up. I was only thinkin' you might be interested in other people who're visiting your friends here.

— I'm not interested in other people's business, said Tancred.

— Well, if you ever wanted someone to keep an eye on things, like, I could do it for you, eh? And it wouldn't even be that much. I'm sure not lookin' to gouge anyone. That's for sure.

— I'm not interested, said Tancred.

And he walked away.

In fact, Tancred had been interested in Delmer's proposition. It might have been helpful to know who had recently visited the Weidens' graves. What had soured the encounter was Delmer himself. Tancred would not, as they say, have trusted the man any further than he could have thrown him. It troubled him that Delmer had seen him near the Weidens' mausoleum.

Delmer, for his part, could not believe his good luck. He'd been hired by – and still worked for – Alton Azarian. His sole responsibility was to tend to the Weiden mausoleum and keep watch. What, exactly, he was looking for was not clear. Azarian had mentioned his sister, Willow. But even after Willow's death, he'd encouraged Delmer to stay on for a while 'just to see what you might see.' And Delmer had stayed on for a number of reasons. First: because at sixty-eight he did not expect to find better – that is, easier, more leisurely – employment. Second: although the work was dull it paid well. And third: the work encouraged his tendency to woolgather.

(Encouraged it? His time in Mount Pleasant was a positive inducement to think about trivial but comforting things. What, for instance, had happened to the old clothes pegs, the ones from his childhood that looked like round-headed men with troublingly long legs? You couldn't convince him that the new ones, with their rat-trap coils, were in any way better, and they were certainly less elegant.)

When von Würfel had come snooping around, Delmer had felt something like delight. What a relief! Something to report to Mr. Azarian, at last – and he had, of course, reported it. On top of that, there was the practical matter: von Würfel had paid him to go on doing what he was already paid to do! The man was a godsend and his money was pure gravy.

Yes, but what was he to make of the young black fellow who'd entered the mausoleum? Tall, guarded, soft-spoken, not the kind to give money without reason. (Also blue-eyed! First dark person he'd seen like that!) Was it a good sign or a bad one that a young black man and an older white one were both interested in dead Weidens? It had to be good, didn't it, that there was what you'd call 'diverse interest'?

Because he hadn't done so in a while, Delmer entered the mausoleum and looked around.

The crypt was nothing but plain white marble, an unimpressive flame, much engraving but not a picture of the dead anywhere around. His favourite graves were those with cameos of the deceased on them. It was really something to see that this corpse had once been pretty or that one thin, that this one had had bad teeth, that one a full head of hair. Pictures made the dead seem like your next-door neighbours, a feeling that brought Delmer a surprising peace.

If there was anything precious in the mausoleum, he was happy to leave it for others. He could not imagine that people with such banal taste in crypts would leave anything interesting. A certificate of some sort, maybe: stocks, bonds, the deed to a ranch or an oil well. Nothing a normal person could use.

After calling Alton Azarian, he dialled the number Alexander von Würfel had left him.

– Is this Mr. von Warmfull? he asked.

– Who is this, please?

– Oh, it's Delmer from down the cemetery. I've been doin' some lookin' out and I caught a body nosin' around your Weidenses' graves.

– Ah, Delmer, said von Würfel. I hope you didn't scare this person off.

– I wouldn't do anythin' like that. I'm not sayin' he's still around but I didn't have anythin' to do with him leavin'.

– Did he see you looking at him?

– No, sir. I was what you'd call discreet.

– And this is the first time you've seen him?

– Yes, sir, and I been out there every day payin' attention. So, I woulda seen him already if he'd been here before. And I woulda called you. It's a lot a work keeping an eye out, eh? I'm not sayin' you haven't been generous, but this keepin' your eyes peeled is a real business for an oldster like me.

– If, said von Würfel, you call me next time you see him and you keep him busy till I get there, I'll give you two hundred dollars. Would that make it worth your while?

– Oh, yeah, that'd do 'er, for sure, said Delmer.

And the following afternoon when Tancred returned to get another look at the mausoleum in case he'd missed a mark or sign, Delmer was there to meet him. Well, not meet, exactly. Distract is more like it. No sooner did Tancred leave the mausoleum than Delmer was at his side.

– G'day, g'day, said Delmer, it's good to see you again, buddy. I spend most of my time here, eh, and you don't see the same person twice. Not wheres I'm concerned.

Politely, Tancred said

– I don't have time to stay and talk.

– Oh, Delmer said, no one's got time for oldsters these days. It'll happen to you one day, son. You'll be old and grey and good luck gettin' anyone to pay attention t' you when you're on your last legs.

– You're dying? asked Tancred.

– Yes, sir, son. I'm goin' t' be six feet under in two shakes of a lamb's tail. That's why I'm spendin' time around here. A man's got to be down in the worst dumps to hang around here, I'll tell you. I'm dying for sure, son, and it won't be long now. Six weeks is all they give me. And I can't help wonderin' what it's goin' to be like when I'm gone and all this is goin' on without me. You ever thought about that, son? I'm not sayin' you *should* be thinkin' about it. You're still wet behind the ears. But the time'll come for you, too, and young people won't want to hear about it any more'n you do.

Tancred was not convinced Delmer was dying faster than anyone else, but he would rather have been played for a fool than to have been cruel to someone in need of company.

– If you don't mind my asking, he said, what're you dying of?

– Oh, I can't say's I mind you askin', son, if you're sure you want to hear about it.

Delmer left him no time to consider the matter. Before Tancred knew it, a half-hour had gone and Delmer had only just got to the story of how his father – Bruce McDougal – had inherited a piece of land in Renfrew. Well, just outside of Renfrew, actually, a ways beyond where the Walmart now stands, not that there *was* a Walmart when Delmer was young, because when Delmer was young what there was was mostly cows and fields, and winter was for seeing how far you could fling cow patties if you'd been drinking, which, be it said in passing, was not a good thing to do outside in winter, because a man could freeze to death in the blink of an eye, if he'd been drinking and throwing cow shit around without a warm place nearby.

Tancred felt almost palpable relief when, as Delmer was wittering on about 'the Valley,' an older man approached and touched Delmer's arm.

– How're you doing, Delmer? the man asked.

– Well, Mr. van Warmer, said Delmer, I'm not doin' so well, eh?

Alexander von Würfel turned to Tancred and introduced himself.

– I know we don't know each other, he said, but could I speak to you a moment?

– I don't have time, said Tancred. Your friend here's been telling me all about his childhood.

As if offended, Delmer said

– You're the one who asked about it, son, but I know when I'm not wanted. You don't have to say nothin' twice for my sake.

He turned his back and walked off in the direction of the office, though he didn't go that far. Rather, he theatrically examined a few of the graves just beyond the Weidens'.

Von Würfel turned away from Delmer and quietly said

– It'll only take a minute. I'd just like to ask if you're looking for the same thing I'm looking for. I mean, where the Weidens are concerned.

– What are you looking for? Tancred asked.

It felt – to von Würfel – as if he were suddenly obliged to irrevocably choose between a discretion that would keep doors closed and an honesty that might open them too wide. His inclination was to secrecy, always, and even here it occurred to him to keep certain details to himself. But he had closed the door on Willow Azarian and that had led to this impasse. If he were to go further, he needed to know about the fifth piece of the puzzle. He did not know if

Tancred could tell him anything about it, but secrecy and discretion would lead him precisely nowhere.

– I'll be honest with you, he said, because I don't want to waste your time. I think there's some sort of secret mixed up in these graves. I've put some clues together and this is the place they lead to. Of course, I could be wrong. It wouldn't be the first time.

For a moment, the men looked at each other. Then, Tancred said

– So, you got Delmer to keep me here till you came?

– Yes, I did, said von Würfel. Yes, I did. He's been keeping an eye out for me, to see if anyone would come around. But no one has. No one but you. Not even any Weidens.

Tancred did not trust von Würfel, but he felt sympathy for a man who was, it seemed, going through a similar struggle to understand Robert Azarian. Then, too, he wanted to know how von Würfel had come to the Weiden mausoleum.

– We might be looking for the same thing, he said.

So it was that the two men, both warily honest, stood in Mount Pleasant, yards from where some sort of thing was meant to be hidden in some sort of way.

Von Würfel lived on Seaton Street not far from Dundas, in a Victorian house, part of a row of Victorian houses. It's here that he took Tancred, rather than to his shop.

In contrast to Von Würfel's Animals and Birds, his home was unremarkable. It was spare, almost Spartan. Here the walls were pale yellow, the trim pale green. The furniture was both rough and elegant: darkly stained wood with white cushions (sofa) or (for the most part) no cushioning at all. Von Würfel's back was too temperamental to take soft surfaces. Even his mattress was hard to the point where, inevitably, the women who slept with him complained about it in the morning.

– Would you like some tea? asked von Würfel.

And having brewed a pot of lapsang souchong – the smell of it like a damp dog by a dead campfire – he brought Tancred to the dining room where, on a long wooden table, the plans for the four pieces he'd made for Robert Azarian were laid out. Beside each of the plans was a version of the object it delineated. Looking at the table, Tancred briefly felt as if he were dreaming. The model of Fallingwater was identical to the one he'd stolen. The painting of Nero was as if altered – its colours more vivid, the smell of the paint more pungent, Nero taller, the raven fatter, Gould's piano softer – but it was remarkably similar to Simone's original. And, of course, as far as Tancred could tell, the bottle of aquavit and the setting for the poem were identical to the originals, both having been done to specifications Azarian had set out.

As if to allay any doubts, von Würfel said

– These are as close to the originals as I can get them.

He then told Tancred the story of his involvement with Azarian and how, after a visit from an albino and a limping, unpleasant man, he'd accepted what he'd suspected from the moment Azarian had commissioned the mementos: the pieces were meaningful. They had significance as a group. Together, the four *meant* something. More lucidly than Simone had, von Würfel went through the significance of each object, explaining each one's numerical correlative. For his solution, von Würfel had unwittingly ordered the mementos according to the Azarians' ages, from the poem meant for the eldest (Alton), down to the aquavit meant for the second youngest (Michael). When Tancred told him so, the man was delighted. It was, he said, further proof of Robert Azarian's subtlety.

Faced with such candour and enthusiasm – and accepting the fact that von Würfel knew at least as much as he did – Tancred was in his turn candid. He told von Würfel all that he knew, including the personal significance of Simone's painting and Willow's screen. He also told von Würfel what the siblings thought the pieces meant: that they, Robert's children, should remain close, that in Babylon it is the idea of home that brings comfort.

– Do you think that's what the mementos lead to? von Würfel asked.

— I'm not sure what to believe, answered Tancred.

— If we go by what's written on the floor of the mausoleum, that solution makes sense. But it feels to me there's more to this. For one thing, it's a game a father's playing with his children.

— Mostly for Willow's sake, said Tancred.

— Yes, said von Würfel, but it's a strange game for a father to play. I think it tells you a lot about Robert Azarian. He must have loved each one of his children, if each of these things has the same kind of meaning the painting has for Simone. But why would he want to keep something valuable from them? Why withhold money or jewels or what-have-you? You can't be generous and miserly at the same moment, can you?

— It would be hard, said Tancred, but isn't it strange that Simone let me take her painting?

— That's not so strange, answered von Würfel. It means there's at least one more who isn't convinced the solution is what's written in the mausoleum. Do you think I could see the ones you have, Tancred? Especially Willow's screen. It's the missing link, for me.

Tancred hesitated.

— I made a promise, he said. Anything I find, most of it goes to Willow's brothers and sisters. I'm only entitled to Willow's share, however much or little that is.

— I see what you're saying, said von Würfel.

He drank his tea, quietly contemplating his options.

— Do you know, he said, by this point, I'm mostly interested in the solution to all this, the real solution, if there is a real solution.

Tancred was now at yet another impasse. On his own, he was unlikely to solve anything. He had returned to the cemetery out of frustration as much as anything else. But if he were to show von Würfel Willow's screen, and if von Würfel solved the puzzle, the man might well keep the solution to himself. On the other hand, if there was a convincing solution to the puzzle and von Würfel found it and shared it, it would free him from the second part of his task.

– I can give you some of my share, said Tancred. The rest isn't negotiable. If you agree, I'll show you the screen.

Von Würfel smiled, recognizing himself in Tancred's dilemma.

– It's hard to take on a partner so late in the game, isn't it? he asked. But I don't want much. How does 10 percent sound? I mean, *if* we find anything. I'm beginning to think this could all be a lot of fuss over nothing. I'll have a better idea once I've seen Willow's screen.

But Willow's screen did not give up its secrets so easily.

Von Würfel had built the thing up in his mind. He assumed that this piece would make sense of all the others. It had to. Willow's screen, the final piece, *had* to take you to the 'treasure' or, at very least, reveal the hidden significance of the Weidens' resting place.

From Tancred's description, von Würfel had anticipated the look and feel of the screen. He'd assumed it would feature a poor painting of a bridge, done by some amateur or other. But the thing itself was breathtaking, as if it had come straight from the seventeenth century: the willows' leaves a delicate cascade of pale green (in the first panels), turning darker (in the last panels); the golden bridge gleaming over waves of silvery water in which golden stones clustered; the golden shore, above which a coppery moon. It was proper *meisho-e*, the painting of a famous scene – in this case, the bridge that joined Kyoto and Nara, a bridge on which von Würfel himself had once stood.

The screen was not from the seventeenth century. It would not have gleamed in quite the same way if it had been, and the orange paper backing would not have been quite so crisp. But whoever had done it knew what they were doing, had mastered the style of Japanese painting. In and of itself, the screen was valuable, easily worth thousands of dollars. Von Würfel found it disappointing that anyone but him should have done it so well, but he comforted himself with the thought that, whoever the artist had been, he or she was almost certainly Japanese. As well, he could not help thinking that Azarian had purposely gone about it so that no one artist had access to all the pieces, no one artist had access to the solution.

He'd been staring at the screen for some time when Tancred interrupted his reverie.

— Does it tell you anything? Tancred asked.

— Not really, said von Würfel. It's a lovely piece of work. I'm sorry Robert didn't ask me to do it. But yes, it obviously points to Psalm 137. Still, what aspect of the psalm are we supposed to think of? What's the connection between the psalm and the bridge?

— The river and the willows, said Tancred.

And because he knew it by heart, he spoke Psalm 137 aloud:

By the rivers of Babylon there we sat down, yea we wept when we
*   remembered Zion.*
We hanged our harps upon the willows in the midst thereof.
For they that carried us away captive required of us a song and they
*   that wasted us required of us mirth saying sing us one of the*
*   songs of Zion.*
How shall we sing the Lord's song in a strange land?
If I forget thee, O Jerusalem, let my right hand forget her cunning.
If I do not remember thee, let my tongue cleave to the roof of my mouth;
*   if I prefer not Jerusalem above my chief joy,*
Remember, O Lord, the children of Edom
*   in the day of Jerusalem who said Raze it, raze it, even to the*
*   foundations thereof.*
O daughter of Babylon, who art to be destroyed;
Happy shall he be that rewardeth thee as thou hast served us.
Happy shall he be that taketh and dasheth thy little ones against
*   the stones.*

— The river, the willows and the stones, said von Würfel.

— And then there's the number 137 to think about, said Tancred.

— That, too, said von Würfel. There's that, too.

CHAPTER FOUR

A BOTTLE OF AQUAVIT

1 Errol Colby Goes Too Far (Conclusion)

The encounter with Detective Mandelshtam had ended in Errol Colby's favour. Or so Colby saw it. He'd had a narrow escape, and other men might have taken the slightness of the escape for proof that more caution was warranted. But Colby was encouraged by his victory, enflamed even. He felt as if his escape proved his cause was just and, feeling justified, he was incensed that Tancred had forced him to try to steal from the Azarians, outraged that his plan had not worked, offended that he'd been condescended to by a rich woman and questioned by Mandelshtam, one of Palmieri's friends.

But, just cause or not, Colby found himself in the same place he'd been: on the sidelines as Tancred went about the business of finding a reward that belonged to him, Errol Colby. Spurred by his recent good fortune, he resolved to do what he now felt he should have done at once. He – with Freud – would administer a beating on Olivier Mallay. They would send a message to Tancred: co-operate or your friends will suffer.

Having made the decision, Colby thought of a few modest constraints. They could not, for instance, kill Mallay. It was important that Tancred should co-operate, not seek revenge. So, he would, he thought, have to keep watch on Freud. The man so enjoyed hurting others it sometimes went to his head, especially if he thought he was being inconvenienced. Colby had seen him kick a junkie so often and so hard the man had ended up in hospital for weeks. Why had Freud gone at him? Because the idiot had complained about his count, a count that *had* been short. And what use was there for a hospitalized junkie? None, none whatsoever. And Freud's reaction to his own carelessness? A shrug.

– Shit happens, Nigs, he'd said.

It would be his duty to see that, at least on this occasion, shit did not. Once they'd got what they needed out of Tancred? Different story. He could think of few things that would please him as much as helping to cripple Tancred Palmieri. Still, best to save that pleasure for its proper time. First things first: get Tancred's attention.

The easy part was finding Mallay's home. A number of people – well, a number of regulars at the Coffee Time – knew Tancred's friend and found him memorable because they'd often seen him with Tancred. Knowing his first name and that he worked at a bakery in Bloor West Village, it took Colby and Freud little time to find the man's home. How? A woman at the third bakery they tried said

– Olivier? Why don't you try his home?

– Do you remember his address? Freud asked.

She did remember his address. And gave it to them! The man lived in a house on Runnymede with his parents, fifteen minutes from the bakery itself. Once they'd found the place, however, things got progressively more frustrating.

To begin with, Colby and Freud rang the doorbell and were answered by a woman with thick glasses, her hair dark with a skunk-like streak of white.

– Who is it? she asked

as if mistaking her front door for a telephone.

– Is Olivier there? said Freud.

– Olivier? said Mrs. Mallay. No, Olivier's not home.

From somewhere inside the house, there came a faint voice.

– *Qui est là, Mathilde?*

Almost to herself, Mrs. Mallay said

– *Je n'sais pas, moi.*

And then asked who they were.

– We're Olivier's friends, said Freud. Where is he?

– I don't know, she said. *Il n'est pas nourrisson quand même.*

With which words she closed the door, leaving them on the front porch.

Freud was put off by her curtness. But the real irritant was the weather. It was cold. They had come in the Volkswagen Colby habitually borrowed from his sister. They'd parked across the street from the Mallays' home and they'd been prepared to wait for hours, but they hadn't reckoned on the cold or on how eccentric the Volkswagen's heating could be. When it was on, it scorched the air in the car, threatening to drive them out. They were comfortable neither in nor out of the car. After four hours of this irritation, Colby suggested Plan B. They'd waited for the man. It was time to rough up Mom and Dad a little and call it a day.

If the suggestion had come from Freud, Colby would have rejected it. He might even have suggested they return some other time with a better car. But in his own mind they had done the honourable thing, waiting for hours so they wouldn't have to hurt Mallay's parents. And given that Olivier's parents were older, it was less likely that Freud would allow himself to lose control. It was one of Freud's virtues that he deferred to the elderly. This was no doubt because Freud's own parents were ancient. His mother had had him, her only child, at fifty. To his mother and father, he was a miracle and they doted on him in a way Colby found amusing.

Plan B seemed solid. But, not unexpectedly, Freud objected.

— I didn't come to kick pensioners around, he said.

Those very words, however, settled the matter. Freud did not want to hurt the Mallays, but he could still serve as intimidation.

— Let's do this, Colby said. Let me handle it. You won't have to do a thing. I mean, unless you want to stay in this car …

No, Freud did not. They waited a few more minutes, as if to tacitly acknowledge the absence of Mallay *fils*. Then they got out of the car and resolutely crossed the street to the Mallays' porch. Colby pushed the doorbell and, when Mrs. Mallay opened the door, he put his foot in and forced the door open, gently pushing the woman back as he did.

— *Mais qu'est-ce qu'il veut, Monsieur l'albinos?* she asked.
But by then Colby and Freud were already in.

Inside, the house was dim, warm, almost humid. It smelled of Christmas ham and old men. To the right of the door, wooden steps led up to the next floor. Attached to the banister was a chairlift. In the lift an old man sat, as if he'd just come down or were just heading up.

– We should help Mr. Mallay down, Colby said.

– But I don't need help, said Mr. Mallay.

Freud, annoyed at having to intimidate the Mallays, lifted the bar on the chair and, as if taking a recalcitrant child from the seat of a Ferris wheel, pulled him from the contraption, hurting him as he did.

In distress, Mr. Mallay said

– Help is not necessary.

His accent was as thick as if he'd immigrated from France the day before.

– Shut up, said Freud.

To the right of the door there was a living room – fireplace, sofa, armchairs and floor lamps whose shades had pink tassels. Freud pulled the old man into the living room and, unceremoniously, pushed him into an armchair. Colby encouraged Mrs. Mallay to join her husband, pointing to the armchair beside him.

– Why don't you sit there, he said. We've got a message for Olivier.

Mrs. Mallay sat in the chair, but it was as if neither she nor her husband could believe the men before them were not actors. It felt as if their living room had turned into a theatre, the play they were watching an absurdist thing with a broken fourth wall. The couple spoke to each other in a kind of running and loudly whispered commentary.

– *Mais qu'est-ce qu'ils veulent, ces messieurs?*

– *Comment veux-tu que je sache? J'les connais pas, moi.*

– *Ils n'ont pas l'air gentils. Ça c'est évident.*

– *Oui, ce ne sont surement pas des gentlemen.*

This whispered talk – rather loud because Mr. Mallay, years older than his wife, was hard of hearing – was too much for Freud. It wasn't just that he'd been talked into abusing geriatrics. It wasn't just that the geriatrics in question were foreigners who very likely wouldn't understand a thing Nigger said. No, on top of it all, Mallay's parents would not even listen to them. It was all, after hours in a ridiculous car, an indignity. He was Nigger's friend and loved him like a brother. Nigger had helped him in the past. So, he did not mind wasting time if Nigger wanted it. But a man has to keep his dignity, whatever the circumstances. And, feeling as if he were in danger of losing his, Freud jumped at Mrs. Mallay, grabbing her by the throat and shaking her.

– Shut your mouth! he said.

This had an immediate effect, though not the one Freud was looking for. The others in the room shut their mouths. They stared at Freud, taken aback. All, that is, save Mrs. Mallay. Mrs. Mallay's mouth opened and her body contorted. Her hand moved up, clutching at something – Freud's hand, perhaps. Whatever it was she was going for, she would never reach it. She had a massive heart attack and died at once, with Freud's fingers still at her throat.

It was a moment before the three men realized that Mrs. Mallay was not doing at all well. Freud, feeling both resentment and disgust, took his hand away from the woman's throat as if it had scalded him. But it was Mr. Mallay who spoke first.

– *Mais vous avez tué ma femme*, he said.

And then, because he did not really believe his wife was dead:

– *Mathilde? Qu'est-ce qu'il y a, ma chérie?*

As if he had been a doctor, Colby put a hand on the woman's forehead. This told him nothing, of course. Her body was still warm. But then Mrs. Mallay's head lolled to one side and, doctor or no, that was enough for Errol Colby.

– Let's go, he said.

And he and Freud cleared out.

Colby's good luck was stubborn. Mrs. Mallay's heart attack accomplished what he'd hoped intimidation would: Tancred began to cooperate with him. But Tancred's change of mind was not a change of heart. Colby was mistaken about the reason for the change.

To begin with, Puli Paulsen had seen Colby and Freud go into the Mallays' home. He did not know Olivier, so the house meant nothing to him. From his own car, half a block away from the Volkswagen, he'd taken photos of Colby and Freud as they stood on the porch, as they entered the house and as they unexpectedly left it not ten minutes later. (Why would anyone wait four hours before conducting ten minutes' business?) He'd then followed the men to Parkdale where they'd spent time in the Skyline before going their separate ways. An unexceptional day, save for a minor episode on Runnymede that faded from Puli's memory. When, a week later, he reported to Daniel, he put no particular emphasis on the photos of the Mallays' home. But Daniel recognized the home of his friend at once. He had been there, days before, at Mrs. Mallay's wake.

– When did you take these? he asked.

Puli turned one of the photos over.

– November 23rd, he said. Between nine in the morning and one in the afternoon.

– A week ago? said Daniel.

– Yes, said Puli. Why?

But Daniel could not say why. He'd been to Mrs. Mallay's funeral and her wake. On neither occasion had Ollie mentioned Colby or Freud. In fact, judging from Ollie's behaviour, one would not have said there'd been anything unusual about his mother's death. A heart attack, plain and simple. The only thing he remembered Ollie saying was: Death being unavoidable, there was no reason to take this one harder than any other. And, as the death of those he didn't know never bothered him, this one would not either.

That was exactly the kind of thing Ollie *would* say, and it must have seemed to anyone who did not know him well that his friends had taken the death of his mother harder than Ollie himself. His grief, which he denied feeling, was expressed (paradoxically) by his good spirits. Daniel could not recall, in all the years they'd known each other, ever seeing Ollie so accommodating, so insistent that people eat or drink. It was as if Mrs. Mallay were still alive, saying, as she had countless times over the years

– *Voyons, Olivier, tu ne vois pas que tes amis ont soif?*

Ollie's father had been a different matter, of course. A man who could not, at the best of times, hide his emotions, Mr. Mallay had been a heartbreaking sight: a seventy-two-year-old man sitting in an armchair, tears running down his cheeks, unable to speak. To think that loving a woman could lead to such suffering. Daniel had turned to Fiona. They'd been married five years – very little time, really, but it was painful to think about a world in which she did not figure.

In the midst of all that grief and remembrance, Daniel had not for a moment doubted that Mrs. Mallay's death had been natural, that her time had come, that there was no more to it than that. So, it was a shock, looking over Puli's photos, to recognize the shadowy figures of Colby and Freud on the Mallays' front porch. He could not believe that a couple as gentle and generous as the Mallays would have anything to do with the likes of Freud or Colby. That could only mean, as far as Daniel was concerned, that they'd been there to see Ollie. But that too was hard to believe. Though by his own admission, he sometimes helped Tancred out, Ollie was not a proper criminal. For one thing, he lacked ambition. No, that was putting it mildly. Ollie was philosophically opposed to ambition.

Beneath these thoughts, a more unsettling idea ran: what if Freud and Colby had something to do with Mrs. Mallay's death? Ollie would have said so, wouldn't he? Hard to say. If Ollie was mixed up with Colby and Freud, he might keep quiet. Or, as this was Ollie, and Ollie was indifferent to mortality, the cause of his mother's death might not have troubled him enough to inspire mention. In any event, he could not stand the thought of questioning Ollie when, as far as he knew, there was no crime and, so, no reason to disturb Ollie's thoughts. Nor, obviously, could he call Colby in. His suspicions or fears could not justify letting Nigger know he was being followed. Yet, given the photos of the two on the porch, it was disturbing to do nothing. So, he chose to speak to Tancred, to find out if Tancred knew anything that connected Colby and the Mallays.

They did not meet in Parkdale. At Tancred's suggestion, they met far from it: way the hell and gone, past Dufferin and St. Clair. And though Daniel loved Toronto – the city of his birth – it was hard for him not to feel that St. Clair, from Bathurst west to Earlscourt, was a test of human patience. Traffic lights every yard or so is what it felt like, with lanes reserved for streetcars and countless offshooting streets you couldn't turn onto. To drive a klick, you needed half an hour, half an hour if you didn't hit one of the taxis careening and caroming along as if St. Clair were meant for bumper cars. Making things worse, as far as Daniel was concerned, was how lovely the street was in his mind: from Wychwood and old churches to Italian restaurants and Pain Perdu, past north-rising streets with their old houses or south-subsiding ones that led to mazes of smaller streets and more elegant homes. It was diabolical that a road should be so lovely in the mind and yet so dire to drive on. But drive he did, Earlscourt being too far to walk.

He and Tancred met not far from Prospect Cemetery at a bakery whose name, Café Pastéis de Belém, suggested something more wonderful than the unremarkable shop above a lawyer's office. As usually happened when they met, it was some time before they'd caught up, caught up not only with the present but also with old matters – this thought bringing forth that one from long ago, that one calling up things they'd spoken about months previously.

It was Tancred who brought up Olivier.

– I swear, he said, Ollie's even stranger now than he was in high school. It's like he's not any more upset about his mom's death than he was about Bazarov's.

– His cat? said Daniel. If Bazarov died, Ollie'd be in mourning for at least an hour.

– Baz the *fifth*, said Tancred. I remember because when the fourth one died, Ollie wanted to drink in the cat's memory. I said, 'Why should we have a drink in Bazarov's memory if death is no big thing?' I was only kidding, but you know how Ollie takes these things. He said, 'You don't have to get sentimental. I just bought a bottle of Stoli Elit. And Baz's death is a good excuse to try it.' So, when Baz the fourth died, we drank three-thousand-dollar vodka.

– Three-thousand-dollar vodka?

— That's not all, said Tancred. It was good vodka, but Ollie didn't like it because Ollie doesn't like vodka. So, he gave the bottle to his neighbour. You know, the Filipino woman he's got a thing for. Only problem is, she doesn't drink. So, she threw the vodka out and kept the bottle. I said, 'Didn't you tell her the vodka was worth three thousand dollars?' He said, 'What's the difference?' I said, 'It's a waste of money. And it's not like you can afford it.' And he said, 'I saved up for it and Jovelyn likes the bottle. What's the problem?'

— He's right, said Daniel.

— I know he's right, said Tancred, but if you're going to pay three thousand dollars for a bottle, you could have got a nicer bottle. It was plain as dirt. Anyway, it's useless to argue with Ollie about anything.

— Listen, that reminds me, said Daniel. Do you know if there's some kind of business between Ollie and Nigger Colby?

Tancred tilted his head, as if he'd missed something.

— What?

— You know I don't like to talk business, said Daniel, but one of our officers saw Nigger and Sigismund at Ollie's house a week ago, just around the time Ollie's mom died. I thought it was a strange coincidence. I've never known Ollie to hang with those two, have you?

— What were the police doing at Ollie's house? said Tancred.

— They were on Runnymede and recognized Sigismund, so one of the officers took some pictures. On a whim, I guess, but Luxemberg's a violent man, so they were interested. They didn't know it was Ollie's house. I'm the one who recognized it.

Daniel pushed one of Puli's photos across the table and watched as Tancred examined it.

— Next time you see him, Daniel said, you should tell him these aren't the kind of people to hang out with. As it is, I can't help wondering if there's any connection between them and Mrs. Mallay's heart attack.

— Can I keep the photo? asked Tancred.

— Sure, said Daniel. If Ollie doesn't know about this, he should.

The following day, it was Tancred who pushed the photo across a tabletop.

– What's this? asked Olivier. Is that Colby and Freud? Then my father wasn't dreaming. You know, Tan, since my mother's death, my father hasn't always been coherent. He was going on about a white man, but he never said albino. And there wasn't any word from the doctor that anything was wrong. She died, that's all there was to it, so I thought he was talking about death, not an albino. I still don't think Colby and Freud had anything to do with it.

The day after that, Tancred pushed the photo across a final tabletop toward Colby, whom he found eating (with Freud, of course) in a booth at Harry's.

– Where'd you get this? asked Colby
as if politely impressed by a trick.

– From a friend, said Tancred.

– You have nosy friends, said Freud.

– This was the day Mrs. Mallay died, wasn't it? asked Tancred.

– We don't know anything about anybody dying, said Freud.

– What are you, added Colby, a district attorney? Like a TV show? You think this is a TV show? Well, listen, Counsellor, how should we know when some biddy decides to kick the bucket? As far as I remember, we were asking for directions, weren't we, Freud?

– We were asking for directions, said Freud.

– Anyway, what's the big deal? said Colby. Bad things happen to good people all the time.

– If she *was* good people, said Freud.

– Exactly, said Colby.

In that instant Tancred accepted that everything Mr. Mallay had told Ollie was true. Freud and Colby were responsible for Mrs. Mallay's death. And it had been his – that is, Tancred's – fault. Ollie had nothing to do with these men.

He was shaken. He'd miscalculated the extent of Colby's drive and competence, and his miscalculation had cost Ollie's mother her life. There was no recourse, nowhere to go for justice. But what he felt more than the longing for justice was the desire that nothing like this should happen again, that none of his friends should ever suffer through his fault.

The other thing he felt was anger, an emotion that was useless to him, interfering as it did with his ability to think straight. Looking at Freud, for instance, he had to shake the terribly strange thought of stabbing the man's face with a coffee spoon.

– I haven't been fair to you, Errol, he said. From now on, we should work together.

– *Now* he wants to work with us, said Freud.

Colby put up a hand to silence Freud and, to Tancred, said

– How haven't you been fair?

– I admire your nerve, said Tancred. I think we'd work well together.

Magnanimous in what he took to be victory, Colby said

– We're good people. We only want what's good.

– Should we bring Mr. Armberg in on this? asked Tancred.

– If we're in on it, he's in on it, said Colby. Mr. Armberg's the man.

– Okay, said Tancred. This is what I know about Willow's inheritance.

Dispassionately, he told Colby and Freud much of what he knew.

2 Castle Rose

On seeing von Würfel's replicas, Tancred had begun to question the need to complete Willow's task. But he'd decided to go on stealing the Azarian mementos because a task's demands are distinct from its reasons. He'd given his word and that was it, at least until (or if) he figured the puzzle out. But for the first time in his life, a vow he'd made clashed with his ideals. His vow had brought pain to those close to him. The moral dissonance was almost unbearable.

He had no choice but to keep Colby close, because it was only by keeping him close that he could be certain Colby did not interfere with Ollie or Daniel. Then again, keeping Colby close was a temporary solution. If Robert Azarian had actually hidden something of value, it was Tancred's duty to give most of what he found to Willow's siblings. He'd already promised some of what was due him to von Würfel. He'd have to split what remained with Colby or even give Colby all that he had promised Willow he'd keep. He could not be sure, however, that Colby would accept less than what he'd demanded: 50 percent of anything they found.

That was out of the question. Willow had not told him what to do with her share. Giving it to Colby was, therefore, not breaking his word. Giving away the part meant for her siblings, however, most definitely was. So, he, a child of Alexandra Park, had become a defender of people who had all the advantages (the Azarians) against the depredations of men (Freud and Colby) who'd had none.

Where was the right way in all that?

Tancred had hoped his accord with Colby would make his life easier. It did not. He now had to hide things from Colby. He could not tell him about von Würfel, for instance, without endangering von Würfel himself. Nor could he tell Colby that the theft of the final two objects was, perhaps, unnecessary. He could not even tell him about the belief of Willow's siblings that they had solved their father's puzzle, because he could not risk Colby's disbelief. In effect, Tancred was forced to be more careful, more diligent, more devious.

But how strange that secrecy should be disturbing. Had he not lived by stealth? Silence is to thieves as water to fish, no? Why should this duplicity now make him suffer? It would not have troubled his younger self. He had changed. He was perhaps changing still.

As if it were a correlative to Tancred's emotions, the building from which they'd have to steal Michael Azarian's bottle of aquavit was itself complex, bewildering and (worse) reputedly impenetrable.

The Chateau Rose Suites, more commonly known as the Hidden Castle or the Hidden Suites or Castle Rose, was an experimental condominium at the foot of Bay Street overlooking the lake. It was 'experimental' in that it was designed by an artist named Yves Rokeby, whose only instructions were that the building be both aesthetically pleasing and safe. At the time it was commissioned – that is, in 2009 – 'safe' was generally taken to mean impregnable to crooks or madmen. Rokeby, inspired by the drawings of M. C. Escher, created a building that was both beautiful and safe.

To deal with appearances first: Castle Rose was a perfectly square building. It was twenty-five storeys high. Its exterior was white marble interspersed with squares of reddish-pink granite, which formed a twenty-five-storey-high red C on the building's north side, an R on its west side and an S on the side facing the lake. On Castle Rose's east side, the squares of granite formed an immense spiral that was meant to represent a rose.

In the building's forecourt, there was a fountain whose white-marble base was like a version of the building behind it: perfectly square, five feet by five feet by five feet. At night, a thick jet of froth-topped water rose, every few minutes, like a blue tree, lit from beneath by blue lights in the fountain.

The forecourt itself led to the only part of the building accessible to the public: a twenty-four-hour Lebanese restaurant on the ground floor called Café el-Bugat, which served what was advertised as the best chicken shawarma in the city. On its walls were half a dozen platinum-framed photographs of a crying woman in a hijab.

As 'el-Bugat' is also the name of a 'festival of weeping women' held yearly in Aleppo, Syria, it was sometimes assumed by those who knew Arabic that either the café's name had suggested the photos or that the photos had suggested the name. But the café's owner, Nadim al-Hafez, was a third-generation Lebanese-Canadian who hadn't known the name's significance. He'd taken 'el-Bugat' from the Cervecería el-Bugat, a tavern he'd visited in Seville. The photographs, meanwhile, were of his mother, Rafqa, a well-known actress who'd translated *A Streetcar Named Desire* into Arabic and had played Blanche DuBois half a dozen times. Each of the photos was of Rafqa al-Hafez in *Streetcar*'s final scene as she movingly depends on the kindness of strangers. This odd disjunction between the café's name and the photos that hung on its walls was entirely appropriate for a business in Castle Rose because …

The simple beauty of the building's exterior was, in a sense, betrayed by its interior. To begin with, every floor of Castle Rose was identical to every other. Though there were two sets of elevators – one accessible from the north, one from the south – the view, once one left an elevator, was the same, northern and southern prospects indistinguishable from one another. In part, this was accomplished with 'mirrors' – that is, the walls, ceilings and floors of the elevators' landings were of a polished silver that reflected as well as if they had actually been mirrors. Then, too, on the landings, there were no doors, doorways, doorknobs or easily distinguished recesses. On reaching a floor of Castle Rose, one had the impression of geometric near-infinity, and it was not uncommon for any who stayed too long by the elevators to become physically ill.

From the elevator, a resident had to push on a hidden panel to reach a hallway, one with proper doors, doorknobs and door frames. Not that this hallway was less bewildering. Here, there were mahogany doors and polished maple floors. None of the doors had any mark or number to distinguish it from the others – just above each of the doors was a small indigo triangle that lit up at the approach of that condominium's owner. A number of the doors, however, were decoys. Some led directly back to the mirrored landing, locking behind the intruder and setting off an alarm. Others led to single rooms whose doors slammed shut unless held open, locking in any who entered and setting off an alarm.

As if this programmatic bewilderment weren't enough, there were a number of further features meant to keep the dweller safe:

1. There were hidden cameras at unpredictable intervals on each floor.
2. Entire floors – two or three, apparently – served as decoys and, once accessed, held intruders until security released them.
3. The elevators looked normal. That is, their panels had numbers on them to indicate specific floors. But an elevator, while indicating it was on its way to, say, the fourth floor, in fact deposited the traveller to a floor whose number was unknowable by residents or intruders. As each landing was unnumbered, to travel in an elevator in Castle Rose was to arrive nowhere certain.

No doubt, there was something nightmarish about Castle Rose. But, for the dweller, the nightmare was countered by a pleasing efficiency. To begin with, a microchip assigned to each condo owner, embedded wherever the owner wished, freed him or her from thought. At the presence of a chip, the elevators went to the appropriate floor, a white circle appeared in a silvery wall identifying the proper panel to push and the indigo triangles above the true doors lit up as soon as a dweller was in the hall that led to his or her condominium.

Then, of course, there were the condominiums themselves. They were glorious, especially those overlooking the lake. One felt, in Castle Rose's tall-ceilinged and broad-windowed rooms, as if one were in the midst of precious things: the distant, low-lying green of the islands, small aircraft gliding like paper planes as they sank onto Billy Bishop's tarred runway, boats scudding on the grey-green waters.

With one's back to the concrete off-ramps, with one's back to the curtain of steel and glass that crept ever closer to the lake, year after year, as if to sever land from water – that is, here, with one's back to the careless and vulgar surge of the city – it was possible to imagine Toronto beautiful.

Of course, to do this imagining from Castle Rose, one had to be extremely wealthy and relatively young. Extremely wealthy because, in 2010, when the condominiums went on sale, each unit, lake-facing or not, sold for two million dollars with one hundred thousand dollars a year in condo fees. Relatively young because Castle Rose did not sell to buyers older than sixty, however wealthy, and contractually obligated owners to sell their homes once they'd passed the age of retirement. Though this age limit was, on the surface, harsh, its origin was humane. The microchip issued to each owner was expensive: ten thousand dollars for the chip and ten thousand for a replacement in the event the original was lost. Thereafter, the price doubled, tripled, quadrupled and so on. The company selling the condos believed that the elderly, being naturally forgetful, were more likely to lose their chips and, so, cost their families money or, worse, compromise Castle Rose's security. Then, too, even with the microchips, the look and feel of the landings and halls could at times bewilder younger owners; many felt it would be cruel to subject the elderly to what was sometimes called by the Hidden Castle's administrators an approximation of dementia. So, from an excess of caution – and some condescension – the condominiums were sold to wealthy and childless people between the ages of twenty-one and sixty.

But, as the Scottish say, the best-laid schemes o' mice an' men gang aft agley. An exception to the age limit was made for Colonel Randall 'Ran' Morrissey. Morrissey, an honorary colonel who'd served three years in the Canadian military, was a braggart and a bully. A white-haired man with jowls like a Boxer (*Canis lupus familiaris*), his chief virtues were monetary. That is, he was a man who'd inherited millions and had, thanks to inspired investing by his money managers, made millions more. Colonel Morrissey was unmarried.

He had no dependants. His only flaw – with regard to the Chateau Rose Suites – was that he was seventy years old at the time he decided to buy a condominium. However, he extravagantly bribed every member of the selection committee, after which the committee discovered in itself a largesse that allowed it to make an exception for him.

In his first year at Castle Rose, Ran Morrissey lost two microchips. The first was embedded in the cap of an eighteen-carat-gold Omas 'Pushkin' pen. The idea, which came from Morrissey's minder, was that the Colonel would pay attention to the whereabouts of a pen that cost fifteen thousand dollars. Not so. Morrissey was worth north of half a billion, so he did not consider the pen expensive or exquisite or any such thing. In fact, one day, needing a ballpoint but having only the Pushkin with him, he threw the pen into the lake in frustration. He then fired his minder, blaming the man for the loss of twenty-five thousand dollars.

The second chip was meant to be embedded in an antique belt buckle. The buckle in question was from the Royal Canadian Corps of Signals: brass from the year of his birth (1940), and at its centre a silvery Hermes stepping on planet earth as if it were a stone in a riverbed. Colonel Morrissey wore the buckle (and leather belt) every day, unfailingly, sometimes even wearing belt and buckle to bed, ever mindful that, should he die in his sleep, it be known that he had been a military man and a patriot. The problem here was that Colonel Morrissey was loath to have anyone tamper with the buckle. His minder's son soldered the chip to the back of the buckle and although it was not noticeable, neither was it secure. After three months, both solder and chip fell off somewhere by the lake.

So, the minder was fired and a third chip was embedded in Ran Morrissey's titanium leg.

3 Colonel Morrissey's Leg

To build an 'impregnable' building is, like it or not, to issue a challenge. So, it's no surprise that, over the years, a number of thieves had tried their luck with Castle Rose. Each and every one of them failed, and every failure added to the building's mystique. There were countless rumours and exaggerations, from the credible ('The place is under constant surveillance') to the fantastic ('No one lives in Castle Rose, it's a trap for thieves, devised by right-wing fanatics').

Despite all this, and a few frustrations besides, Michael Azarian's bottle of aquavit was – thanks to what amounted to luck (or destiny) – the easiest of the Azarian mementos to steal.

Frustrations first.

Errol Colby now took it for given that his opinions were crucial. He'd never been much of a thief but his newfound faith in himself seemed to make his own views irresistible to him. He listened to Tancred's account of Castle Rose but he couldn't help expressing skepticism.

– I've heard all the stories you have, he said. But there's no such thing as a place you can't steal from.

– I say that we just walk in and see what happens, said Freud.

– That's what I say, too, said Colby.

It was mid-afternoon on a weekday. Colby, Freud and Tancred were in the apartment where Tancred kept the mementos he'd got. The November light was unsoftened by leaves or clouds or smog. Nor was it intensified by snow, there being little. The light was what one might call raw, and it seemed somehow meaningful to Tancred, as if the sun were trying to suggest something.

– So, one of you is just going to walk in? asked Tancred.

– I'll do it, said Freud, since you're such a pussy.

Freud's effort was pitiful. He followed a well-dressed woman into Castle Rose and was immediately found out when, in the elevator, the woman was politely asked (over the intercom) if the one with her was her guest. When the woman said he was not, the elevator rose to a floor where it was met by security (two tall young men in light-blue uniforms), who respectfully accompanied Freud out of the building while politely suggesting he get lost or there would be serious consequences.

A fiasco, but a predictable fiasco. Tancred had left Freud and Colby to break in on their own. He'd gone, instead, to meet with von Würfel, gone to explain to von Würfel why he'd been avoiding him (because of Colby), why he was determined to steal the bottle of aquavit (to fulfill his promise, yes, but also to keep Freud and Colby close) and why he was now unsure of himself (Castle Rose was intimidating even for one who loved a challenge).

– You mean Chateau Rose at the harbourfront? asked von Würfel. That's a hell of a place, I can tell you. I think I've been there more than anyone who doesn't actually live in it.

– Why? asked Tancred.

– Business, said von Würfel. Business, business, business. It sometimes feels like I've preserved a pet for everyone in the place. Cats, mostly. The Chateau Rose is like a mortuary for cats! But you know the rich, Tancred. They *are* different from us. It isn't just that they have more money. It's that they've got less imagination. When one of them does something, the rest feel obliged to do the same thing. They all collect cars, boats, buildings, paintings ...

– But what about the place? asked Tancred. How can I get in?

– I think it's going to be difficult, said von Würfel. I knew the man who designed the Chateau Rose. We were close friends, and I'm pretty sure that if Yves designed the place so thieves can't get in, then thieves can't get in.

Von Würfel looked out at Dundas, at the cars passing by, at a light November flurry – a scant dusting that made you think of eyelashes. The two were quiet until, suddenly, von Würfel began to laugh.

– What is it? asked Tancred.

– I just remembered the Colonel, said von Würfel.

How strange the things that stick in a mind! Von Würfel had got in the habit, after delivering one of his preserved pets to a tenant in Castle Rose, of having Lebanese coffee and a slice of aish el-saraya, an exquisite bread pudding with pistachios for garnish, at Café el-Bugat. For a time, it seemed as if he was in el-Bugat every few days. Naturally, he began to recognize the regular patrons. And, of those, 'the Colonel' was hardest to miss. This was largely because the Colonel was white-haired and strikingly thin. He walked slowly, with a limp, and he was inevitably followed by someone younger. And whenever the Colonel entered Café el-Bugat, he called out

– Can't a veteran get a tea in this place?

as if daring someone to deny him.

Von Würfel assumed the café's owner and the two young women in hijab who worked there must have dreaded these entrances. But he himself found the Colonel amusing. The man had immediately struck him as a fairground version of a soldier, something you'd see if you were watching Punch and Judy. His monologues – which one couldn't help overhearing, as he tended to shout – were mostly about his exploits against 'the enemy,' the 'enemy' sometimes shifting from continent to continent, country to country, but ever a force for wickedness. At times, the Colonel seemed preoccupied by the Middle East: Iraqis, Iranians, Saudi Arabians. At others, it was Asia that bothered him: the Vietnamese, the Indonesians, the Chinese. All of this was as one might have expected. The Colonel was like a man cursing whichever group happened to be in the day's headlines. But one afternoon, von Würfel heard him lay into the Welsh.

– Lying bastards! I wouldn't trust a Welshman as far as I could throw him! Bunch of singing pansies! By God, there isn't a Welshman born that's fit to clean my stinking shorts!

Despite himself, von Würfel was curious. In North America, there are, after all, very few occasions on which to hear the Welsh vilified. Not that he sought these occasions out, you understand, but after finishing his aish el-saraya and coffee, he introduced himself to the Colonel. And, well, one thing you could say about the man: he was neither discreet nor delicate. The heart of the story – matter-of-factly related – was of one evening in Cardiff when the Colonel had picked up a lovely Welsh streetwalker (in a fashionable district, mind you!) who, at the business end of the evening, turned out to be the possessor of a penis. Having gallantly (but now regrettably) paid in advance for his night's entertainment, the Colonel was damned if he wasn't going to fuck the Welshman. And you can be sure he got his money's worth. But thereafter, he resented what he took to be a general Welsh tendency to deceptiveness.

– Fair enough, von Würfel had said
because he could think of nothing else to say. But after that the two had often spoken.

Whenever they were in el-Bugat at the same time, Ran Morrissey called him over to sit with him. Von Würfel assumed Morrissey would make a tedious companion. But if you could get over the shouting and the fact that he was a bully who liked to lord it over his minder and that he did not like to listen, Ran was entertaining. And he was generous. After their second or third coffee together, von Würfel understood exactly why the Colonel was welcome at el-Bugat. He saw Morrissey leave a hundred-dollar tip on a bill for two coffees and a shot of arak.

Morrissey was generous – or forthcoming – in other ways as well. It was he who'd explained the security system at Castle Rose to von Würfel, as proudly as if he'd conceived it himself. Just as proudly, he'd shown von Würfel his prosthetic leg, with its embedded microchip.

– He showed you the leg? asked Tancred.

– He did, answered von Würfel. It was titanium, strong as hell, made by the Swiss. You're not going to steal it, are you? I'd feel terrible if you did. Ran Morrissey's a good man. I mean, he's capable of good. That's about as much as I need from anyone.

– Have you met many who're incapable of good?

– Yes, said von Würfel. Yes, I have. But you have to remember there's a difference between doing good and thinking you're doing good. Almost everyone *thinks* they're doing good. But we know too little, Tancred. I mean humans know too little. When a man has so little idea what the consequences of an action will be, how can he know if he's doing good or not?

— I hadn't thought about it that way, Tancred said.

— When I was your age, said von Würfel, I assumed everyone could tell good from bad and that that was enough. As I've got older, I'm sure it's *not* enough. I'm convinced it takes a certain amount of faith to do good, Tancred. Not faith in God. I mean, faith that the actions you take will have the outcomes you desire.

— Don't you believe in God? asked Tancred.

— I'm afraid it's worse than that, said von Würfel. I believe God is an impediment to good. All those people acting in his name don't bother to think their actions through. They're incapable of good, if you ask me. No, that's not right. I shouldn't say so. There are any number of them who accidentally do good. And that's something. What I mean is it's more difficult to do good with God in the equation. But I admit I'm a pessimist in these matters, Tancred. I believe we do good or evil indiscriminately because we haven't a vantage from which to judge our actions *before* we've committed to them. Then again, the world works very well without our knowing all the consequences of our actions. So, perhaps I simply haven't found a church to suit my needs.

To Tancred, Ran Morrissey did not seem like a good man at all. He was loud, obnoxious and rude to the women who worked in el-Bugat.

On the other hand, it had been easy to recognize him. Von Würfel's descriptions of Morrissey's person and personality had been exact. And they had immediately brought to mind Willow's description of the one-legged man who lived beside her brother. Nor did Tancred have to wait long before Morrissey put in an appearance. On the first day Tancred was at el-Bugat (along with Colby and Freud), the Colonel entered and said, in an unpleasant tone:

— Can't a veteran get a tea in this place?

Colby had leaned forward and said

— Is that him?

– Yeah, said Tancred.

Freud, contemptuous, barely lowered his voice:

– I say we just kidnap him, take the leg and get on with it. What are you so worried about? If the shoe was on the other foot, I bet he'd kidnap you.

It was going to be tricky stealing the old man's leg. Then it was going to be a problem returning it. But it made more sense to borrow Morrissey's leg than it did to kidnap him. For one thing, they did not know if the chip was still in the prosthetic leg. Nor did they know if it was possible to get into Castle Rose with the leg but without the Colonel.

Then, too, there was the minder: a woman in her forties by the look of her: slim, red-haired, quiet. She seemed shy or perhaps she was simply embarrassed to be in the employ of a man like Morrissey.

(She reminded him of an evening spent with a woman he'd loved, an evening when she'd coaxed him to a reading at the harbourfront. They'd heard, amongst other things, a Christian with blond hair and pale skin who was dressed in a suit. Tancred had not understood a word of the man's work – something about someone named Ubu – but he had been in love and happy, and it suddenly troubled him to think they'd have to deal with Morrissey's minder, that they'd have to get her out of the way.)

It was three in the afternoon. The view from Café el-Bugat was monotonous. The fountain in the square was all you could really see. But the café, with its floor-to-ceiling windows, was filled with light. Tancred, Colby and Freud were at a table in the middle of the café. The Colonel and his minder were near the entrance.

– What's the problem with this city? shouted Morrissey. I thought Rob was going to clear away the streetcars. He's doing his best. I'm not saying he isn't. But this city won't be worth a damn until it gets rid of those things. It's those councillors that're dragging their heels and making things hard for him. And don't you dare tell me a man like Rob can't be intoxicated every now and then and still do a job. I can't count the number of men served their country drunk out of their minds. Damned fine men. Better'n this country deserves.

To Colby and Freud, Tancred said

— Stay here. I'll let you know when to come over.

Tancred had dressed well: a suit jacket, slacks, an expensive sports shirt. He had also, perhaps optimistically, brought along a golf bag in which there was a 4 wood and a 7 iron. He'd brought it in the hope he'd need a place to hide the Colonel's leg. Pausing by Morrissey's table, he said

— I couldn't help overhearing you, sir. Are you a military man?

Ran Morrissey looked him over. He did not, in principle, approve of black people, but he liked any who noticed he was a soldier. He said

— Who the hell are you?

— My name's Matthew Lemon, said Tancred. Ex Queen's Own.

— A rifleman? said Morrissey. Where'd you serve?

— Darfur, said Tancred.

— Really? said Morrissey. Damned good idea to send black soldiers to Africa. What can I do for you?

— I'm sorry to interrupt, said Tancred, but you remind me of a colonel I served under. Maybe you know him? Colonel Hugh McKenzie.

— Name sounds familiar, said Morrissey, but I can't say I know him. I was a colonel myself, you know.

— You were? said Tancred. I wonder if I could buy you and your companion a drink?

— You're missing the service, aren't you? Well, well, well. I wish there were more young men like you. No one gives a monkey's about serving their country. Not these days. I couldn't refuse a young man a chance to buy me a drink. I'll have an arak. But my minder here will have nothing. I can't have her getting drunk, you know.

The minder spoke up.

— I wouldn't mind a coffee, she said.

— Where are your manners? asked Morrissey. It's rude to make a stranger pay for your coffee. Don't I pay you enough?

– It's my pleasure, said Tancred. By helping you, she's helping the military. She's doing us all a favour, the way I see it.

With that, he ordered a Lebanese coffee for the minder and an arak for the Colonel and a double arak for himself.

– A double? said the Colonel. I was just saying how much I like a man who holds his liquor.

When the order came, Tancred made a show of pouring a little of his arak into the Colonel's glass, as a mark of respect. Or so he said. But what he did was slip a Rohypnol he'd palmed into the man's drink. He did the same with the minder's coffee. He was careful about it, but he needn't have been. He had encouraged the Colonel to tell him about his time in Europe. Which the Colonel did. The minder, who must have heard Morrissey's stories innumerable times, was staring at Tancred's face, caught by something about it. Tancred smiled politely at her. Morrissey, for his part, barely took a breath. It was only at Tancred's insistence that they drink to the country they all served – Canada – that the Colonel downed the arak in one motion, as if afraid the drink would distract him from his tale.

– Hmph, he said. This tastes odd. Does it taste odd to you, Matthew?

Twenty minutes later, he was slurring his words, for all appearances tipsy. His minder, too, had begun to wobble. It was then that Tancred called Colby and Freud over.

To any who were observing, it would have looked as though a group of acquaintances were talking as they drank themselves legless. But it was late afternoon. There were only two other patrons in the café. The waitresses were eating a late lunch at a table toward the back and the owner was nowhere to be seen.

Tancred had it in mind that he and Colby would walk the Colonel to the washroom and take his prosthetic leg from him there. When it came to the moment, he feared that taking Morrissey anywhere would create too memorable a spectacle. But crawling under the table to take the man's pants – and leg – off would no doubt have been worse. So, although it felt undignified, he and

Colby – each with an arm around the old man's waist – guided the incoherently muttering Colonel to the washroom, passing beside the waitresses, who did not look up from their meals.

The Colonel's stump was sheathed in soft leather and as the limb came away there was a sound like a muffled finger pop. At that, the Colonel said in a loud voice

– For the love of God, man, drink your juice!

But that was all he said before falling over and banging his head on the clean, white-tile floor. There was no blood, but the bump would leave a bruise on the man's forehead and Tancred was sorry for it.

It was almost as arduous putting the man's pants back on. It took both Tancred and Colby to hold him up and buckle his belt. But the walk back to the table was somewhat easier, perhaps because they were frankly carrying him, now that he was without a leg – a leg that was nestled in his waistband, the artificial foot with its shoe peeking up above his belt like the head of a large black goose. Tancred and Colby each held one of the Colonel's arms around a shoulder as well as holding him up by the waist. It was awkward, but it was done quickly, the two men working well together.

Once they put him down, the Colonel might have fallen from his chair, had Freud not caught him. But Freud did catch him. And so, on one side of the table, backs to the restaurant as if looking out at the fountain, were Morrissey and Freud. Facing them were Colby and Morrissey's minder, she with her head on the table, slumped forward on the straight-backed chair.

– I'll be back in a few minutes, said Tancred. Don't let either of them hurt themselves. We may need them again, if I can't get in.

– Don't you worry about us, said Colby.

He was unhappy at having to babysit the Colonel. But Tancred – who believed it would not take him long to either reconnoitre or be found out by security – had no sympathy for him. He slipped the Colonel's titanium limb – its black shoe now like a monstrous headcover – into the golf bag where it almost disappeared. Then he walked through the el-Bugat, the glass doors at the back sliding open to allow him entrance to Castle Rose.

Tancred was not distracted by the idea of being caught. It made no sense to worry about that and he never did. He was, if anything, self-conscious about the clothes he was wearing. It was November. There was snow on the ground, and although he'd brought an overcoat with him, he'd left it in the café. The clothes he'd chosen were a kind of calculated risk. If one didn't consider the time of year, Tancred looked a certain type of fashionable. If one did, he looked eccentric, which, he imagined, was unexceptional at the Hidden Suites.

The lobby was elegant and yet it was disconcerting. Its walls were covered by tall, wide slabs of maple cladding. It was as if one were inside a pale wooden box. The place was lit by a row of halogen bulbs each at the end of its own black rod. There were two elevators – side by side – whose doors were panelled with dark wood. Above each elevator, there were not numbers but letters of the alphabet. The letters lit up, as if the elevator were travelling from floor to floor, but they did not light up in sequence. Going by the letters, it appeared the elevator was moving randomly up and down, and it was a surprise when its doors slid open.

He entered the first one that came and, once inside, did nothing, pushing no buttons though there were buttons (with numbers on them!) in a panel of what looked to be pink stone beside the doors. The elevator closed and ascended. When it got to his floor it opened and Tancred stepped out, though it was disconcerting having no way of knowing what floor he'd been taken to.

The landing, with its myriad infinities, was exactly as unpleasant as von Würfel had said it was, but he was there only momentarily. As soon as the elevator door closed behind him, a circle of light appeared on the wall to his right. He pushed on the circle. A panel in the wall gave way and he entered a hallway. As he did, small orange lights (one-inch circles a foot or so apart) appeared above the coppery quarter-round. They led past a number of doors, above which pale blue triangles had lit up. In the triangles were names. The lights above the quarter round led beyond a door that said 'Azarian' to the next one down in whose triangle was the name 'Morrissey.'

As he approached Morrissey's condominium, Tancred suddenly wondered if he would find the door to the Colonel's place locked. But it was not and Tancred stepped into a spectacular room. It was on one of the upper floors of the building, apparently. The first thing one saw were large windows that looked out at the islands and the lake – the lake that was, just then, illuminated by a reddish, mid-afternoon light. The room was at least a thousand square feet, with a wooden floor and light blue walls on which the Colonel had four glass showcases. In each there was a faceless mannequin dressed in full, formal military regalia.

The condo was on two levels. To Tancred's left there were steps leading up. In other circumstances, he might have explored the rest of the Colonel's home. But, uncertain that he would ever again find – let alone return to – this floor in Castle Rose, he decided instead to break into Michael Azarian's place at once, to go in though he had no idea if anyone was home.

If he'd stopped to think about it, Tancred would have found the situation absurd. It was a cold November day, but he was dressed as if he were off to play golf. He had with him, and could not leave behind, a golf bag in which he'd hidden the artificial limb of an old man he'd recently roofed. And now he was about to break into a home that might be occupied by one (or many) he did not want to hurt. His adrenalin came in waves and he was calm.

Stepping back into the hallway, he saw that the lights above the quarter-round led in two directions: toward Azarian's door and away from it. He stopped in front of Azarian's and turned the doorknob. The door was locked but with a lock so easy to overcome he felt as if it were cheating to use the pick attached to his own keychain. To think that so much thought had gone into making Castle Rose unbreachable and here he was before a lock he could have opened with a hard plastic card. Then again, gated communities were, once you got past the gate, the easiest to rob, because the dwellers, convinced of their security, ignored basic precautions. It was difficult to blame them, though, 'security' being, for the most part, a trick of the mind.

He was in Azarian's home. The place was exactly the same as Morrissey's. Had there been anyone on the first level, he'd have been seen at once. But there was no one. From Azarian's windows, the view was as spectacular as it had been from the Colonel's: the islands in the distance, the lake in afternoon sunlight, one of the ferries moving on the water. The difference was, of course, in the décor. Here, there was furniture and a sense that the place was lived in: a sofa, a coffee table, two paintings of toy horses by Harold Town and, beneath the paintings, a wooden credenza.

On top of the credenza, as if it were nothing special: a bottle of aquavit.

Despite himself, Colby found it all impressive. From the moment Tancred left them to look after Morrissey to the moment he returned with the bottle of aquavit, no more than ten minutes passed. Having seen how efficient security was at Castle Rose, he and Freud could not help feeling respect for Tancred. They might have felt more, but there was something about Palmieri that curdled closeness. The man kept things to himself – which led Colby to be cold in turn.

The other reason for his coldness was the nagging thought that Tancred would have to be forced to give them what was theirs: that is, the money Colby knew they would find once all the clues had been unravelled. He and Freud were at a disadvantage. They were not as clever as Tancred. Colby was not into the kind of games clever people played. His mind immediately shut off when people talked about chess or computer games or anything that involved numbers or logic. All his life he'd hated mathematics. And why wouldn't he? For years and years his mother had tried to beat math into him – drunk out of her mind, smacking his hands with a ruler every time he got 'six times seven' or 'nine times five' wrong. (God knows, he always got those things wrong.) Now, of course, now that he was in his twenties, he regretted his lack of talent. He did not regret his inability with numbers. No, it was not numbers that mattered but, rather, what lurked behind them: the calculating mind. That was the thing to admire and fear. And Tancred was one of those who calculated.

Well, what about it? There were ways of dealing with men who thought too much: leverage, something to catch their attention, something to keep their brains occupied. Which is why, when Tancred returned to el-Bugat with the bottle of aquavit, Colby said

– Looks like you had the easy part.

– Good thing we know how to handle deadbeats, said Freud.

The Colonel and his minder were both somewhere between co-operative and unconscious. The pale woman was now sitting with her head on Colby's shoulder. The Colonel was face down on the table, still mumbling, with Freud holding him steady. One of the waitresses had come over to see if everything was all right. When Colby said, 'The Colonel's been drinking,' the woman had walked away, almost apologetic, as if she'd interrupted a ritual she knew well.

Now, Tancred called a waitress over.

– How much do we owe you for everything? he asked.

– Fifty-five twenty-two, she said.

Tancred paid.

– Listen, he said, do you know these people?

– Who? said the waitress. The Colonel? Yes, I know him.

– Good, said Tancred. I bought him and the lady a drink, but it looks like I shouldn't have. They're both out of it.

Tancred withdrew the Colonel's artificial limb from the golf bag.

– I don't know how this came off, he said, but I think he's going to need it.

He handed the leg to the waitress.

– Maybe you could bring them some coffee so they can sober up.

He gave her a twenty.

– I'm sorry for the trouble, he said. Usually guys in the military can drink.

The waitress, caught completely off guard, said

– Yes, yes, I'll get coffee

and, distracted, took the leg with her to the back of the café.

To Freud, Tancred said

– Lie him down on two chairs. He'll get hurt if he falls.

Freud grudgingly allowed Morrissey's body to sprawl over the chairs. Colby put the minder to lie forward with her head and upper body on the table. The three men then went out of Café el-Bugat without waiting for the waitress's return.

4 A Discovery That Comes with an Address

Who were Errol Colby and Freud Luxemberg, or *why* were they who they were?

It would have been difficult for Tancred to think of more difficult or more unappealing questions. Who is anyone? Why is anyone anyone? These were the kinds of questions it was better not to ask because they almost certainly had no answers, and thinking about them only added to the uncertainty.

For all his frustration and unease at the questions, however, their answers were vital to him. Just how dangerous were Colby and Freud? They'd had a hand in Mrs. Mallay's death. He was almost certain of it. But if he'd decided to keep them close to discover the kind of men they were, he'd have been disappointed. Colby and Freud were all manner of men. They were threatening and obsequious, ignorant and perceptive, concerned and callous. It was as if you could pick and choose among their characteristics and create your own Errol Colby, your own Freud. At times it wasn't clear to Tancred that either man was any particular man – which only proved how useless thinking could be. For all his cogitation and consideration, it was a safe bet that Colby and Freud were dangerous and would be happy to have him out of their way.

But what was he to do about it?

They had returned from Castle Rose with Michael Azarian's bottle of aquavit. None of them could find anything remarkable about the bottle itself. The numbers on the label had been changed from proper dates to the two numbers (1889, 4185) that made the bottle part of Azarian's puzzle, one more clue that led to Mount Pleasant Cemetery. They spent a while, the three of them, trying to understand what Robert Azarian had meant by the bottle, if he'd meant anything at all.

Colby and Freud scrutinized the clues. They walked around the Japanese screen. They picked up the bottle of aquavit. They approached the painting and listened to its 'boring' music. They contemplated the model of Fallingwater. Tancred, for his part, sat in one of the two chairs in the apartment thinking about Colby and Freud until, without warning, Freud's face reddened and he began to shout in Colby's direction, though what he said was meant for Tancred.

– This is bullshit! He's fucking with us! He knows something!

– I told you everything I know, said Tancred.

– You shut up! I'm not even talking to you!

Tancred got up from his chair and stepped away from the mementos. Freud, furious, moved toward him.

– You sit down or I'll knock you down!

Incongruously, this was the moment Tancred recalled his mother's belief in the sacredness of human life. He remembered her words in part because it suddenly seemed to him that Freud was an animal, something like a large dog baring its teeth. And Freud sprang at him, helter-skelter, a cliché out of a class in jiu-jitsu, his fists up.

As if the apartment were a dojo, Tancred calmly stepped forward, took Freud by the coat and threw him to the floor. The floor trembled, tipping the bottle of aquavit over. Tancred then punched Freud as hard as he could in the face, catching him on the cheek, the sound of it a moist *thuck*. Freud put up an arm, late. Tancred hit him again, this time catching him over the eye. Again, Freud tried to protect himself, late. Tancred caught him square on the nose, breaking it.

It was over in moments, but the man was alarming. It had taken three painful knocks to the head – painful to Tancred – just to calm him down.

– You didn't have to do that, said Colby. Why'd you do that?

Freud got up off the floor.

– I'll kill you, he said.

But his words came out somewhere between a complaint and a question.

Tancred said

– It's time for you two to go.

– You really shouldn't have hit him, said Colby.

But Freud allowed his friend to coax him out of the apartment, leaving Tancred to clean up, to soak his hand in ice water, to wonder about who, among his friends, Colby and Freud knew. (Ollie, Daniel, Fiona?) Maybe he shouldn't have attacked Freud. But it would have been worse, he thought, to let them think he was intimidated. Then there'd have been no stopping them. No, decidedly, they were not the kind of men one treated kindly.

Though he wasn't fastidious, Tancred hated blood. It always got to unexpected places. Now, for instance, he found two drops on the Japanese screen, though Freud had been a few feet away from it. But as he was wiping Freud's blood from the screen and the floor, his thoughts turned to Alexander von Würfel, the one who, curiously, hadn't painted the screen, though he'd made all the other mementos.

How careful Robert Azarian had been, not wishing anyone to know all five clues. Then again, why did he allow von Würfel to make four of the five pieces? A previously vague idea came back to Tancred with unexpected clarity. Willow had assumed that the hints they needed were in the five objects her father had bequeathed to his children, in the congruity of the pieces.

But what about von Würfel? Was he – that is, the man himself – a clue?

Von Würfel's initials had been on the one piece he hadn't actually made: the Japanese screen. The man's name must have been a hint. Willow had come to think otherwise, largely because the 'signature' had read a(ɯ), not a(vɯ) or av(ɯ). But also because, having discovered nothing significant about von Würfel, she had lost interest in the man, had begun to search for some other meanings to the a(ɯ).

Indeed, Willow had found another meaning. The signature was not an a and w, as she'd imagined, but an a and ɯ, the ɯ being the first letter of the Armenian alphabet. It stood for

առաջին

or 'aɍaǰin,' the Armenian word for 'first.'

– You see? Willow had said. The 'a' stands for Alton and the 'ɯ' stands for 'first.' My father was saying 'Alton (first)' but I don't understand why.

When Tancred related Willow's words to him, von Würfel understood perfectly.

– That makes sense, he'd said. It means Alton's clue comes first.

Tancred had nodded in agreement at the time, but now he was not sure. There was something about von Würfel – had to be. The maker was tangled in the things made.

So, what was it about von Würfel? First and most obviously, the name was German. So was the name Weiden, which was, as Willow had told him, the German word for willow. Less obvious, but maybe as significant: Alexander von Würfel was *English*. He did not himself speak German. So, there was, in von Würfel himself, a conjunction of German and English. When Tancred thought about that and held Psalm 137 in mind, one phrase stuck with him, the same phrase Ollie had pointed to:

We hanged our harps upon the willows in the midst thereof ...

Which is to say:

We hanged our [something] upon the [Weidens] in the midst thereof ...

He found the 'something' easily enough online:

An den Wassern zu Babel saßen wir und weinten, wenn wir en Zion gedachten.
Unsere Harfen hingen wir an die Weiden, die daselbst sind ...

So ...

We hanged our Harfen *upon the* Weiden *in the midst thereof ...*

Somewhere among the Weidens there was a Harfe or Harfen. Maybe. If Robert Azarian had been thinking as Tancred now imagined he had been, if Alexander von Würfel was in fact a clue to a puzzle whose solution, strangely enough, von Würfel himself was seeking.

Tancred felt ridiculous breaking into the cemetery. It was two in the morning. He was walking with a stepladder that hung awkwardly from his shoulder. The night was cold – minus something or other – so he'd dressed warmly: gloves, boots, a toque, a pullover, a black overcoat. His getup felt lumpish, as if parts of himself didn't quite fit.

No doubt, there were security guards around, somewhere. But he neither saw nor heard anyone else. He was among the dead and it felt that way.

Over the weeks, he'd examined all the gravestones around the Weiden mausoleum and knew them well and was almost certain there were no HARFEN among them. So, Tancred began his search inside the mausoleum. The light from the flame was inadequate. It illuminated the words that surrounded it but not much more. In fact, the dancing shadows it cast made reading the names on the walls difficult. Even more disheartening: each of the four walls of the mausoleum was fifteen feet wide and ten feet high, and each of the rectangles bearing the name WEIDEN was four inches by five inches. That meant that each of the walls – save the one with the door in it – had, in theory, 1,080 engraved rectangles to be examined.

There being no sure way to proceed, Tancred chose to begin with the wall that had the fewest WEIDENs in it; that is, the wall with the door. Here, there were a mere thousand or so rectangles. But each and every one of them contained the name WEIDEN. This it took him some forty minutes of mind-haltingly dull work to ascertain: flashlight in hand, himself atop the stepladder or bent from the waist or down on his knees. After half an hour, Tancred was far from sure that what he was doing was sane, let alone sensible.

The second wall he chose was even more tedious to do. He was now tired and warm. The flame, though modest, was enough, when coupled with his going up and down the stepladder, to heat the mausoleum. So, after examining another thousand (plus) white-marble rectangles, he was uncertain if he'd missed something or not. His mind was now so used to seeing (and his fingers feeling)

WEIDEN, he wasn't sure it would register anything else. He regretted not asking Ollie – who had returned home to care for his father – to help him. This was just the kind of thing Ollie would have been happy to do. And Ollie would not have cared if they found a rectangle with the name HARFEN carved in it or not. The more futile an endeavour, the more it suited Ollie's view of the world.

But Tancred was fortunate. He did not have to examine all four walls. The third one he came to, the wall facing the door, was the one on which he found – seven rows down from the top of the wall and five columns from the right-hand edge – not the name HARFEN but the word HARFE: HARP, a single harp among the willows.

Though he had spent an hour and a half systematically looking for it, Tancred was dumbfounded to discover this HARFE on the wall. It seemed improbable – and somehow sinister – that he should be the one to find it. Or had Willow's siblings come to it before him? And then, the discovery felt unreal: too simple, too obvious, though it hadn't been simple or obvious until the moment he saw and touched the engraved marble for himself.

But he'd been right! His and Robert Azarian's minds had taken the same path and had come to the same place. Yes, it was marvellous, but his moment of wonder was brief. Having found a rectangle with HARFE engraved on it, Tancred wasn't sure what to do. The rectangle was indistinguishable from those around it, save for the different engraving, and even that was visible only if you shone the light directly at it.

He blew on the rectangle. He wiped it with his elbow. Then Tancred pushed on the stone. It gave way, slightly. A curious feeling: like he was falling into the wall. He pushed again, harder. This time the stone went in easily and kept going until there was a click and it sprang back, some four or five inches out from the wall. The name HARFE had been engraved on the face of a secret drawer. In the drawer, there was a black-leather Hermès envelope in which Tancred found two things: a small gold key and a thick piece of yellow paper – like a canary's breast – on which the words

Crédit Suisse
Fairmont Le Montreux Palace
Avenue Claude Nobs 2
Montreux, Suisse
Box #742015

were printed in black ink.

Just like that, after stubbornly following an intuition, Tancred had proven Willow right. Her father had meant her to find something, and that something was (apparently) in a box at a Crédit Suisse in Montreux. Whatever the thing was, however, its existence inaugurated another task. He would have to go to Switzerland.

First, of course, he'd have to deal with Colby and Freud.

As he walked from the cemetery, the half moon seemed to be sticking out of a black pocket. It was still cold but Tancred was now too distracted to care. Another thought had come to him: wasn't it strange that if Willow had connected 'Weiden' – her own name in German and the name of her father's friend – with Psalm 137 she could, on her own, have discovered the drawer in the mausoleum? The four other clues were redundant – perhaps only a spur to Willow's mind – and each was useless on its own. It seemed her father had wanted Willow – Willow alone – to find the key and the address. You couldn't help wondering why or feeling sad now that she never would.

5 Daniel Has a Word with Delmer McDougal

– I don't really *have* an impression, said Puli. I guess the least you could say is that your Colby guy isn't exactly predictable. One minute he's at the cemetery, hanging around looking for something. Yeah, that's him in the picture. Sorry. I couldn't get a clear shot of him. Anyway, then he's in Parkdale. Then he's at the harbourfront having a drink with buddy there who's dressed like he's going golfing. They were in the Lebanese place on Queen's Quay. It's got great *aish el-saraya*. You should try it, Dan.

Daniel thanked him.

– You did good, he said. I've got what I wanted.

– Thank god for that, said Puli. I can't stand surveillance when it's cold out.

But what, exactly, had Daniel got? Photos of Nigger Colby, Freud and Tancred. Photos that were upsetting because, now, he knew something was up. Despite telling Tancred that Freud and Colby might have had something to do with Mrs. Mallay's death, there Tancred was hanging out with them like they were friends – an idea Daniel found impossible to accept. There was nothing honourable about Colby, and Freud was a sociopath. Perhaps they had something on him. It was impossible to tell from photos what exactly was going on.

(How surreal to see Tancred with a golf bag. Tancred hated golf.)

There was no doubt about it: he'd have to speak to Tancred. Friend to friend, first. There was still no reason for official involvement, but Tancred's life now impinged on Daniel's professional imagination. Meaning that, until now, the detective in him had never had to think about Tancred Palmieri. Before he got in touch with Tancred, though, he would visit the places where Puli had taken pictures of Freud, Tancred and Nigger: Café el-Bugat, Mount Pleasant cemetery, an apartment building on Winnett.

The first place he went – to get it out of the way – was Mount Pleasant. He disliked the cemetery and hated the thought of spending time there on a day off. To think that there were people who loved to walk about among the gravestones, cenotaphs and mausoleums. Some, it seemed, came to pay their respects to the famous dead, like Glenn Gould. But of what good is the place where a man's bones lie rotting? In Gould's case, why not leave it at the recordings? There was more of Glenn Gould in one measure of the *Goldberg Variations* than there was in all this well-kept necropolis.

Then again, Daniel's father was buried in Winnipeg and Daniel resented the distance. It felt as if Baruch had disowned him in choosing to be buried so far away. So, perhaps there was some significance to a resting place? No, none. As far as he could tell, the earth did not mind where petals fell. Why should he care what ground his body nourished? And yet, he missed his father, his ashes even.

Mount Pleasant was its late-autumn self: trees mostly leafless, with here and there a burst of yellow or orange from persistent fronds, a thin layer of snow on the ground, the sun bright, the feeling in the cemetery one of almost circumspect calm, as if Toronto's dead were, even for corpses, well-behaved.

Daniel found the Weiden mausoleum easily. It was close to the cemetery's main office and pale smoke rose from its narrow chimney. He looked into the mausoleum and saw nothing obvious – that is, nothing to explain Nigger's interest in the place, nor anything to explain Tancred's. It was white marble. There was a perpetual flame and biblical engravings on the floor and the name Weiden was carved thousands of times into the walls.

It was impressive, in its way, but not the kind of thing to attract drug dealers, you'd have thought: too elegant, too subtle. Then again, Colby had been at Simone Azarian-Thomson's home, with its paintings and expensive rugs. So, maybe there was a connection between this place and that one.

As he stepped out of the mausoleum, he was met by an older man in a long, grey coat.

– G'day, g'day, said the man. There a bar in that place there?

– A bar? asked Daniel. Why would there be a bar in a mausoleum?

— Oh, jeez, don't ask me, eh? Your average person'll drink Jaysus knows where. But I seen so many people go in there, that iron grille's like a screen door in a windstorm.

— Really? said Daniel. How many people are we talking about?

— I'm not sure just how many . . .

— I wonder if you could describe some of them for me, said Daniel.

He showed Delmer McDougal his ID, which Delmer examined closely.

— Police, eh? Well, I guess it's to be expected. Somethin' must be goin' on.

And because he was, when faced with the police, honest and forthcoming, Delmer told Daniel everything he knew about Alexander von Würfel, about a 'dark fella' whom he described well enough for Daniel to recognize, about an albino and a blond man with a limp.

— What do you think they were after? asked Daniel.

Delmer was suddenly thoughtful.

— Well, I'll tell you, son. In my experience, it's usually about Liz. The Liz on a twenty, I mean. If it's not about Lizzie, it's about love. I been runnin' 'round for pret' near seventy years an' I can count on one hand that's missin' three fingers when it's been about anythin' else.

— Can you tell me what the men were like?

— The one fella, the old gent, he's a talker. Paid me to keep an eye out. Wanted to know if anyone ever came 'round. Gave me his number an everythin.'

Delmer took out his wallet and from one of its pouches extracted a piece of paper with von Würfel's number on it.

— The dark fella, said Delmer, he wasn't a talker. But he an' your von Waffle went off together. For my two cents, they were both lookin' for something an' they seemed to get along pretty good.

— What's so special about this place? asked Daniel.

— I don' know, said Delmer, but I'll give you another number you should call.

On the other side of the paper with von Würfel's name, Delmer wrote followed by a telephone number.

Astonished by this sudden connection of Colby, Tancred and the Azarians, Daniel said

– How do you know Mr. Azarian?

– How do I know 'im? said Delmer. I been workin' for 'im for years, eh? Everything goes on aroun' here, he knows about it.

Bay Street around King – its towers like vast and trunkless legs of glass – was exactly where you'd expect to find the offices of Azarian Holdings. And from Alton Azarian's office, you could look out onto other tall buildings or down to the lake. It was the kind of view that must often have elicited the words

– You have a lovely view!

But Daniel found it tiresome, evoking as it did not loveliness but a child's version of power: the king of the castle sniffing at a parade of rascals.

– You have a lovely view, he said.

– Thank you, said Alton Azarian.

He was around six feet tall and, you could see, kept himself in good shape. No doubt, thought Daniel unkindly, he spent a lot of time in front of mirrors.

– What can I do for you, Detective?

– It seems there might be a connection between the Weiden mausoleum and the things stolen from your sisters . . .

– From my sisters *and* my brother, said Alton. My brother's just had a bottle of aquavit stolen from his home. But what's the connection with the Weidens, do you think?

– It's mostly my intuition, at this point, said Daniel. A man I saw at your sister's home was recently seen at . . .

– No, I'm sorry, said Azarian, I'll stop you there. I was just curious about what you knew. There is a connection between the things our father bequeathed to us and the Weiden burial ground, but it's all part of a game. My younger sister, Willow, who we all loved, had it in her head that the things my father bequeathed us were part of a treasure hunt. My father encouraged her to think so. He wanted something to take her mind off the hard drugs she was using. She was not well, Detective. She was an addict. But she must have been well enough to encourage people to help look for this treasure of hers. The only real mystery, as far as I'm concerned, is how these people found the mausoleum when Willow never did.

Daniel was going to ask about McDougal, but Alton Azarian anticipated the question.

– I hired Mr. McDougal to keep an eye on the Weiden plot. I mostly hired him because I don't trust the staff at Mount Pleasant to take care of the mausoleum as my father wanted. But, to be honest, I was also hoping Willow would find her way there. The message about family was for her. My father meant her to think about family. He meant her to choose family over drugs.

– How many people did your sister talk to about this?

– That's hard to say. My sister was a heroin addict, Detective. She wasn't discreet.

– Do you know any of the people she encouraged?

– Not at all. I'm not an addict. But I did look into it.

Azarian took a business card from his wallet and read the names written on the back.

– Alexander von Würfel, Tancred Palmieri, an albino named Errol Colby and a man named Freud Luxemberg. Shady characters, Detective. My sister and I didn't share the same social circles. I don't mean that as criticism. I loved my sister. Her death was a blow to all of us but to me especially, because my father asked me to take care of her and I couldn't.

– I'm sorry for your loss, said Daniel.

– Look, Detective, this treasure business was a game. It was a game with a purpose, but there's no treasure. I know that for certain. Some people may have it in their heads that my father left money lying around, but he wasn't that kind of man. He was an honest, hard-working businessman. That's all he was. And no businessman I can think of would bury money without knowing it was going to be found. That just doesn't make sense.

— I'm sure you're right, said Daniel, but that means someone or some people don't know they're chasing a will-o'-the-wisp. So far, you've been lucky. None of your siblings have been hurt. But if people believe you and your siblings are keeping something from them, someone might get hurt. You've already lost a number of precious things, no?

— You're absolutely right, Detective. I'm glad we spoke. I feel confident you'll sort this out. But I'm afraid I have an important matter to attend to. So, if there's anything else you need from me, any other information, just call my secretary. We can make another appointment or, if you like, I'll call you myself. Is that all right?

— I'm sorry to have taken your time, said Daniel.

But Alton Azarian's attention was already elsewhere. His suit was elegant. His shirt was white as February snow. He was speaking into his phone, and Detective Mandelshtam had been dismissed.

— Oh, said von Würfel, that explains everything.

— What does it explain? asked Daniel.

They were in the back of Von Würfel's Animals and Birds. It smelled of formaldehyde. At a long table, Mr. von Würfel was working on a badger that had been the pet of a man from Sutton. The animal was beautiful — its eyes open as if it were still alert, its ears forward so as not to miss the answer to some crucial question.

— It explains, said von Würfel, why Delmer was always there when there was someone near the mausoleum. One wouldn't expect that, if he'd really been walking around without a destination. Delmer must have stayed close to the mausoleum.

— That's true, said Daniel.

Von Würfel sighed.

— I've found, Detective, that you can't depend on anyone these days. People have become so deceitful. It's why I prefer animals.

Anyway, I apologize for not telling you sooner about my involvement with the Azarians. It's because I've learned to mistrust men that I kept quiet.

– What about Tancred?

– I don't know much about him, Detective. We've met once or twice, but he's not talkative. I like him. My impression is that he's driven by the right impulses.

– Do you think Tancred believes there's a treasure?

– To be honest, Detective, I'm not sure it matters to him. My impression is that he's doing this for someone or something else. I think what matters to him is the doing, not the finding. But I'm speaking about things I don't know. You'd have to ask Tancred.

– Where can I find him? asked Daniel.

– I haven't got a clue, said von Würfel. We're not that close.

– So you have no idea who stole the Azarians' pieces?

– I'd certainly tell you if I knew, Detective. But I have the copies I made and Tancred's seen those. I can't say if he's a thief, but there's no reason for him to have stolen them.

– How do I know you're not telling me this because you mistrust me?

– I can't help you there, Detective.

For Detective Mandelshtam, an unexpectedly difficult question: should he meet with Tancred or speak to him on the phone? In the end, he decided they should meet. Phoning him was not the act of a friend, and it felt as if a long, potentially awkward phone conversation would have done damage to their friendship. An interview in person, being more official, carried less emotional weight – for him, at least, if not for Tancred. Besides, he wanted to see Tancred's face. Knowing him as well as he did, he was certain he'd get at least a hint – from his expressions – of the kind of trouble he was in.

On this occasion, they met nowhere in particular: a Starbucks at Dovercourt and Dundas. They were both uncomfortable and neither could hide it. Daniel led with a joke about a filthy bus terminal (a crusty bus station) and a lobster with breast implants (a busty crustacean) but Tancred had heard it and managed no more than a perfunctory smirk.

– I hear, said Daniel, you're treasure hunting. You don't have to say anything, Tan. Just let me get a few words out. You've never stolen anything in 14 Division before. Not that I know of. So, I've never had to say anything to you. But now I do. I'm going to have to look into all this more closely and I've got to do this by the book. The way I figure it, you're the one who stole a model from Mrs. Azarian-Grau, a painting from Mrs. Azarian-Thomson, a bottle from Michael Azarian and a screen from Willow Azarian. I don't know why you stole them. When I spoke to Alton Azarian he told me there's some idea out there that his father left treasure somewhere around the Weiden plot or in the Weiden mausoleum in Mount Pleasant Cemetery. The thing that upsets me more than having to go after you is that, from what I can tell, you're doing this with Nigger Colby and his psychopath. I'm worried about you, Tan. This isn't how the Tancred I know operates. So, I assume there's something wrong.

Daniel had planned to observe Tancred as he said all this but, of course, he hadn't been watching him at all. He'd been thinking how difficult all of this was, difficult to accept that he and Tancred were on opposite sides of a fence. He'd kept his head down, but he looked up to say

– Fiona and I have about fifty thousand dollars in a joint account. It's my money, mostly, but I asked if she'd mind if I gave it to you and she had no problem with that at all. I didn't tell her why. I didn't have to. Look, I know you're going to turn it down. It wouldn't be you if you didn't. But I'm asking you this one favour. Please, Tan, if you've got problems you can solve with money, please think about it. No strings attached. We both love you and we couldn't forgive ourselves if anything happened to you. So, I just want you to consider it. For our sakes. It's not going to change how I handle the theft of the Azarian things. I'm going to do the best job I can. You know that. Anyway, that's all I've got to say, really.

Tancred, moved by his friend's offer, said

— Why didn't you just arrest me, Danny? I'd have understood.

— For petty theft? I don't have proof. If there's any to find, I'll find it. But it's the Nigger thing that bugs me. He and Luxemberg are idiots, but idiots can be dangerous. If you're into them for a few thousand, I'd rather deal with that. *If* the problem's money.

— Errol thinks this is about thousands of dollars, maybe millions. He's convinced I know something about Azarian's money.

— Do you?

— I'm not going to tell you, said Tancred. I don't want you on this side of the fence. But the thing is, Errol and Freud tried to get to me through Ollie.

— I thought so.

— So, I'm co-operating with them. I don't have a choice.

Though he knew how Tancred would answer, Daniel asked nevertheless

— Have they done anything I could pick them up for?

— I want you to know, said Tancred, and be sure you tell Fiona, that I'm sorry to have put you through this. I promise you, Dan, if it'd been the kind of thing that could be solved by fifty thousand, I'd have taken your money. But it's not that kind of thing.

— Let's promise, said Daniel, that until this is all over, we're not going to see each other. I'm not going to call. I don't want you to call me. Because if you say something that helps me catch you and Nigger, I'll use it.

— It's a deal, said Tancred.

As they'd done all their lives — but now with a hint of self-mockery — they shook pinkies, though neither man would have thought for a moment of breaking his promise. Then they spoke of other things.

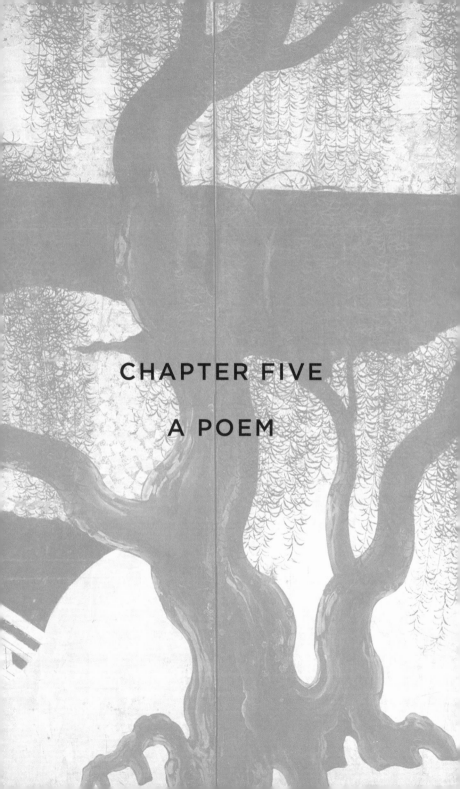

CHAPTER FIVE

A POEM

1 Alton Azarian Clears Things Up

It was dumbfounding to enter the apartment on Winnett and find it empty. There was not a thing left: none of the Azarians' pieces, no furniture, not even the plastic cutlery Tancred had brought or the futons and bedsheets he and Ollie had been sleeping on.

Tancred's first thought was that Colby and Freud had taken everything. But why would they have taken his table, his chairs, his bedding and futons? That made no sense. Even the Azarian mementos were useless to them, as neither Colby nor Freud had the least idea how to interpret them. His second thought was that von Würfel had raided him. But that made even less sense. Von Würfel already had copies of the Azarian pieces. Daniel's was the next name to come to mind, but it was there only a microsecond. This kind of thing was so unlike Daniel it was impossible to believe he was involved. That left, in effect, only the Azarians. So, when there were three firm knocks at the door, Tancred tried to imagine which of them it might be.

His first impression of Alton Azarian was of fashionable clothes, the smell of a cologne that wedded patchouli and cocoa, and a recent haircut that had something of a pompadour to it. He was not young. His hair was so black it looked as if it had recently been fitted to his scalp. The skin on his face was facelift-taut. In kind lighting, he might have passed for sixty. He was at least sixty-five, though, and Tancred's first impression was of a man afraid of death.

With him, a discreet but looming presence: a tall, muscular man in a black suit, his delts and traps built up so that his head seemed perched on a mound. A chauffeur, as it turned out.

Alton Azarian introduced himself and extended a hand.

– I assume you're Tancred, he said, and I imagine you were expecting me or, at least, one of us.

– I wasn't sure what to expect, said Tancred. Come in?

– No, no, said Alton, there's nowhere to sit. I'm inviting you to Scaramouche. I've made a dinner reservation for us. Is that acceptable?

The restaurant was not one Tancred would have chosen. It was intimidating, with its wood-and-glass decor and windows that looked down onto the lights of the city. The place evidently put Alton Azarian at ease, however. The man ordered two bottles of a Quintarelli Alzero, one for himself and one for Tancred.

– It's a little overpriced, he said, but I like the wine.

Azarian recommended the lamb for Tancred and had filet mignon himself. When they'd finished eating, he ordered a Château d'Yquem. The man had eaten little – not more than a quarter of his steak – and he'd drunk half a glass of the Alzero. The meal had been for Tancred's benefit, it seemed. Perhaps Azarian had meant to reassure him. Or perhaps he was trying to put Tancred in his place, using generosity as a weapon. A shame, since Tancred – who rarely drank alcohol – could not have told a thousand-dollar bottle of wine (the Alzero) from a chalky plonk.

– I want you to know, Azarian said, that I'm not obliged to you. I don't owe you anything. A part of me feels you exploited my sister. On the other hand, while she was alive, Willow must have thought highly of you, and Simone was impressed as well. We're all impressed by you. If I ever need a thief, I know whom to call. On the other hand, please don't take this the wrong way, but I think you'd make a lousy detective. There's so much you don't understand.

Azarian wet his lips with the Sauterne.

– In light of Willow's admiration for you, he said, my siblings and I agreed it would be fair if I filled in the blanks for you. For Willow's sake. So, to begin with ...

Immediately after their father's death, Alton had hired a private investigator to keep an eye on Willow – not to snoop on her, exactly, but to make sure she wasn't hurt. That hadn't worked out. Willow had noticed him and, assuming he was up to no good, she'd had him beaten up by one of the albino's associates, the one named Freud Luxemberg. Still, the investigator, poor man, hadn't been useless. Before being roughed up, he'd been pretty thorough. They knew, for instance, where Willow went for heroin, who she associated with and, most importantly, that no one believed Willow was wealthy. Her siblings hoped none of the sociopaths who hung around Parkdale would believe her ravings about treasure.

– Do you believe in this treasure? asked Alton.

For a moment, Tancred considered telling the man about the 'harp' he'd found in the mausoleum, just to see the look on his face.

– I don't know what to believe, he said.

– Then why were you looking around the mausoleum?

– I promised Willow I'd look into this business. She's the one who told me about it.

– It's good of you to keep your promise. But why didn't she go there herself?

– I don't know, said Tancred. But if you knew she was an addict, why didn't you have her committed?

Alton pursed his lips and shook his head.

– I loved my sister, he said. We all did. We pleaded with her to get help. We tried an intervention. It's not that we wouldn't have had her committed. But it would have been our last resort. It would have been humiliating for all of us.

Alton believed that the worst idea his father ever had was to use his bequests as clues in a treasure hunt. His children – all save Willow – understood why he'd done it. He'd told them why. He'd meant to keep Willow occupied, to take her mind off his death, to take her mind off drugs, to bring her back to her old self. To be fair, the idea had been intermittently successful. When Willow was not high or incapacitated, she was at least engaged by something.

None of them had taken the decline of Willow's mind into account, however. The younger Willow would have found the 'treasure' their father had left in no time. But the woman she'd become was confused, deluded, unable to properly read the clues.

– You never really met my little sister, said Alton. Willow was the smartest person I've ever known. And I've known some brilliant people.

Alton – too optimistic – was convinced she would eventually arrive at the mausoleum. But it occurred to him that Willow, who'd never been good at keeping secrets, might point the wrong people to the mausoleum, and he wanted to know who any such wrong people might be. So, he'd hired Delmer McDougal to keep an eye on it and on the grounds around it. The mausoleum was not only a message to Willow. It was also a shrine to the Weidens, his father's closest friends. It was right that it should be protected from desecration.

– This is where you come in, said Alton. You, von Würfel, Mr. Colby and Freud Luxemberg. None of you have any idea you're on a wild goose chase. You have to admit it's a little amusing, Tancred. But now that the police are involved, I think it's a good time to put an end to it, don't you?

For the first time that evening, Alton smiled.

– By the way, he said, congratulations on stealing Michael's bottle of aquavit. I've always thought those crooks at Chateau Rose were self-important frauds. The Hidden Castle. As if anyone could build a place that's 100 percent secure. I was hoping someone would steal that stupid bottle. I assume it was you?

Tancred said nothing.

– My father was unpredictable, Alton said. He was a business-man. He thrived on being unpredictable. But he wasn't a fool. He wouldn't have left scads of money around just in case someone found it. It's inconceivable. In any case, he told me there was no treasure. He told me what he was doing and why he was doing it. And just before he died, he gave me the solution to the hunt and asked me to keep an eye on the mausoleum.

As Alton saw it, the final proof his father had *not* hidden treasure was the fact that each of the mementos he'd left were treasures in themselves, much more valuable as testaments to his love for his children. Each was like a message from the grave. Did Tancred know the poem he – that is, Alton – had inherited? No? Well, no matter. Alton knew it by heart and he wrote it out on a sheet of paper he got from the maître d':

None of the dead are lonely,
or so the breeze would have it.
Rather, far, the civilized wit
than fortunes won without it.
Hours from you, my porcupine, though
four of your quills pierced
three of my vines.

When your fingers have plucked
each of the strings
south of my dying equator,
the oceans will wave their
seven blue veils but
nine will comfort you, later.

The most obvious thing about the poem was, of course, the clue provided by the first letters of its first words: North 43, West 79. Any fool could see it for what it was: a designation of latitude and longitude. An invitation to keep looking for a place.

– But you didn't think the other words in the poem were meaningless, did you?

No, the other words were not meaningless. Each word and line had significance beyond the clue it provided for Willow. He would not go into it because, frankly, the poem's meaning was personal. It was not for Tancred's consumption. However, the poem itself was a paean to family, and its cleverest lines referred directly to the Weidens:

the oceans will wave their
seven blue veils but
nine will comfort you, later.

Here, the 'oceans' were Mr. and Mrs. Weiden because Robert Azarian had often mocked his friends (lawyers both) for their supposed depths, sometimes calling them Mr. and Mrs. Pacific or Mr. and Mrs. Atlantic. His words had taken on special meaning when, at Nicole Azarian's funeral, the Weidens and their children had dressed in blue. Though Robert Azarian had been grief-struck, he'd seen how the Weidens were dressed, and their gentle eccentricity had moved him. They – at the time seven of them – had brought him comfort. But *nine* Weidens – the number of Weiden graves before the mausoleum – would be the ones to comfort the Azarian children, now that Robert was dead.

– I know what you're thinking, said Alton. You're like Simone. You're convinced there's something more to all this. But you've got to keep in mind that the last words my father told me were: 'Remember, Alton, there's no treasure, except for Willow.' He said it over and over – no treasure, except for Willow – until I told him I understood. But it wasn't until after we read the will and I thought about this whole treasure business that I realized he'd given me the answer in advance. He wanted Willow to look. It was something to keep her occupied. And, in the end, it did keep her occupied. Intermittently. Not that the occupation did much good.

Tancred again thought of telling Alton about the black-leather envelope. The man was so smug, so certain he knew what others did not.

– You must be wondering how I found you, said Alton. The landlord contacted me. He'd been trying to get in touch with Willow and called my office on the off chance we were related. I didn't know what to expect when I got there, but it all comes down to fate, doesn't it? I was meant to find the things you'd stolen. In any case, my brother and my sisters have their mementos back. So, I consider this whole business over. We'd all like to be left alone now, Tancred. Willow is dead. I assume you know von Würfel and the others. I'll leave it up to you to tell them what I've told you. Should any of you bother us further, you'll find that we know how to defend ourselves.

Alton Azarian again allowed the wine to touch his lips before setting his glass down.

– There's one more thing, he said. I'm afraid it's unpleasant, but we've got to get it out of the way. When my sister died, she left a lot of money to you in her will. She left you fifteen million, an exorbitant amount. You haven't heard about this because you're a difficult man to find. So much the better, as far as I'm concerned, because I've contested the will. I believe if she'd been compos mentis, Willow would have left that money to her family, to her nieces and nephews. I'm very much opposed to giving you *any* money, because I think you've taken advantage of circumstances. I'm not saying you took advantage of her or that you deliberately got her to put you in her will. But you end up with money you don't deserve and I don't think that's right. I spoke to the others and they all feel you should get something, especially if it means avoiding lawyers' fees.

– What do you suggest? said Tancred.

– I'm just coming to that, said Azarian.

Tancred saw that the man had somewhat lost his composure. As Azarian reached into his jacket pocket, his hand shook slightly, but he managed to extract two envelopes. Placing the first one before Tancred, he said

– This is a cheque for ten thousand dollars.

Alton Azarian then put the other envelope down on the table beside the first.

– And this, he said, is a document saying you voluntarily give up all rights to property or funds left to you in my sister's will. If you sign this, I'll sign the cheque and we'll be quits. Ten thousand dollars. I think it's fair. Very fair.

Tancred took the elegant white-and-gold ballpoint Alton offered him and signed the document. He then waited as Alton slid the cheque toward him.

– This isn't necessary, said Tancred.

And slid it back.

– Are you sure? asked Alton.

– I'm very sure, said Tancred.

Alton Azarian relaxed. You could see the tension leave him. He signalled for the bill.

– Is there somewhere I can drop you? he asked.

Tancred shook his head.

He wondered how men like Azarian sustained their fantasies of 'fairness,' but he wasn't offended. He hadn't expected money for keeping a promise. So, *not* getting money caused him no bitterness. He thought about stealing Alton's pen and wallet, just to throw them away. The thought had nothing to do with money or retribution, however. It had to do with Alton Azarian's presumption, his social standing. For a moment, it was as if the wealthy really were his natural enemies, like cats to goldfish, as Baruch Mandelshtam might have said. But he felt petty thinking about things that way. Alton was Willow's brother and, if for no other reason, worthy of, well, not respect, exactly, but something.

As he walked down Avenue Road, Tancred's thoughts turned to the Azarians. How different the three he'd met actually were. What was it that linked such disparate personalities? Was it only father and mother? How did consanguinity play out?

It was an impossible question to answer, at least for him, but it was a diverting one. By the time he got to Harbord Street, he was reminded of his mother's belief that 'we are all God's children.' An amusing thought: God as absent parent. The idea led him to reflect on how much (or little) one can know about a being one has never met.

His own father, for instance.

Did his father ever think of him as he walked whatever streets he walked? He must, surely. Though, perhaps his father was one of those men who did not consider children their concern, a quick spasm being all they knew of duty. In any case, it had been a very long time since he'd longed to know his father. And that was it, wasn't it? If God was a father, He was a bad one, one who'd had His divine moment and left. And when his time was through and death came, Tancred could not imagine wishing to see Him.

– Too late, he said aloud

thoughtful, as he walked along Harbord, past dark houses and brightly lit, empty buildings, the city so quiet it was as if he were no more than a moment in its endless conversation with itself.

2 Freud Out for Revenge

It had been difficult for Colby to push Freud from the loft on Winnett. Then it had been difficult to keep him from going back. Freud had hated Tancred from the beginning, Tancred and Daniel being among the older kids who hung around Alexandra Park when Freud was growing up. Now – with both his eyes black and his nose bound by surgical tape that held a protector in place – his hatred bordered on obsession. He no longer cared about addicts or the handful of dollars he earned bilking them. He wanted so badly to pound Tancred into the dirt that Colby had to calm him down, incessantly.

– I don't care what you do to him, Colby would say. I care about *when* you do it! Once we've got what we want, you can murder the prick. But wait till then!

– How do you know we're going to get what we want? Freud asked.

They were in the Coffee Time at O'Hara. The place had felt inhospitable since it had been renovated. For years, it had been an overheated and sour concern, a convenient place to use the washroom or to eat doughnuts. Its new incarnation just did not feel right. They were at a table by the window in armchairs. Still, from where Colby sat, he could look across at the Dollarama with its green-and-yellow sign, the store filled with what he imagined were low-income mothers with children trailing behind them, outpatients from CAMH and people in need of sweets, toys and knock-off knick-knacks. A good place, one that made him happy, reminding him of the dollar stores of his childhood where, when his father had been more vicious with him than usual, his mother might buy him a plastic something to keep him quiet.

– If we don't get what we want, he said, we'll kick the shit out of him together.

– He could use a beating, Freud answered.

– Well, there you go, said Colby. It'll be like we did him a favour.

Both of them laughed but, in fact, Colby was almost as angry as Freud. It had been days since they'd seen Tancred, and his absence was exasperating.

– Serious question, he said. What do you think about Palmieri?

– How's that a serious question? asked Freud. He's an asshole.

– I don't mean his personality, said Colby. I mean his juice.

– He's not connected. What do you care?

– I don't know, said Colby. I just never really thought about it before. It's good to know what you're dealing with. If you corner a rat, it'll attack you, won't it?

Freud pushed hair away from his eyes and said

– My uncle used to say that. He used to work for Beaver Exterminating and he was always talking about rats. But I worked with him one summer, eh? And I was down in a basement over on McCowan. More rats than you can shake a stick at and I got one in a corner, just like they say. And the fucker did run at me. And you know what? I kicked it to fucking death, that's what.

– Your answer to everything is 'Kick it to death,' said Colby.

– You think I'm wrong?

– No, I think you're right. But it's about timing. That, plus you got to know what you're dealing with. A rat's different from raccoons.

– Palmieri, said Freud, is a rat *and* a coon.

– Jesus! said Colby. Show some respect for black people.

– Sorry, Nigger, said Freud.

For a moment, they were quiet. Anyone passing their table at Coffee Time might have taken them for men slightly younger than they were – for twenty-year-olds, say. They drank coffee from paper cups, two doughnuts on white porcelain plates before them: toasted coconut for Colby, double chocolate for Freud.

Their quiet was interrupted …

– Speak of the devil! said Colby.

… by Tancred himself.

Freud thought of getting up to deck him. His bile and anger rose. But along with them came a tincture of doubt. He wasn't afraid of Tancred exactly. His desire to hurt him ran so deep he felt something like embarrassment. His body, however, remembered the pain of having its nose broken. So, he was involuntarily hesitant, as when you've been sick on vodka and, a few days later, someone offers you a vodka and orange.

Tancred took a chair from a neighbouring table and sat beside Freud, as if nothing had happened between them.

– Sorry I've been away these last few days, said Tancred. Things have happened.

– What kind of things? asked Colby.

– Alton Azarian took back all the pieces we stole.

– And how'd he do that?

– The lease was in Willow's name. The landlord contacted him and he told the landlord to put the apartment up for rent. Then he came in and took back the screen, the bottle, the model and the painting. Everything.

– You expect us to believe that?

– I don't expect anything, Tancred answered. You can go and see for yourself.

– I told you he doesn't take us seriously, said Freud.

From the pocket of his coat – which was draped over the back of his chair – Colby took out a handful of photographs.

– I was going to save these till later, he said, but why shouldn't you see them now? After all, you love photos, don't you, Tan?

He moved his chair closer to Tancred's and spread out the half-dozen photos they'd taken of Daniel's wife, Fiona.

The photos were, on the surface, banal. They'd been taken one mid-afternoon at the corner of Dundas and University. Colby and Freud had waited for her, apparently. Then, pretending to be tourists, they'd asked if they could take a few pictures. You could see by the expression on her face that Fiona was annoyed, but she'd allowed it. (Tancred recognized the look. He and Daniel called it 'English Disapproval.' It was similar to 'English Annoyance,' which was itself similar to 'English Outrage.') The most disturbing photo was of Freud standing behind her, out of her line of sight, leaning down so his face was just over Fiona's shoulder – eyes closed, tongue lolling out to one side as if he were a hanged man.

The effect of the photographs on Tancred was gratifying to Colby and to Freud. It was as if Tancred's face had gone blank – amusingly blank, as far as Freud was concerned. But Tancred's reaction was only part of Freud's pleasure. The other part came from seeing again the face he'd made behind Fiona's back.

Tancred said

– Why'd you do this?

– Your friends are our friends, Tan. We want everyone to get what they deserve.

Freud guffawed.

– You should see the look on your face, he said. Classic!

Tancred took up the photographs, then looked at his companions: two men in their early twenties, his contemporaries, both of them from places like the one where he'd grown up.

– These don't make any difference, Tancred said. I don't want anything to happen to my friends but ...

Colby interrupted.

– Neither do we, he said.

– I don't know about that, said Freud. Why should I care about his friends?

Tancred said

– These don't change anything, because I think I figured the clues out.

– How'd you figure them out? asked Colby.

Tancred pointed to his cranium.

– Kidneys, he said. It's got to do with the word *Weiden*. *Weiden* means willow in German. The mausoleum's got the word *Weiden* written on it thousands of times. But I'm thinking there's got to be at least one time where there's the word *Harp* because in Psalm 137 there's a harp among the willows.

– Really? said Colby. You think *that's* the answer?

– Why would I make something like that up?

– He's got you there, said Freud.

– Azarian has a man working there in the day. So, we'll have to look at night. And I need your help. We're going to have to look at thousands and thousands of pieces of marble. It's going to take a while, even with three of us.

Petulant and unconvinced, Freud said

– I don't like cemeteries at night.

– Why not? said Colby. You afraid of ghosts? Remember Russ Baker, the guy used to deal acid? Know what he does now? He's an accountant! Makes more money than when he was dealing. Last year he got a house on Springhurst. Got it for nothing 'cause the place is haunted. It's straight-up haunted, too. One day, he goes down the basement and he sees this little girl in a dress just standing there looking at him. His wife's seen her, too. I said, 'Did you know it was haunted before you bought it?' He says, 'Yeah.' I said, 'Are you crazy? Why'd you buy it, then?' He says, 'You know how many people got killed by ghosts in T.O. last year?' I said, 'How many?' He says, 'Not a fucking one!' You see what I'm saying?

Tancred said

– You need to bring ladders and flashlights. The walls are about ten feet high. I'm going in around one in the morning.

– You sure about this harp business? Colby asked.

– No, I'm not sure, said Tancred. But it makes sense and it's all I've got.

– Okay, said Colby. We'll meet you in the cemetery around one.

When Tancred had gone, Errol said

– Freud, man, you should come with us.

– Why? I don't like cemeteries.

– Yeah, but if we find something, like if we find money, we'll just take it. We won't need Palmieri anymore. And if we don't find anything, I think it's time you got some payback. Know what I mean? I'll make sure he doesn't sucker-punch you. Either way, you won't be wasting your time, okay?

Freud was pleased at the thought of punching Tancred's face in.

– You want another doughnut, Nigs? he asked.

– Nah, maybe more coffee, answered Colby.

3 An Even Number of Endings

The Azarian business ended exactly as Baruch might have predicted. The wealthy had got their way as usual, wasting resources as they went. Daniel, a detective, had been sent to investigate a petty theft. A few more thefts had occurred and then, as things were getting interesting, he was dismissed – that is, the Azarians had magnanimously informed the police that their services were no longer needed. The family had recovered the stolen mementos on their own.

Interesting timing: he'd been waiting in the Café el-Bugat for half an hour when dispatch told him the news. Michael Azarian had not called and would not show. As Baruch might have said, consideration was for peers, and he, a member of the police, was no peer to the Azarians. Daniel had felt slightly put upon, but he got over the bitterness quickly. The matter was closed and, appropriately somehow, the strangest case he'd been involved with was over before it had really got going.

Daniel had finished his aish el-saraya and coffee when an older gentleman walked into the café. As if he were peeved, the man shouted

– Can't a veteran get a tea in this place?

Daniel recognized him at once. It was the man in Puli's photo, the one with whom Tancred had spoken. Up close, he looked to be about seventy, and he had a prosthetic leg. The most striking thing about him, however, was a purplish-black bruise on his forehead – it looked as if he'd recently been in a fray of some kind and he'd come out the worse for wear. Though there were tables free, when the man saw Daniel he hobbled over, accompanied by a younger woman who unobtrusively helped him walk.

When he got close, the man stared at Daniel, wordlessly. Nor would he move on when his minder tried steer him away. Finally, he said

– Do you know me?

– It's not the same man, said the woman.

– I'm afraid I don't know you, Daniel said.

– Well, said Ran Morrissey, I admit I can't tell the difference between one black man and another. But you look like the one who bought me the best drink I've ever had.

– We were drugged, said the woman.

– He was a military man, said Morrissey. There's no chance we were drugged. That was the best arak I've ever been served. It was like the opium I had in P.E.I. I didn't know arak could be so strong.

– But I had coffee, said the woman, and I passed out.

– So you say! So you say! said Morrissey. But what looks like coffee is sometimes tea! You asked him for arak, I remember.

– But what about your bruise?

– Did you or did you not ask him for arak? asked Morrissey.

The woman said nothing and Morrissey, confident he'd settled the matter, retired to a table somewhere behind Daniel's. After a moment, Morrissey began talking loudly about the American economy and the fact that the United States had foolishly elected a lackey to lead it. Barack Hussein Obama! It was a miracle the apocalypse hadn't come at his inauguration. It was only a matter of time, of course. Only a matter of time.

Mystified by the encounter, Daniel left the Café el-Bugat and walked to his car, thinking about how peculiar human beings sometimes are. Of course, he worried often, in these days before the birth of his and Fiona's child, about all the malice on earth, the terrible things his child would face. Baruch had, perhaps, felt similarly at his – that is, Daniel's – birth. Which would, no doubt, explain Baruch's rage to make the world a better place. At any rate, it comforted Daniel to think so.

In fact, Daniel was suddenly sanguine about the world. The man with the bruised forehead was as far from Baruch as he could imagine. But the difference was, momentarily, unimportant. The man was human and fallible and Daniel was moved by this fallibility, by the fate they all shared, by the thought that there was so much they could not know.

There were, no doubt, worse ways to feel when one had failed to solve a case.

It was December 4th. No, it was December 5th, one in the morning. What else? It was cold: four or five degrees Celsius at most. What else? Nothing else. Of the moments before Colby and Freud came, Tancred had no memory. No memory of the drive to Mount Pleasant, no memory of going over the fence and drawing his ladder after him, though, of course, he had done these things. His awareness began with the appearance of the two. No, not with their appearance; rather, with the sound of them – loud whispers getting louder as they approached, then silence as they saw him.

When he was certain Colby and Freud had seen him, Tancred stepped into a Weiden mausoleum that he had, the night before, prepared for them.

– I hope we're not doing this for nothing, said Colby.

– I hope so, too, said Tancred.

He explained again why they were looking for the name Harp or Harfe on the walls of the mausoleum. When he'd finished, he said

– I'm going to do this one.

He stepped up his ladder, turned on his flashlight and made as if he were closely examining the marble around the entrance to the mausoleum.

Though they were skeptical, Colby and Freud in turn climbed their ladders and began to inspect their walls. The light in the mausoleum was bronze and yellow, the beams from three flashlights creating elongated circles and shadows on the marble.

After a half-hour of a silence broken only by Freud's grumbled complaints, Colby shouted

– Jesus!

startling the other two.

– What the fuck? said Freud

who'd almost fallen off his ladder.

– Jesus! Colby said again. I found it!

As Tancred had done before him, Colby pushed on the rectangle with the word HARFE engraved in it. The rectangle went in and then opened out like the drawer it was. Colby took out the same black-leather envelope Tancred had found, extracting from it a silver key and a white business card on which an address was darkly printed:

> *Royal Bank of Canada*
> *2 Bloor Street East,*
> *Toronto, Ontario*
> *Safety Deposit Box #15011985*

Colby was careful not to show the contents of the envelope to Tancred. Instead, shining a light on the business card so Freud could see it, he said

– I knew Willow was right! I *knew* it!

– Can I see that? Tancred asked.

Colby considered the question.

– No, he said.

Summoning all the outrage he could, Tancred said

– I'm the one who solved the puzzle

and took a step toward the two, as if he intended to press the matter. Freud happily stood between Tancred and Colby, flashlight ready as a weapon. Tancred said

– Don't make me break your nose again.

Worried that Tancred would be more than Freud could handle and too excited to get into it, now that he'd got what he wanted, Colby held Freud back.

– Not worth the trouble, he said. He's got nothing.

Then, to Tancred:

– We'll look into this and get back to you.

Warily, but as if disappointed, Tancred stepped back, waiting for Freud to come at him.

It was not difficult for him to feign disappointment because he *was* disappointed. He had, of course, switched card and key himself. Colby and Freud would find, in the RBC safety deposit box, five precious stones that he'd stolen years previously. The stones were worth between fifty and a hundred thousand dollars, depending on how one disposed of them. (Depending!) They were beautiful. He'd grown particularly attached to the carbonado – a black diamond with a ruby flaw. It was against his principles to make a fetish of the things he stole – that is, he liked to imagine that his relationship to objects was so pure it verged on indifference. The black diamond was an exception, but he had given the five stones up, knowing that whatever was in an Azarian safety deposit box had to be valuable enough to convince Colby that Tancred had not tricked them, that they were not being played. So, Tancred had given up his most valuable pieces, unsure if what waited in Montreux would compensate him for the loss.

Then again, he'd had no choice. As he warily watched Colby and Freud leave the mausoleum, he remembered the photographs they'd taken of Fiona. If anything, he wondered if he should not have left the men more.

Tancred had bought his ticket to Switzerland and had almost managed to stop thinking about Colby when, three days before he was to go, he ran into him at Ali's.

– It's Tancred Palmieri, said Colby. How you doing?

Tancred feigned displeasure.

– I'm still waiting to hear what you found.

– Oh, that? said Colby. It was nothing. A lot of trouble for nothing. A diamond and a couple of pearls. You know how much we made, Tancred? A thousand bucks. Willow's dad was a cheap motherfucker. I'm glad she didn't live to find out. It would've killed her.

Tancred said

– A thousand dollars?

– I'm sorry about that, said Colby. I really am. If you want, I'll buy you a roti.

Tancred looked at him witheringly, then walked out of Ali's.

So, in principle, all had gone well. He'd solved Azarian's puzzle. (It seemed.) He'd outsmarted Colby and Freud. (Perhaps.) He was free (almost free) of his obligations to Willow. Yet from the moment he'd put the jewels – no, not all the jewels, the black diamond specifically – in a safety deposit box, something vague preyed on his attention. He had not taken something into consideration. But what?

In different circumstances, needing to talk, he'd have spoken to Daniel. Now that Alton Azarian had reclaimed the stolen mementos, now that Colby was satisfied he had got what was meant for him, now that neither Ollie nor Fiona were at risk, why shouldn't he sit down with Daniel and tell him everything? No reason. Yet he didn't, promising himself, rather, that he'd speak to Daniel when he got back from Montreux. It was only then, after all, when he'd learned what the Azarian business had been about, that the story would have its end.

The evening before he left for Europe, Tancred had supper with von Würfel.

– It was very clever of you to get that right, said von Würfel, but even more clever of Robert Azarian. It's an elegant solution to an elegant puzzle. Having caught the … the geometry of the man's mind, I'd have expected nothing less. Do you have any idea what's in Montreux?

– No. Do you want to come with me?

– No, no, not at all, Tancred. I hate spending time in planes. It takes my bones days to recover whenever I visit my daughter in Halifax. Going to Geneva would cripple me. I hope you find something useful, like money. But I'm inclined to believe what Alton told you. His father was a shrewd businessman. It's hard to credit that he'd leave millions somewhere inaccessible.

– What do you think it is?

– If I had to guess, I'd say an heirloom, something to remind his children of himself or their mother. On the other hand, a mind as lovely as Robert's might just leave money, because he'd have had no reverence for it. So, it could be millions and millions. I feel as if I've come to know Robert through all this. And I think of him as an artist. I want you to know that if your share's something you don't want, I'll buy it from you.

– That's good to know, said Tancred. But if it's something I don't want, you can have it.

– Do you know, said von Würfel, I'd like another memento of the man. I feel like I'm having a relationship with a friend who's in some distant country. Very odd, don't you think?

– It's not odd for me, said Tancred. Willow's in the same place.

– Yes, of course, said von Würfel.

On Tancred's way home, the night was cold and there were patches of hard snow on the ground. The sky was cloudless and the moon was bright. Save for the cars, the streets were quiet and there were few people about, though it was still early and, passing this or that bar or restaurant, there would be the occasional exhalation of sound and warmth, as if the buildings themselves were breathing. It was a night made for contemplation. So, no surprise: the thing that had troubled him, the thing just out of his mind's reach, came to him at last. Rather, it was shown to him. As he passed a dispenser for the *Sun*, he saw a picture of his black diamond on the tabloid's front cover. It was not the main story, but the diamond was there beside the words

FAMILY'S JEWEL RECOVERED

He bought the paper and read the story in a coffee shop in Liberty Village.

Tancred had left five gems in the Royal Bank's safety deposit box. Each of the stones was in its way valuable but the diamond, stolen from a home on the Bridle Path, was well-known. It had its own personality – a carbonado, expertly cut but with a rare flaw: a naturally occurring, ruby-red crescent at its centre, like a waxing or waning blood moon. It was a striking gem. Which is why Tancred would never have taken it to a dealer. In fact, Tancred was so used to dealing with fences that it had not occurred to him that Colby was not. Then again, as far as Colby knew, the gems had been left by Robert Azarian, and Robert Azarian had been a very wealthy man.

Why would he have left stolen property to his children? Rather than fencing the gems, Colby had taken them to a well-known jeweller who, after buying four of them, had expressed doubts about the carbonado.

The man had then asked Colby if he could do tests on the diamond to see if it was real. When Colby returned to collect either the diamond or money for the diamond, the police had been there to take him in for questioning. No doubt – though Tancred had no way of knowing – Colby had told them all about the Weiden mausoleum, about how he'd found a black-leather envelope, and so on. None of that was in the *Sun*, however. The black diamond was worth, at a conservative estimate, somewhere north of a hundred thousand dollars on the legitimate market. That, as far as the *Sun* was concerned, was the most important thing.

Even to Tancred, it seemed incredible that he could have been so thoughtless. Had he wanted Colby to be caught? If so, why? It would have been senseless to wish him jailed, because bringing attention to Colby would have been bringing attention to himself. But if he hadn't been thoughtless, what had he been? The answer – the only other answer he could grasp – is that he had been, unwittingly, an instrument of fate.

He'd been so troubled by what he'd read that, instead of taking East Liberty to Dufferin, he'd turned from the coffee shop right toward Mildred's, the restaurant, instead of left onto Hanna. That is, he'd gone toward the steps leading down to King Street and it was there – on steps he rarely ever took – that he was shot.

In the moment itself, he had no idea what had happened. But, of course, a number of things had happened at once. He'd felt, strangely, as if his arm had grazed the branch of a thorn tree. He'd heard the *pap* of a gun firing or a truck backfiring. He'd heard a human voice. All of this before he had a chance to look up. But when he did look up, his being shot was no longer the issue. He was being shot *at* and the second bullet missed his feet, sending bits of cement and cement mist up from the step beneath him.

It was then – thinking himself already dead – that Tancred's instincts took over. He felt exhilarated. The one shooting at him – Freud, as it turned out – was coming up the steps, drawing closer.

Tancred heard bits of imprecation

– *Something* fuck … *something* fucker …

before the gun loudly clicked, misfiring.

At the sound of the misfire, Freud, his rage almost palpable, swore.

– You cunt!

he said, referring perhaps to Tancred, perhaps to the gun.

Without thinking, instinctively Tancred ran down the steps at him. Freud again tried to fire but, again, there was an unsatisfying *click* which was, perhaps, the last sound he heard in his life. Holding the guardrail for support, Tancred launched himself at Freud, both feet catching the man solidly in the chest. Freud, gun still in hand, fell back – almost as if diving backward – onto the cement steps, his body awkwardly landing on the concrete: gun beneath him, forehead bloodied, neck broken.

Tancred – still exhilarated – walked down to see what had happened. Freud's head was at an unnatural angle to his body, resting on its own shoulder, fresh blood coming through the bandages on his nose.

A moment before, there'd been rage. Now there were only subsiding spasms.

Tancred continued down the steps, leaving Freud's body where it had landed, as if its state had nothing to do with him.

But, of course, Freud's death was his doing.

Yes, certainly, Tancred had accepted the idea that his life was dangerous. But dangerous to *him* is what he'd imagined. *That* danger had made for a kind of excitement. Something like this was a different proposition, more difficult to accept.

But what had he done wrong? Freud had shot him, grazing his arm before the revolver had misfired. In the instant Tancred had charged at his attacker, he had been wholly, unthinkingly himself.

He could not have done other than what his instincts demanded. Where, then, was there blame? He'd been the cause of Freud's death, but he hadn't chosen to be.

Distraught, Tancred went about preparing to leave. He tidied his apartment, which took no time at all, there being so little to tidy: a table, four chairs, a couch, the painting of Oshun given to him by his mother, a bed, a handful of dishes, knives and forks, a vacuum cleaner, and little else. He packed his small black bag and set it beside the door. Then he lay down, fully clothed, and tried to sleep.

But sleep was a thing he would not do for some time.

So, although it was midnight, he took the 504 to Dundas West and, because he suddenly found it intolerable to be alone, he went on to Runnymede and woke Ollie up.

The temperature had fallen. It was now so cold that even Ollie, who did not like to acknowledge the seasons, wore mittens.

Of course, it was also possible that Ollie was wearing mittens because they were the last pair his mother had made for him. Mrs. Mallay had been a persistent but indifferent knitter and, all his life, Ollie's mittens had looked like hybrids of tuning forks and pot holders. Not that this had ever made the slightest difference to Ollie. His love for his mother being, as he called it, 'unexceptional,' his affection for her 'by-products' could not be considered exceptional either. Though many had tried, it was impossible to tease him about his mittens or any such thing.

Runnymede was like an abandoned street as they walked, without destination, toward St. Clair. The Christmas lights on the houses and evergreens made it seem as if the world were quietly confident of some great thing. But to Tancred, the many lights – blinking in sequence or constantly shining – stopped time in its tracks, one Christmas being like any other.

– I don't know how long I'll be gone, he said. It depends what I find. A week, most likely.

217

— Freud decided to shoot you, Ollie said. I understand you running at him. I'd have done the same thing. Why not face death if it's coming? It just happened to be Freud's death, not yours. What could you do about that, Tan?

— It's not like I ran over a dog, Ollie.

— It's not like you killed anyone. Freud did something unexpected. The gun did something unexpected. You did something unexpected. And he died. Nine times out of ten, you run at someone with a gun, you die. This was time number ten. It's okay to feel guilty, because you are who you are. But you're wrong to think you caused Freud's death, even if you did cause it.

— That doesn't make sense, said Tancred.

— Sure it does, said Ollie. You were the instrument, that's all.

— Whose instrument?

— No one can say that, Tan. If there's a god, you were god's instrument. If there's no god, you were chance's. I don't know why people don't worship chance. It's as powerful as any of the gods and it doesn't need money, doesn't punish, doesn't care what you eat on Friday. I'm not a believer, but if I was going to be, I'd worship chance. You could have churches that look like dice.

Despite his mood, Tancred smiled. He briefly imagined a white, square church with a ⚁ on its side. The idea was absurd, incongruous and maybe unholy, but it was also appropriate. It was exactly the kind of church Ollie would frequent.

— I'll keep an eye on your apartment, Ollie continued. And if you think you're not coming back for a while, I'll just bring everything here.

— You sure your dad'd be okay with that?

— My dad? My dad's waiting to die.

— That's terrible, said Tancred.

— Why? Ollie asked. He loved my mom. It'd be weird if he didn't want to die. Anyway, all I'm saying is he's got other things on his mind. He wouldn't notice even if I put all your stuff in our kitchen.

4 A Palace in Montreux

The man who walked the streets the following morning was not the man who'd spent hours drinking tea with Olivier the night before. For one thing, it occurred to Tancred that he did not know who, if anyone, was after him or what they might be after him for: questions about Freud's death or Colby's arrest or even the theft of the black diamond. Although he was booked on a flight from Montreal to Geneva – as close as one could get to Montreux – he wasn't sure it was wise for him to leave.

The biggest change in Tancred was that he now knew for certain he was not a man who could kill without remorse. Or was it, rather, that he could not kill *Freud* without remorse?

His flight left from Montreal at six in the evening.

At six in the morning, he left Ollie – his friend nodding off in an armchair – and went down to the lake, walking along the shore in an effort to recover some sense of normalcy, the lake being a good companion in troubled times. It was its winter self – gunmetal grey, the water quietly shushing as it brought its small warmth to shore.

Tancred suddenly wondered what it would be like if he never saw Lake Ontario again. Not just its water, waves and stone breakers, but all the ways the sight of it made him feel, the things it evoked. This morning, for instance, walking by the shore was like biting into a hard apple while someone held open the door to a fridge full of rotting plants.

But he saw the lake again that same day.

He had decided sometime before to take the train to Montreal, there being no direct flights to Geneva from home. He had his train ticket already. So, he went by rail. Five mournful hours. His views of the lake were a kind of peekaboo: the water – ruffling, greyish-blue with smooth stones beside it – disappearing behind buildings or towns, appearing again briefly here and there, in the distance, before going away for good somewhere east of Kingston.

A curious coincidence: the train from Geneva to Montreux seemed, at times, an iteration in a different key of the trip to Montreal. For long stretches, the train ran beside the greyish water of Lake Geneva. The lake would disappear, then reappear farther along. Despite the similarity, however, the trip from Geneva to Montreux was like the beginning of an erasure. The 'old world' – its buildings, the Alps beyond the shore, the houses like chalets – was unlike anything he knew. It was, in theory, beautiful, but it did not move him. It obscured – in his mind – the place from which he'd come.

On his arrival in Montreux, the world seemed endlessly grey, not just because the sky was overcast but because he could barely stay awake. And although he wanted nothing more than to open box 742015 at the Crédit Suisse, he went straight to his rooms on the sixth floor of Fairmont Le Montreux Palace and slept for ten hours straight, waking too late to visit the bank.

(He dreamed the same dream over and over. He and Freud Luxemberg were on a train from Geneva. They were having a conversation about sugar, a conversation so vivid that, each time Freud said the word *sugar*, Tancred's mouth watered as if he were biting into the pith of a sugar cane. As they spoke, Tancred found it unsettling that Freud's head was in such darkness that it was, effectively, hidden. Then, when the train stopped in Gare de Montreux, Freud refused to get off. It was only then Tancred saw that Freud's neck was broken and his head lay almost sideways, his temple flat on his shoulder. Embarrassed to see Tancred looking at him, Sigismund Luxemberg retreated to the shadows and said

– See you later, Tan.)

That night, Tancred ate a hamburger at the hotel's American-style bar before returning to his room, turning on the television and falling into a deep sleep punctuated by bursts of jazz.

Montreux was, for all intents and purposes, a way station. From the window of his room, he had what might be called a magnificent view: the grey lake, the snow-topped Alps, the clean streets of the city. Yet it felt to Tancred as if he were stuck in a postcard. It was all repulsively quaint. He felt the heaviness of his body. It was a relief to do his one duty: go to the bank, extract whatever was in box number 742015 and go somewhere – not home – for a time.

At the Crédit Suisse, there were no difficulties. He was shown to the safety deposit boxes. The key fit perfectly, and from the narrow, silvery compartment he took five black-leather envelopes, each bound to a white envelope by a coppery clasp. Tancred chose not to open the envelopes in the bank. He put all of them in the pocket of his coat and returned to his room where, on a desk at which a famous writer had, it seemed, written famous books, he opened each of the envelopes in turn.

He was surprised by what he found, neither pleased nor displeased. In each of the black envelopes there was a bank book and in each of the five accounts there were one hundred million American dollars. Along with each bank book, there was a bank card and for every bank card a PIN printed on a square of thick yellow paper. In each of the white envelopes, there was a letter addressed to one of the Azarians by their father. Willow's was the only letter of any length, though. It was three pages long, written in an almost conspicuously precise hand.

Willow had reckoned that the amount her father left his children had been short a billion dollars. She'd been wrong, but Tancred imagined she would not have cared about her overestimation. By coming to Montreux, Tancred had inherited a hundred million dollars, an almost inconceivable amount to one who had little interest in money or possessions. Even minus the ten million he would give to Alexander von Würfel – if von Würfel wanted it, the amount being awkward to declare or to hide – it was more money than Tancred knew what to do with. Out of curiosity, he went down to the lobby of the Fairmont Le Montreux Palace, put Willow's bank card in an automated teller and withdrew five thousand Swiss francs. The machine dispensed his money, then asked if he wished to do anything else. When he did not, it returned his card with an officious *click*.

Not knowing what to do with the money but needing some proof that it was real, Tancred bought a cup of coffee and a croissant at the hotel's café. He left a twenty-franc tip for the waiter and returned to his room. Numb from all he'd been through, he did not know what or how to feel. Relieved? Perhaps. Happy? No. Happy for Willow then? Yes, because although she was not there to live it, Tancred's discovery meant that of all Robert Azarian's children, she'd been the one he had trusted most, despite her addiction.

Robert Azarian admitted as much in his letter:

My Dearest Willow,

Though I am no longer with you as you read these words, I want you to know that you have always been in my thoughts and that I love you. None of your siblings will take this treasure hunt as seriously as you. I've taken pains to see that they do not. I have written this letter to you, confident that you will be the one to find the funds in these five accounts.

I imagine you will have a number of questions for me. Nothing would make me happier than to answer them all. But I will limit myself to the ones you may not be able to answer on your own.

Why have I created this final hunt?

Because, my poor Willow, I have been worried about you. I know you have done your best to hide your sickness, but how could I not know my daughter is dependent on drugs? We have spoken about these things. There is no need to rehearse our conversations. In the end, I did all of this because I hope it will take your mind off your heroin or your alcohol or whatever it is you have turned to. If you are reading this letter, then you have found the clarity I have hoped you would attain.

Why have I left so much money?

These past few years, I have seen that my children have all done well — even Michael — and that they have all the money they need. Alton has been a great success. I am proud of him. But I have long felt that more money would only give you all more headaches. I am proud of what I have accomplished, Willow. But I have made more money than any man needs and I worry that all of this will make you children miserable.

I have given much to charity, because I believe those who have have a duty to those who do not. We've spoken of this, you and I. But the funds in these accounts represent money about which I cannot come to a decision. I have hesitated between charity and my children.

Your brothers and sisters would, I believe, take the money without thinking about the consequences. But money has never mattered to you. That is why I want you to decide what to do with it. If you are thinking straight enough to find these accounts, you will be thinking straight enough to decide how they should be dealt with. I have no preference. If you decide to give your brothers and sisters their share, I will be happy. If you decide to give some their share and leave others without, I will be happy. If you decide to give everything to the grand-children, I will be happy. If you decide to give it all to charity, I will be happy. I have left letters for Alton, Gretchen, Simone and Michael to the effect that you are the only and final arbiter of the five hundred million dollars in these five accounts.

There is no way you can disappoint me. Do as you see best.

It is my hope, Will, that you'll have enjoyed this little puzzle. I can just imagine you annoyed when you realize you could have solved this without the help of your siblings' clues! Did you discover the meaning of my a(ш)? It was redundant. So, I am willing to bet you did not!

(Here is another hint: the ш rhymes with origin!)

I want you to know, my dearest Will, that I have worried about you, as any father worries about a child in need. I never wanted my worries to be a burden. Perhaps I was wrong to keep them to myself. In my life, my only regret is that I have not been a better father to you.

All my love,
Dad

On reading this – and after looking at the notes Robert Azarian had left for his other children – Tancred was overcome by disappointment. How banal that at the end of his (and Willow's) search there were dollars: no enlightenment, no truth, nothing noble. What a tiresome way to learn again that all earthly journeys end in earthly things. Then, too, what was he to do with a hundred million dollars? The amount was overwhelming to someone who knew how to live without much. It might as well have been play money.

Willow's wishes had been clear. He was to give whatever he found to her siblings. Would she have felt the same after reading her father's letter, he wondered. He could see the truth of her father's thinking: Alton most certainly did not need another penny. And he understood why Robert Azarian had discouraged his son from looking for more of it. More complicated was the thought of what might happen when he sent the money to Willow's siblings. In his letters to Alton, Gretchen, Simone and Michael, Robert Azarian let his children know that he had deliberately left the decision about their inheritances to Willow, that her decision about it was his. But they would question the disappearance of Willow's share, wouldn't they? Alton had got himself in knots over the money Willow had left him in her will: fifteen million, the amount he'd seen on her bank statement. Alton's knots would have more gnarls and ramifications if he knew that Tancred would decide what to do with Willow's share.

But Alton's feelings were none of Tancred's business. He'd done everything Willow had asked of him. He would do this, too, and deal with Alton – or any of the others – later, if he had to. For now, there was only one question: where to go. When he thought of destinations, the word *déboussolé* came to him – literally, to be without a compass. Not only confused or disoriented, but with no direction.

For days, he stayed in Montreux, staring at the mountains, trying to imagine a place – a place other than home – that would suit him, a place from which he might find the way home.

Tancred chose Key West for two reasons. First, he remembered Willow's stories of being a child on Grinnell Street. So, Key West, at least, was connected to someone he'd cared for. Then, too, Key West was in North America. He could eat the things he was used to.

But he was in exile and it was even more painful than he'd thought it would be. He longed for his friends, for places, for a host of things: roti at Ali's, the fairgrounds of the CNE, the feeling of being on the 504 and on the way home, standing where King, Queen, the Queensway and Roncesvalles converged and trying to guess which would come first, the King car or the Queen car. A thousand memories and impressions came to him. Toronto became more real to him, more vital, the longer he was away.

Why stay away, then? Why not return and face the consequences of his actions? He hadn't murdered Freud. Freud had tried to murder him. Why should he end up in exile for doing what any creature would have done in his place?

That was the question and he could not answer it.

He could not answer it and then, while walking toward the ocean one day, he remembered the voice of Mrs. Luxemberg calling her son home from her doorway, her accent, the lilt of it.

– Siggy! Siggy! *Komm Heim, mein Schatz!*

It was a terrible thing to recall, but it brought Tancred to the edge of an understanding. He and Freud were connected not only by Freud's death. They were connected by something deeper – anger, resentment. But whereas Freud had attacked and hurt people face to face, he had buried his frustrations. In silence and darkness, he had got back at those he could not see, who could not see him.

The worst of it was that, for all these years, he had hidden his own emotions from himself with noble ideas, with ideals he had inherited from Baruch and from the shady world he'd found hospitable: the rules of his trade, the desire to defend those he could, a code of honour. He had used strong principles and fidelity to blind himself.

In killing Freud Luxemberg, he had, from a certain angle, killed a version of Tancred Palmieri.

And yet he was not dead.

One night, he was sitting at a restaurant called Azur. He'd just got the menu when he heard the couple at a table beside his speaking French. There was a man and a woman, both in their thirties, not much older than he was. The woman, in particular, looked familiar, and it was a moment before he realized she resembled Anne Sylvestre, the singer. But her hair was short, where Sylvestre's (on the cover of *J'ai de bonnes nouvelles*, one of his mother's favourite albums) was long, and this woman's eyes were dark beneath dark eyebrows. Her companion was tall and handsome, his hair combed back, grey at his sideburns. He spoke French with an American accent and his voice was deep.

– *Comment était la salade?* he asked.

– It was good, Harry, she said. *Goutes-donc ma langue. Il doit y rester un soupçon.*

They kissed and then Harry laughed.

– *Tu as raison*, he said. *Il reste la saveur de ciboulette et lavande.*

Slightly embarrassed, Tancred asked about the menu, in French.

– Oh, said the woman, you speak French!

– I'm Canadian, said Tancred.

They invited him to join them and, over dinner, he spoke to them about his homesickness. In that way, his home came flooding back to him – whole, a gift, not lost but waiting.

After dinner, Tancred walked the half-mile to the harbour, then along the seafront, looking out toward Cuba and South America. It was New Year's Eve and warm, and the streets and bars were filled with revellers waiting to ring the new year in.

Tancred, staring at the ocean, was thinking about how to change his life.

To do that, he'd have to accept who he had been.

And what did he hope for? That he might be virtuous without the blindness of virtue, that he might discover the good but without the arrogance of those who assumed it was theirs to possess.

The first step, at least, was clear. He needed help. He would write to Daniel and tell him all that had happened: from meeting Willow at the Green Dolphin to finding millions in a Crédit Suisse in Montreux, from leaving the carbonado for Colby to knocking Freud down the steps at King and Atlantic. He would leave no important thing out. He would abandon discretion.

Then he would take the letters and bank cards he'd found to Simone Azarian-Grau. She should know what her father had done and why. They all should. He would not keep their money, though it was clear they did not need it. It was not up to him to decide how others should be charitable. And if Alton objected to his keeping Willow's share? He would stand up to him. It was not Alton's right to decide how *he* should be faithful to Willow.

In the midst of these resolutions, Tancred thought of Ollie. What is it Daniel had said about him? That it was difficult to imagine Ollie being a father because it was difficult to imagine a man choosing, moment after moment, to be a father, to be virtuous. But Ollie had learned to make a habit of the things he'd chosen to be. He would follow Ollie's example and choose a life away from exhilaration and adrenalin, until the new life became a habit.

And where was home in all this?

He had once wondered if home were people or a place. It was, of course, both and neither. Each person who lived in Toronto held a facet of the city. Naturally, he did as well and, to see himself clearly, to begin the new life, he would have to be in that place that held the old one, that held those who knew him.

Others, it seemed, could leave home to become different.

Not him. He needed the strength he drew from home in order to change. More than that, it now seemed to him that good and evil changed according to the place from which one judged them.

It was a cloudy night, but every now and then the moon came out. He could hear revellers singing in the distance. Not 'Auld Lang Syne' or anything like it but, rather, something recent that Tancred recognized but did not know.

He was twenty-eight years old, homesick but hopeful. For a moment, with moonlight trembling on the black ocean, he was reminded of Toronto as it is when one looks back from the night ferry to Ward's Island. For a moment, he did not miss home because it flared up within him.

It was as quickly gone, however, and as he walked back to the house he'd rented on Petronia Street, he felt nothing that could be put into words.

Ocala, Florida, 2016
Quincunx 4

A NOTE ON THE TEXT

The Hidden Keys was inspired by a reading of Captain George North's *Treasure Island.* The text incorporates snippets of – or allusions to – the following books:

La chanson de Roland, Anonymous (Somewhere, circa 1115)
The Marble Flea, Mikhail Bulgakov (Moscow, 1975)
Naked Lunch, William S. Burroughs (Paris, 1959)
Our Mutual Friend, Charles Dickens (London, 1865)
Le Platane, un discours sur les arbres, Denis Diderot (Paris, 1757)
The Waste Land, T. S. Eliot (New York, 1922)
Montreux, an appreciation, E. M. Forster (Lausanne, 1957)
Rouge 23, an unproduced screenplay, W. Alex Irwin (Toronto, 2012)
Critique of Pure Reason, Immanuel Kant (Riga, 1781)
The Sinking of the Odradek Stadium, Harry Mathews (New York, 1975)
Treasure Island, George North (London, 1883)
Le Naufrage du Stade Odradek, trans. Georges Perec (Paris, 1981)
Impregnable Rooms: The Architecture of David Rokeby (Toronto, 2007)
Institutions and Power, Elaine Stasiulis (Toronto, 2014)
From Ritual to Romance, Jessie L. Weston (Cambridge, 1920)

The couple described in the final chapter of *The Hidden Keys* are Harry Mathews and Marie Chaix. Harry, Marie and the restaurant they frequent exist, but all three have been altered to suit the needs of the author.

The city of Toronto, as depicted in *The Hidden Keys*, is not entirely true to life.

The city of Etobicoke, as depicted in the novel, is not true at all.

ABOUT THE AUTHOR

André Alexis was born in Trinidad and grew up in Canada. His debut novel, *Childhood*, won the Books in Canada First Novel Award and the Trillium Book Award, and was shortlisted for the Giller Prize and the Writers' Trust Fiction Prize. His previous books include *Asylum, Beauty and Sadness, Ingrid and the Wolf* and *Pastoral*, which was also nominated for the Rogers Writers' Trust Fiction Prize. His most recent novel is *Fifteen Dogs*, which won the Rogers Writers' Trust Fiction Prize and the Scotiabank Giller Prize.

Typeset in Albertan and Gotham.

Albertan was designed by the late Jim Rimmer of New Westminster, B.C., in 1982. He drew and cut the type in metal at the 16pt size in roman only; it was intended for use only at his Pie Tree Press. He drew the italic in 1985, designing it with a narrow fit and a very slight incline, and created a digital version. The family was completed in 2005, when Rimmer redrew the bold weight and called it Albertan Black. The letterforms of this type family have an old-style character, with Rimmer's own calligraphic hand in evidence, especially in the italic.

Printed on Zephyr Antique Laid paper, which was manufactured, acid-free, in Saint-Jérôme, Quebec, from second-growth forests and printed with vegetable-based ink.

Edited and designed by Alana Wilcox
Cover design by Ingrid Paulson
Cover image is *Willows and Bridge*. Japan, Momoyama period (1573–1615), early 17th century. Pair of six-panel folding screens; ink, colour, copper, gold and gold leaf on paper. Image (each): 61 5/16 in. ×11 ft. 6 9/16 in. (171.8 x 352 cm). Mary Griggs Burke Collection, Gift of the Mary and Jackson Burke Foundation, 2015 (2015.300.105.1, .2). The Metropolitan Museum of Art, New York, NY, U.S.A.. Image copyright © The Metropolitan Museum of Art. Image source: Art Resource, NY.

Coach House Books
80 bpNichol Lane
Toronto ON M5S 3J4
Canada

416 979 2217
800 367 6360

mail@chbooks.com
www.chbooks.com